Doctor's Daughters

Doctor's Daughters

A NOVEL BY
Frank G. Slaughter

Thorndike Press • Thorndike, Maine

Library of Congress Cataloging in Publication Data:

Slaughter, Frank G. (Frank Gill), 1908–
  Doctor's daughters.

  1. Large type books. I. Title.
  [PS3537.L38D6 1982]   813'.52   82-3362
  ISBN 0-89621-355-2 (1. print)   AACR2

Large Print edition available through arrangement with Double-day & Company, Inc.

Cover design by Holly Hughes.

Doctor's
Daughters

Chapter 1

The clock over the marquee covering the main entrance to the tower of Biscayne General Hospital on downtown Miami's bayfront said exactly eight twenty-five. Lynn Rogers stopped before the bank of newspaper vending machines just outside the door. Dropping in two coins, she took out a copy of the Miami *Herald* for the morning. The story she sought was on the front page, amidst accounts of turmoil and disturbance all over the world, proving once again the power that went with the name of Dr. Theodore Malone, even by proxy.

The headline was large and black: "WORLD-FAMOUS HEART SURGEON UPSTAGED – BY HIS DAUGHTER."

Father's going to see red, Lynn thought as she stepped out of the stream of early morning pedestrian traffic entering the great hospital, and paused in the shade of a huge

7

It isn't often that Miami's famous heart surgeon, Dr. Theodore Malone, is upstaged by anybody. Last night the feat was accomplished in a surgical miracle by his own daughter, Dr. Lynn Rogers. John Myers had already been pronounced dead, being without pulse, when a Rescue Squad ambulance brought him to Biscayne General's new Critical Care Unit last night, after a robber in Myers' South Miami home had stabbed him in the chest.

In Critical Care, nobody is presumed to be dead until every possible means of resuscitation has been tried and fortunately the chief resident, Dr. Peter Shelbourne, was on duty. Seeing the location of the wound in John Myers' chest, he correctly diagnosed that his pulseless state might be caused by cardiac tamponade − medical term for the blood accumulating in the tough pericardial sac surrounding the heart. A stab wound in that vital structure had literally throttled the organ because it no longer had room to beat.

Inserting a large needle through

Myers' chest wall into the pericardial sac, Dr. Shelbourne drew blood, giving the patient's heart room to beat once again and, literally, snatching him from death. On hand for the emergency, too, was Dr. Lynn Rogers, a cardiac surgeon in her own right as well as a trained "Intensivist" − the name of the new specialty of Critical Care.

Rushing Myers to the operating room suite of the famed Malone Heart Institute, newly added as the twenty-first and twenty-second floors of the Biscayne General Tower, Dr. Rogers made an incision into Myers' chest wall − with this reporter watching from the gallery − exactly twenty minutes after the patient arrived at the hospital.

What followed was literally a miracle, performed under a microscope. When the stab wound proved to involve the main coronary artery supplying blood to the anterior part of the heart muscle, Dr. Rogers used gossamer threads of nylon in the meticulous technique of microsurgery. Literally operating under a microscope, she sewed the cut ends of the severed artery back together, re-establishing the circulation to a large section of John Myers' heart and restoring his life in an hour and a half of surgery that left this reporter limp from the drama of life-or-death suspense.

It was another first for the famed Malone Institute and marked the debut of a heart surgeon fully capable of stepping into her father's shoes.

The paper under her arm, Lynn Rogers walked through the revolving doors into the hospital and crossed the vast lobby toward the Hospitality Shop which occupied one corner of the ground floor.

"Morning, Mabel," she greeted the switchboard operator. "Your grandson's doing fine. I looked in on him before I left last night."

"Thanks, Dr. Rogers. He wouldn't be, though, if you hadn't noticed how blue his skin was last week and talked your father into doing the emergency operation on his heart."

"Don't thank me, Mabel. Two fine doctors named Alfred Blalock and Helen Taussig were the first to use that operation on 'blue babies,' when I was still a high school senior. Has Mrs. Downing come in yet?"

"Five minutes ago; the water ought to be boiling by now."

Everybody on the morning receptionist desk knew Lynn Rogers stopped by the Hospitality Shop whenever she could – unless her father was operating early – for a cup of coffee with Meg Downing. Wife of the Collier Professor of Medicine, Dr. Harris Downing, who occupied one of the endowed chairs on the medical school faculty, Meg was godmother to Lynn and her twin sister, Lisa, younger than Lynn by five minutes.

"That was a nice story in the *Herald* this morning about the operation you did last night," Mabel added. "It's time somebody started giving you credit around here."

"It was touch and go for a while. Have many visitors checked in at the seminar registration desk yet?"

The question gave Lynn an excuse to glance at the corner of the hospital lobby and waiting room that would serve during the next several days as the center of activity for doctors attending the biennial seminar of the Malone Heart Institute. But the tall figure of her ex-husband, Paul, was not in the line at the registration desk.

"Dr. Paul Rogers was the first to register this morning. It seemed like old times to see him come in." Mabel pretended not to

11

notice Lynn's interest in the activity at the seminar registration desk. "He's got a tan and looks relaxed and younger, something he hardly ever did when he was your father's chief assistant in the Institute before —" The switchboard buzzed sharply, drowning out the final words but Lynn knew they would have been "— you and him were divorced."

Had it really been two years, Lynn asked herself as she continued on toward the door to the Hospitality Shop storeroom and Meg's tiny office? Disturbed by the memories, she didn't at first notice a tugging at her long white coat until it came again. Looking down then, she saw a small boy with an anxious look in his eyes.

"Please, lady," he said. "Would you tell me where the bathroom is?"

"It's around the corner and to the left where the sign says —"

Lynn didn't complete the directions, for the look of distress in the boy's eyes told her the state of emergency was beyond his comprehending them. Taking the small black hand, she led him around the corner to the two public toilets that served the waiting room. The door to the one marked "Men" was propped open with a scrub bucket, while the floor was being mopped by an attendant. Pushing open the door of the adjoining one, she glanced in to make sure it wasn't occupied before directing the boy inside.

"Take your time," she told him. "Need any help with your buttons?"

"No'm." The boy scurried into the room. "I kin make it."

"I'll stay here and see that nobody bothers you."

He came out a few minutes later, beaming.

"Feel better?" Lynn asked.

"Yes'm. A bad man tried to rob our house last night and stabbed my daddy in the heart. But a heart doctor operated on him and he's going to be all right."

"I operated on him myself."

"You a surgeon?" the boy asked incredulously.

"Yes. Another ten minutes and your father might not have made it to the hospital alive."

"Mama and me rode in the ambulance. I'm gonna be a doctor when I grow up."

"Good for you. We need more good doctors."

And I need a little boy about your age, Lynn thought as she watched the small figure trot across the lobby toward a sofa where a young black woman – whom Lynn recognized from having spoken to her after the operation last night – was nursing an infant. Turning in the direction the small boy had gone, she crossed the lobby to the sofa where the mother was sitting.

"I checked on your husband by telephone before breakfast, Mrs. Myers," she said. "He's doing fine."

"Thank you, Doctor. They let me see him for a few minutes early this morning."

"Did the police catch the robber?"

The young mother shook her head. "It was one of them Cuban convicts Castro sent over here so he could clean out his jails. I gave the cops a description of him but I guess all them Cubans look alike. They won't never catch him."

Lynn didn't need to be reminded that John Myers' wife spoke the truth. The flood of Cuban refugees from the jails of Havana and elsewhere on the island had been encouraged, even helped by their government, to migrate to Florida. Finding little welcome among the respectable and industrious earlier émigrés, they had sent the crime rate of South Florida soaring. Nor had the smaller flood of Haitians escaping the brutal dictatorship that had ruled that troubled island for so many years helped either.

"Your little boy tells me he's going to be a doctor." Lynn changed the subject.

The young mother smiled and rubbed the boy's shaven skull, then sobered. "Not much chance of that for black folks," she said, "'specially when them Haitians that've been flocking in here are willing to work for slave wages. John says if Mr. Artemus Jones hadn't organized the International Agricultural Workers' Union down here year before last, he probably wouldn't have a job and we'd have to go back to being migrant workers. We lost our first baby several years ago when it was born in a tar paper shack out in Texas where my husband was pickin' tomatoes down near the Rio Grande."

"I lost my first child, too; he didn't breathe well after he was born," said Lynn. "The doctors tried to save him but it wasn't any use."

"I'm sorry to hear that, Doctor. I guess if the union hadn't been organized here in South Florida so farm and packing house workers could live in one place all year, I'd have lost John last night, too. Even then, he wouldn't have made it if you hadn't happened to be right here in the hospital."

"I'm glad I was," said Lynn as she started back across the lobby toward the back door of the Hospitality Shop and Meg Downing's always bubbling coffeepot. "Let me know if you need anything."

It had been her turn to need two years ago when little Paul was born but all the resources of the great hospital had proved to be in vain. Allen Potter, the Chief Anesthesiologist, had used the most advanced techniques for treating the so-often fatal hyaline membrane disease that kept vital oxygen from penetrating the air sacs of little Paul's lungs. Even the most heroic efforts had failed to save the child, however. And when Theodore Malone, denied a son from the pregnancies that had produced three daughters − the older two, twins − blamed the death of his only grandson on Paul Rogers' genes, Lynn had been too distraught to contradict her father and had half believed the untruth.

Actually, she knew, the schism between her and Paul had begun to develop shortly after their return to Miami and Biscayne General from Johns Hopkins, where they'd been married when both were senior medical residents. Theodore Malone demanded absolute loyalty from his assistants and Paul had given it — with little left for his wife, as so often happened in medical marriages.

When, following the baby's death, Paul had been told by the dictator-head of the prestigious Malone Heart Institute that he would never be the successor to the founder and presiding surgical genius of the Institute, the impending break in the marriage had come to a head. Shortly after the divorce became final, Paul had accepted a position as Chief of the Department of Cardiovascular Surgery at the newest of Florida's medical schools in the teeming Tampa-St. Petersburg area. Lynn, in turn, had gone on to become Research Director of the Institute.

"Dr. Rogers," the telephone operator called to Lynn before she could reach the door to Meg Downing's office at the rear of the Hospitality Shop. "Your father would like to see you in his office."

"All right, Mabel."

Lynn hadn't expected the summons to the twenty-first floor quite that soon but she had known it would be coming, once her father saw the story in the morning paper. Changing her course, she went to the express elevator that led directly from the lobby to the two new floors housing the

Malone Heart Institute.

"Go right in, Dr. Rogers," said Essie Taft, Malone's faithful secretary and worshiper for the past twenty years. "He's expecting you."

"Thanks, Essie. I'm sure he is."

Theodore Malone was standing before the broad office window that gave an excellent view of Biscayne Bay, the hotels of Miami Beach to the east, and the shining white cruise ships docked side by side awaiting the afternoon's influx of passengers which had made Miami the Caribbean cruise capital of the United States. He was holding a cup of coffee in his hand.

"You sent for me, Father?" Lynn asked.

"Want some coffee?" Malone never wasted his driving energies on mere words.

"I was on my way to have a cup with Meg Downing in her office. Think I'll wait."

Theodore Malone wheeled upon her, as he might have done a nurse in the operating room who had given him the wrong instrument. At almost fifty-nine, he was a handsome man, tall, a little heavier than he should be, somewhat florid of countenance, and always commanding in appearance. Ever since a spinal cord tumor operation had left his wife, Mildred, paralyzed from the waist down and incapable of sex, Malone had lived in the penthouse apartment of Biscayne Terrace next door to the hospital. A former luxury hotel, the massive structure of stucco and tile had long since been turned into a group of condominiums surrounded by luxuriant gardens and graveled pathways leading directly to the grounds of the tall hospital tower adjoining it. Lynn herself lived there, in the apartment she and Paul had shared before the divorce.

Barely a year ago, Lynn's twin sister, Lisa, now head of the new and widely acclaimed Critical Care Unit of Biscayne General, had also moved into the Terrace Tower. The department Lisa headed, along with the newest and most sophisticated Hyperbaric Laboratory in the world, was housed in the specially constructed two-story wing attached to the massive hospital tower; it also contained the CAT scanner, newest of the sophisticated machines for studying the interior of the body.

"If the Miami *Herald* can be believed, you covered yourself with glory last night — upstaging your father," Theo Malone said heavily. "It's too bad you didn't choose to wait."

"I did what had to be done, when you didn't answer your beeper. The Miami

19

Herald reporter you gave the run of the hospital so he could write up your operations coined the term 'upstaged,' not I. He must monitor the Rescue Squad radio channel twenty-four hours a day. He was here before we took John Myers to the operating room."

"How did you happen to be on duty in Critical Care? That's Lisa's bailiwick."

"She had a date and asked me to sub for her."

"Sleeping around again, I suppose?"

"If she was, she was only following the example you set for us when we were teenagers and Laurel was barely finishing junior high school."

Theo Malone chose to ignore the thrust. His amatory proclivities were no secret at Biscayne General and he made no apologies for them.

"Did you have to rush?" he demanded. "Once the pericardium is aspirated many stab wounds of the heart need no further treatment."

"With the anterior circumflex coronary severed, I hardly think so. Besides, you didn't answer your page," said Lynn curtly. "Of course, it's sometimes hard to hear the beeper, when it's on the floor under a pile of clothing."

"You still took a risk in suturing a main coronary vessel. I doubt that I would have taken the same chance."

"You wouldn't have because you haven't had enough practice in microsurgical techniques to put the cut ends back together successfully," Lynn said bluntly. "You *did* send me to St. Louis to learn the technique, remember? So you can't actually fault me for knowing what to do."

"I stopped in Critical Care on the way up and your patient does seem to be doing well," Theo Malone admitted somewhat grudgingly. "But he still could develop a clot at the suture line and suffer a sudden large infarct."

"That's why he's being watched around the clock, by nurses, residents, and the computer. If it does happen, you may still get to do the new operation on him."

"Perhaps while the seminar is going? I hope you're thinking of that possibility."

"I am — with good reason, when the man's life is at stake. I do commend you for your concern, though," Lynn added dryly. "Don't forget that you also taught me never to leave anything to chance."

"What does that mean?"

"We're giving John Myers heparin to

decrease the likelihood of a clot. As a precautionary measure, I also took out a piece of his long saphenous vein from the upper thigh and did a by-pass to carry blood around the wound in the artery in case a thrombus forms at the suture line."

"I trained you well," Theo Malone conceded, then changed the subject abruptly. "You're a handsome woman, Lynn. Why haven't you married again?"

"Because you drove away the man I love."

"He couldn't give you a viable son."

"That was no more Paul's fault than it was mine — or yours."

"Mine?" Malone demanded with some indignation. "Why?"

"You could have devoted just a little of the Institute's money and time to the study of hyaline membrane disease. Instead you allocated the entire research budget to new operations on the heart just to make headlines and cover yourself with glory. With money for research someone might have discovered how to obtain the surfactant they're using now to let oxygen get through the walls of a newborn's air sacs. To say nothing of the simple fact that a few injections of betamethasone, when I went into premature labor, could have insured that I would have a baby able to breathe for itself."

"You can't expect me to solve all the problems of medicine," Malone said shortly and Lynn had the satisfaction of knowing she had finally reached him where he could be hurt.

"No, I suppose not," she admitted. "After all, you couldn't even raise three daughters to love you as a father and not hate you for deserting their mother."

"All three of you had a beautiful home, the best schools, clubs, clothes, everything a girl could want."

"Everything, except a loving father who appreciated what we did. Do you remember the day I came home from the swimming meet in junior high and told you I'd won the butterfly class? No, of course you don't because you never even listened when we talked to you."

"I was probably busy thinking about an important case."

"You'd come home for dinner – one of the few times I remember ever seeing you at the dinner table. I was riding my bicycle up the drive on the way home from the club and saw your Jaguar in the driveway; even then you had to drive the sportiest car in town. Seeing it made me happy, though, because for once I could brag a little to you about something I'd done. You met me as I was coming up the drive and I remember calling to you that I had won the butterfly. Do you know what you said?"

"I don't remember. I must have had a medical problem – "

"Miami had good surgeons, even then; you didn't have to do all of it yourself. 'That's nice, dear,' you said in the same tone you would have used to one of your Golden Retrievers if it had brought you a wild duck you'd shot. I knew you hadn't even heard me, just like you weren't around to listen when any of us, including Mother, needed the advice of a man, a father, or a husband – none of which you were."

"Lynn! Stop it!" Malone's voice was sharp now; the same tone he used to his staff. "Nothing is to be gained by rehashing what's done and over with."

"Maybe you're right. Do you need me any more?"

"I want to ask a favor of you."

"Like what?"

"Would you see that your mother doesn't come to the reception tonight?"

"Why?" Lynn gave her father a startled look – tinged with anger. "You know it's

24

one of the only chances she ever gets to see her old friends, since that spinal cord tumor put her in a wheelchair for the rest of her life — and made her give you the divorce you wanted."

Theo Malone didn't flinch at the accusation. "I just think it would be less embarrassing for Mildred if she isn't there."

"You still haven't told me why."

"I'm going to announce my marriage to Elena Sanchez tonight and present her as my wife to the people at the opening reception of the seminar."

"You're going to do what?" Lynn stared at him in disbelief.

"Elena and I were married when we went to the State Medical Association meeting in Jacksonville a couple of months ago — by the Bishop of St. Augustine."

"Doctors don't marry their mistresses! It isn't good for their image."

"Don't be snide!" Theo Malone snapped. "Elena and I would have been married a year ago, if she could have gotten the approval of the Vatican."

"Don't tell me you're becoming a Catholic, too?"

"Of course not. Now will you persuade Mildred not to come tonight?"

"I'll warn her – I owe her that much, but she's going to have to decide this for herself. Besides, I've got to talk to Lisa and Laurel about it. Perhaps you'd rather none of us came at all."

"On the contrary. People will talk if you don't."

"People will talk, my God, how they will talk!" Then she sobered. "That doesn't bother you, does it?"

"I don't give a damn what anybody says or thinks, but I did feel an obligation to let Mildred know ahead of time."

"I suppose even the Great God Malone would be expected to have that much feeling, I'm glad to see you're that human. But why flaunt your mistress before your peers and their wives tonight and humiliate your wife – to say nothing of your daughters?"

"If you have to know – Elena is two months' pregnant."

"Why would you legalize this child when you didn't give your name to your other bastards?" Lynn asked, then added before he could answer, "It's inflation, isn't it?"

"What the hell are you talking about?"

Lynn shook her head slowly, almost with an expression of disbelief – but not quite. "I knew inflation was eating into the endow-

26

ment fund of the Institute. The Sanchez family is one of the richest in Little Havana. How much did you get for your dowry?"

Theodore Malone had the grace to flush at the note of contempt in his oldest daughter's voice. "Elena's father is giving two million to the endowment fund."

"Your services as a stud come high," Lynn commented acidly, but Malone chose not to answer.

II

Damn, was Lisa Malone's first thought, when she saw the "Out of Order" sign on the service elevator. *Now I'll have to run the gauntlet of a lot of male conventioneers on the way to breakfast when I look exactly like a hooker going home from an all-night job. Which is what I really am,* she admitted, as she pushed the regular elevator button — *except that I don't get paid.*

This time she was lucky. When the elevator stopped it was empty, except for a popeyed young man and a mousy-looking girl, probably on their honeymoon and a little hung over from sex and the bottle of wine the hotel thoughtfully placed in the rooms of the just married.

The elevator didn't stop again until it reached the lobby. When the honeymoon couple got out, Lisa held the "Lower Level" button down so the doors would close immediately.

The lower level was mostly devoted to expensive boutiques, gift shops and jewelry stores, plus the inevitable barbershop and beauty parlor. The stores had not yet opened so traffic was at a minimum as she made her way rapidly through the almost empty corridors to the ramp leading upward to the circular driveway that gave access to the marquee and the lobby.

"Get me a taxi, Amos – quick," she told the uniformed black doorman, who was somewhat startled by her sudden appearance from the stairway to the lower level.

"Right away, Doctor," he said and blew his whistle, summoning a cab from the ranks of those waiting on the street outside.

"Nemmind, Dr. Malone," Amos said as Lisa fumbled in her evening purse for a coin while he was opening the door of the cab. "You and Dr. Shelbourne saved my nephew from bleedin' to death a month or so ago, when the Rescue Squad brought him to the Emergency Room after he got in a fight with some other teen-agers. It's me that owes you."

As Lisa got hurriedly into the cab, with no concern for the liberal display of shapely nylon-clad thigh revealed by the short evening dress she wore, two men stepped through the outer door.

"Did you see that?" she heard one of them say. "I wonder how much she gets a night?"

"That's no hooker!" his companion answered. "She's one of the Malone twins, both doc —"

The closing door of the cab shut off the final word but Lisa didn't bother to resent the implication of the first man's statement. Ever since a sudden rush of sex hormones with the onset of puberty at thirteen had brought a rapid change from a gangling teen-ager into a lithe blond beauty, she'd been accustomed to the open admiration of men wherever she went.

As identical twins, she and Lynn were practically the same person but some things hadn't quite turned out the same where both were concerned. The chameleonlike blooming following puberty had turned Lynn into a stately beauty along the lines of their mother's Colonial Virginia heritage. But although the gene pattern passing to both of them was the same, Lisa had instead acquired a vibrant sensuality that made the two, however identical in physical characteristics, as different as day from night.

"Biscayne General! The Emergency Room entrance," Lisa told the driver and leaned back in the corner of the cab.

Getting stoned with Roberto Galvez last night had been a mistake, Lisa decided as the taxi turned right off traffic-clogged Biscayne Boulevard into a less congested cross street leading to the bayfront and the massive tower of Biscayne General with the lower height of the Biscayne Terrace condominium complex adjoining it. Still it had been an evening to remember, for as a Fellow in Cardiac Surgery at the Malone Heart Institute – before returning to Caracas and a lucrative practice doing coronary bypass operations on oil-rich millionaires – Roberto had always found easy access to prime Colombian marijuana. Besides, he was a tiger in bed, a combination Lisa hadn't found very often with anyone else.

A binge like last night was hard on a girl's constitution, though. Especially when thirty-odd minutes from now at nine o'clock – in her capacity as Director of the brand-new Critical Care Unit – Lisa was scheduled to host the first of the hour-long biennial seminars of the Malone Heart Institute scheduled for the next few days. So even though her head was splitting and her mouth tasted like a dirty sock, what was she doing in a taxi at eight-thirty in the morning, clutching an evening purse and wearing a considerably rumpled short formal summer dress? Not that she'd been in it much of the night.

Fortunately, as a safeguard against just such an emergency as was happening this morning, Lisa kept a complete working outfit of white Dacron slacks and blouse, plus white shoes, in her locker in the Nurses' Lounge adjoining the Critical Care Unit where the first hour-long meeting of the three-day seminar would be held. With luck, too, a quick shower would erase some of the cosmetic damage resulting from smoking hash, drinking vodka, and making love repeatedly with Roberto Galvez.

The evening had begun with vodka gimlets almost exactly twelve hours ago in Sloppy Joe's Bar, and had been terminated somewhere around two in the morning by mutual exhaustion. Roberto – *damn him,* she thought – hadn't even been gallant enough to get up when the hotel operator

31

had rung the phone at eight for the morning call Lisa had left last night. But she really couldn't blame him for she'd barely had time to dress and grab a taxi at the marquee of the downtown luxury hotel where the Venezuelan surgeon was staying.

"Seen the morning paper yet?" the taxi driver asked.

"No."

"Biscayne General certainly made the headlines last night."

Lisa didn't ask why. With her head throbbing and her stomach in spasm, this was no time to encourage a talkative taxi driver.

Unfortunately that didn't stop him. "A robber stabbed a fellow in the heart and the Rescue Squad that brought him to the hospital had given him up for dead. But a smart young doctor in what they're now calling the Critical Care Unit got his heart beating again so one of the heart surgeons could operate."

"Was the surgeon Dr. Malone?"

"This was a woman; I think her name was Rogers. Can you imagine a woman operating on a heart? The paper says she used a microscope to sew a big artery back together and save the patient's life."

Good for Lynn, Lisa thought. At last she'd

had a chance to prove what everyone in the hospital already knew – except her father, who refused to let her operate alone – namely, that she was as skilled a cardiovascular surgeon as he was. Not that Theo Malone would ever admit it.

When the taxi came to a stop in front of Biscayne General, Lisa pulled a five-dollar bill from her purse. Handing it to the driver, she opened the door and dashed up the short walk to the somewhat secluded side entrance to the new wing that housed the Critical Care Unit and the even newer Hyperbaric Laboratory. She was almost at the door when it opened suddenly and a tall man in a white Navy summer uniform stepped out.

Moving as fast as she was, Lisa had no time to stop before crashing against him and would have fallen into a Spanish bayonet bush with its murderous thorns, if he hadn't caught her just in time. The tight embrace of two muscular arms kept her from tumbling into the shrubbery but was, it seemed to her, prolonged slightly more than was needed, especially when his hands settled on two strategic areas of her body.

"You've had your feel, so let me go," she snapped.

The arms in the short-sleeved white uniform released her but not before she glimpsed a shock of red hair and blue eyes in the midst of an attractive masculine face that was now split by a broad grin. Hurrying through the door he held open for her, she raced for the Nurses' Lounge, hoping to reach it before anyone else saw her wearing a frock that was anything but suitable for holding a medical seminar early in the morning.

The lounge was empty and Lisa started pulling off her dress as she moved toward her locker. Tossing off the rumpled garment she shrugged herself out of the slip. Reaching into the top portion of the locker, she found the bottle of vodka kept there for emergencies and, unscrewing the top, took a long swallow, shuddering as the fiery liquid poured down her gullet into a still queasy stomach. With the second swallow, she gave a silent prayer of thanks that, since vodka was odorless none of the doctors who would shortly be gathering in the Critical Care Unit for the seminar would be able to smell it on her breath.

Shoving the vodka bottle back into the locker, Lisa kicked off her shoes and, clad now only in sheer bra and equally sheer pantyhose, reached back to unhook the bra and hang it over the open door of the locker before removing the remaining garment. No time was left to admire in the full length mirror on the shower door the lovely body Roberto Galvez's skillful hands had caressed last night. Or the blond waves that, thankfully, fell into place in the morning with a few strokes of a hairbrush. Mildred Malone had given her own aristocratic Virginian features to her twin daughters, almost as their only maternal heritage. But the slim torsos with just the right fullness to the breasts, the firmness of rounded hips and long slender legs that made them both startlingly beautiful had come from their father.

Stepping into the shower, Lisa turned on the cold water and leaned back so the pulsing stream wouldn't touch her hair. Gasping from the shock of the cold, she quickly lathered her body and turned in the shower stream to rinse it before shutting off the water. Emerging from the stall, she seized a large nubby towel from a rack beside it and started rubbing her body to a lovely pink glow. The cold water had erased much of the dregs from last night's debauch, too, even as the vodka found its way into Lisa's bloodstream and sent her finger ends tingling.

While brushing her hair, Lisa briefly debated taking another swallow of the vodka but decided against the idea. Many of those attending the Malone Institute Seminars had served as residents or Fellows at Biscayne General. Which meant she already knew most of those who might come to her opening hour, titled "Critical Care Services," in the newest department of the hospital. A few had even known her rather intimately, so it was just as well, she decided, not to risk a slurring of speech or a slip of the tongue.

Her skin glowing from the cold shower and the vodka, Lisa stepped through the door into the Critical Care Unit at exactly nine o'clock to face a small audience of doctors gathered for the opening hour of the Malone Institute Seminar.

Chapter 2

"I'm glad Lisa managed to get you assigned to her Critical Care Unit, Laurel." Mildred Malone watched her youngest daughter gulp down the last of her coffee before standing up to smooth the doubleknit white fabric of her new hospital resident's uniform over hips that needed no girdling.

"I don't get to see many patients with tropical diseases in that department but, after the year I spent in Zaire with the WHO, it will be a relief not to face a hundred stool specimens lined up on a laboratory shelf every morning."

Like the Malone twins, Laurel had inherited her father's height rather than her mother's petite figure. All three, however, had received the genes necessary to replicate the delicately cut features and beauty that characterized the Virginia aristocrats of the Randolph family, one of the noblest in the Colony. Laurel carried her figure well, too.

Though not a beauty by the standards of Colonial Virginia, she was nevertheless handsome by any other, with her deep red hair, mobile features, dark intelligent eyes, and sharp wit.

A champion swimmer since high school, Laurel could have gone on to a professional career in sports, but like her two sisters, had chosen to study medicine, after graduating from the University of Miami. She had not chosen Johns Hopkins as they did. Intrigued by tropical medicine, she had spent the four years needed for the Doctor of Medicine degree at the prestigious School of Tropical Medicine at Lousiana State University in New Orleans. After two years of residency following graduation, plus a year with the World Health Organization, Laurel had recently returned home to start a final year of residency in the field at Biscayne General.

"Are you going to see your father?" Mildred Malone asked.

"If he summons me. One doesn't enter the royal presence without an invitation."

"Theo's not as bad as he's painted by a lot of people. It's just that he always wanted to be a leader —"

"And when you couldn't produce a son for him — probably more because of the arrangement of his own X and Y chromosomes than yours – he shed you. Not that he hadn't already ditched you long ago for a series of mistresses, culminating with that Sanchez bitch."

"Now, Laurel!" her mother chided gently. "Elena comes from an aristocratic Cuban family. Before they were driven out by Castro, the Sanchezes were prominent in financial and social circles in Havana. Besides, your father is a passionate man and, after my operation, I wasn't –"

"The phrase is 'a good lay.'" Laurel leaned down to kiss her mother fondly. "There must have been some sex in our family back then to produce three daughters, so let Father have his mistresses. After all, Dex Parnell may be his son, too. Helen was the first one Father took though God only knows how many he's had since."

"I don't hold Helen or any of the others against Theo," her mother protested. "Especially after he made Dexter his personal lawyer."

"Only because you don't graduate from the Harvard Law School at the head of your class without knowing how to find the best ways to foil the IRS. 'By, Mother. My thirty-six-hour stint on duty doesn't end until seven. I only ran home to put on fresh whites because a lot of eligible male doctors will be attending the seminar and I don't want to bring discredit on my beautiful twin sisters by comparison. By the way, I promised Dex I'd stop by the house in Coconut Grove on the way to Biscayne General and swab little Dexter's throat for streptococcus."

"Dear me," said Mildred Malone. "Has he got that again?"

"It's probably only a cold, but you know Kelley. With five kids, plus another *in utero,* even a sneeze is a disaster."

Outside in the bright Miami sunlight, Laurel paused for a moment to allow the beauty of the bay separating the larger city from Miami Beach to soak into her being. Mullet were jumping in the sheer joy of being alive and far out in the bay a girl in a white maillot was swinging in wide circles at the end of a long ski-rope, drawn by a swift runabout. Laurel herself had spent many a happy afternoon skiing on Biscayne Bay, though usually much farther south in the waters around Key Largo, where Theo Malone owned a waterfront cottage.

She'd missed all this during the year she'd spent in far away Zaire at the station maintained there by the World Health

Organization. It was particularly pleasant now to be able to swat one of the mosquitoes buzzing in the luxuriant garden facing the street, without having to examine it closely to see whether it was one of the ubiquitous Anopheles Gambiae variety that made the malaria parasite a constant threat in Africa. Pausing to pluck a brilliant red hibiscus blossom from her mother's favorite plant, she stuck it into her hair above her left ear before sliding under the wheel of the new compact she'd purchased the day after returning to Miami. Then pulling out into the street before the house, she headed southward toward the tall white column of Biscayne General and the first of the day's emergencies.

II

At exactly eight-thirty that same Friday morning, Dr. Mortimer Weyer had parked his battered Volkswagen behind the storefront building housing the Liberty City satellite clinic operated by Biscayne General and the Miami Health Department. Located in the midst of an inner city area that had been devastated by its largely black inhabitants during the riots of May 1980, following the death of a black man at the hands of the police, the clinic occupied almost the only undamaged building in an area of more than a dozen blocks. A scene of nearly complete desolation, it was proof that angered citizens could create almost as much destruction in a few days as any aerial bombardment.

As Mort Weyer extricated his stocky frame from the confined space of the small car, he could see by the long line of patients waiting in the warm June sunlight outside the clinic door that his second day on a new job would be fully as hectic as the first. Turning the corner on his way to the front of the building, he almost stepped on an old man slumped against the trunk of a mango tree heavy with the ripening yellow-green fruit.

From long experience, Mort could recognize the type without asking; large cities such as New York − from whence he had come two days earlier − were full of them. Living on welfare or Social Security checks, plus the food stamps unscrupulous grocery stores were willing to exchange for cheap muscatel or the sweet port that packed over a third the alcoholic wallop of straight 86 proof whiskey, they belonged in a class by themselves.

Something else about this particular unconscious derelict aroused Mort Weyer's instinct as a highly trained and conscientious doctor, however. Moving along the line of waiting patients, none of whom seemed to be ill enough to demand immediate attention, he paused beside the old man and knelt to feel his pulse. His eyes were shut and he breathed with, to Mort's trained eyes, an alarming slowness. When the doctor reached down to lift the scraggly, bearded chin, the snoring stopped but he still showed no sign of returning consciousness.

"How long has this man been here?" he asked the waiting crowd.

No one answered, until a voice at the end of the line drawled: "He was here sleeping it off when most of us arrived, Doc. Haven't you been away from that fancy center over on Biscayne Boulevard long enough to recognize a wino when you see one?"

Mort gave the speaker a hard, even glance, then blinked, for the man was something to see. Six and a half feet tall at least, he wore platform shoes with purple uppers, purple slacks and tee-shirt, and a large purple cap.

"How about helping me take him into the

clinic, friend?" Mort said quickly.

"Looks like Whitey goes to the head of the line like always." The tall black's drawl was deliberately provocative as he uncoiled his long body into a standing position. "Even if he is a derelict."

"People don't use words like derelict unless they made it well past the fourth grade. What's your name?"

"Artemus Jones, shop steward for the International Agricultural Workers' Union. Around here they call me the Purple People Eater." The black man made no move to answer the request for help.

"If you don't want to help a sick old man, I don't give a damn." Taking the comatose patient under the armpits, Mort lifted the pitifully thin body to cradle it in his arms.

Not at all to Mort's surprise, the tall black moved quickly to lift the lower part of the inert body. Between them they carried the comatose man into the building, depositing him on a table in one of the clinic's two examining-treatment rooms. At the same moment, a plump, black nurse in a tight, white nylon uniform arrived, panting.

"Sorry I'm late, Dr. Weyer," she said. "Had to take my little boy to the day nursery first."

"That's all right, Mrs. Bullock." Although this was only his second day at the clinic, Mort had recognized that she was a capable nurse. More important, she knew most of the patients and their histories by heart, a great help to a physician on this sort of a job.

"Do either of you know who he is?" Mort asked.

Artemus Jones answered. "His name is Jacques LeMoyne but we call him Jock. Papa Doc Duvalier ran him out of Haiti years ago but he managed to bring a lot of money with him."

"What's he doing here, then?"

"Old Jock loves people almost as much as he does whiskey, so he lives in Liberty City and helps folks that can't help themselves. He's been dried out at Biscayne General so many times, his liver's as tough as shoe leather."

"Mr. LeMoyne has had a lot of hospital admissions for cirrhosis, Dr. Weyer, but he still won't stop drinking," the nurse confirmed.

"Why waste time on an old Whitey wino?" Artemus Jones demanded contemptuously as Mort was making a rapid but thorough examination of the sick man. "There are sick people outside."

Mort wheeled upon Jones and, seeing the hot anger in his eyes, the tall man — though obviously no slouch himself physically — drew back a step.

"What did *you* come here for?" Mort demanded. "You look healthy enough to me."

"A shot of methadone. I like it better through the needle."

"I don't give a damn if you mainline it, Jones. The nurse will give you the shot, then get the hell out of my clinic."

"Hell, Doc, I didn't mean anything," Jones protested. "You're new here so maybe you don't know the sick are to be taken in order of — "

"I'm not treating somebody that's fool enough to become addicted to narcotics before a man who's obviously dying of circulatory collapse and needs help immediately." Mort turned to the nurse. "Get a Rescue Squad out here right away to take him to Biscayne General, Mrs. Bullock."

Mort Weyer's angry voice was heard by everybody in the building and even outside, for he knew from experience that if he didn't establish his authority immediately as director of the clinic, he'd only have trouble later on.

"I'll get the Critical Care Unit at the

hospital on the phone," the nurse promised. "The clinic clerk will call the Rescue Squad. They should be here any minute."

Mort picked up the phone when it rang and said: "This is Dr. Mort Weyer –"

"Peter Shelbourne, Critical Care," said a brisk voice. "Can I help you, Doctor?"

The tone was faintly patronizing and Mort understood why. To a resident physician at Biscayne General, any doctor on duty at the Liberty City satellite clinic – even though it was part of the hospital – had to be a lesser being. An older physician putting in the years necessary before starting to receive Social Security or draw from his Keogh Fund would be likely to take such a job. Or perhaps an FMG – Foreign Medical Graduate – waiting to take the necessary examinations for licensure in the United States. None of that made any difference to Mort, however, who already had Board certification in Internal Medicine besides completing an additional two-year Fellowship in Cardiology at Bellevue Hospital in New York City.

"I'm sending you a man named Jacques LeMoyne," he told Dr. Shelbourne. "He's in bad shape."

"Old Jock usually is, Dr. Weyer."

"This time don't make a snap diagnosis of cirrhosis of the liver and put this guy away on a medical ward, where a few hours from now you're going to be surprised to find him dead." Mort's tone was curt. "There's no smell of wine on his breath and he's on the verge of circulatory collapse — "

"What's your diagnosis, Doctor?" The resident's tone had changed abruptly to one of interest and respect.

"I'm not sure; may be toxic shock from something. But if you don't want to find him on a slab in the hospital morgue before the day's over, I'd suggest putting him on a respirator and having a pacemaker standing by, too. Something's knocking the hell out of his circulation but I can't tell what it is with the resources at my disposal."

"Will do," said Dr. Shelbourne. "We'll keep you informed."

"I'm coming over for the Malone Institute reception tonight," Mort added. "Am I correct in understanding that all of the staff is invited?"

"Everybody and his girl friend."

"I'd like to take a look at LeMoyne then — if he's still alive."

"You've got the run of the hospital, Doctor," said Shelbourne. "By the way, where did you take your residency in Internal Medicine?"

"At Bellevue with a two-year research Fellowship in Cardiology under Eric Sondheim."

"Take my advice and don't mention Sondheim where the Great God Malone can hear you," Shelbourne warned. "Ever since Sondheim published that paper last year denouncing vascular surgeons for doing too many coronary by-pass operations, Malone practically has a stroke when his name is mentioned."

"Thanks for the warning. As it happens, my name was on that paper – as one of the co-authors."

He heard Shelbourne whistle softly into the telephone. "One more question – and no offense. What's somebody with your training doing at the Liberty City clinic?"

"Put it down to love for my fellow man, Doctor, and thanks for the tip. I'll try to stay out of Malone's way."

Mort wasn't surprised that a resident at Biscayne General had been impressed with the name of Dr. Eric Sondheim. Acknowledged by most of his peers as one of the foremost cardiologists in the country, Sondheim's insistence that a sizable number of coronary-damaged patients could live functional and effective lives both before and after infarct, with practically no restrictions on their activity, had earned him the concentrated enmity of operation-conscious heart surgeons everywhere.

Actually, Mort himself couldn't have explained exactly why he'd taken the job advertised in the JAMA for a doctor in a worker's clinic in Miami, except that it afforded him an opportunity to return to the place where he was born. The faintly remembered land of palm fronds, bright sunlight, and rippling waters seemed a paradise after the realities of dreary Bellevue spread along the banks of the heavily polluted East River in New York City. Plus the fact that the job in the clinic, however menial for a Board-certified specialist, would let him put away enough money in a year or two to open an office for private practice in one of the Miami suburbs.

The Rescue Squad arrived in time to break off Mort's reverie and the two attendants skillfully transferred the sick man to a rolling stretcher, sliding it into an ambulance whose red lights were still flashing.

"Watch out for respiratory failure; he's near circulatory collapse," Mort warned them. "You may have to use the pacemaker."

"We'll put him on the respirator as soon as we get him in the ambulance and zap him if his heart stops, Doctor," the medical technician who rode inside the ambulance promised. "Jock's an old friend, but most of the time he smells different – like a winery."

"What you smell on his breath now is ketosis. It can be almost as dangerous to him as arsenic."

III

After Lynn Rogers left her father's office, Theo Malone rang for a fresh cup of coffee. Essie Taft brought it immediately, heavily laced with the cream forbidden by the diet Dr. Harris Downing was trying, with little success, to make Malone follow. As he stood at the window drinking the coffee, the world-famous heart surgeon had no eyes for the beauty of the bay and the riot of spring color in the well-kept gardens around the hospital and the adjoining Biscayne Terrace Condominiums. Rather, he was anticipating the gasps of amazement and admiration – from the male contingent at least – when he presented his lush, young Cuban mistress, now his wife of two months, to those assembled that evening for the first social event of the seminar staged every two years by the Malone Heart Institute — the informal reception for guests, their wives, and visitors.

Buoyed by the thought, Malone turned to his desk and the high-backed chair that was like a throne — as indeed it was for the ruler of the new two-floor addition to the great hospital. The feeling of exhilaration drove from Theo Malone's mind all memory of Dr. Harris Downing's warnings about his blood pressure on his last physical examination. And, particularly, the need for moderation in the control of his so-often explosive temper, to say nothing of his rather hyperactive sex life, against which Downing had also advised.

At almost fifty-nine, Theo Malone told himself once again, he was in the prime of life and of his meteoric career. Two things only remained to crown that career. First was the arrival of a patient at the hospital whose heart was beyond repair. And, second, was the birth, some six months from now, of a son to bear his name.

Construction of the two new stories atop the hospital tower to accommodate the

Malone Heart Institute had come about over the considerable objections of both staff and medical school faculty. They could do little to block it, however, for the addition itself had been made possible by the gratitude of a billionaire patient, whose pain from angina pectoris had been relieved by a coronary by-pass operation under the skilled hands of Dr. Malone himself.

To the patient, removing the agonizing pain with its fear of impending death had seemed a miracle, although the operation involved only an ordinary procedure in cardiac surgery, similar to thousands being performed all over the country every year. This fact Dr. Malone had carefully kept from the happy and grateful billionaire – hence the gift for establishing the Institute.

Heavily endowed from the same source, as was the expense of construction, the Institute itself had cost the university and the medical school nothing. Yet other surgeons on the staff and faculty could see no reason for the separate operating rooms, laboratories, and even an intensive care unit, particularly when these facilities were used solely by Malone and his personal staff of residents and Fellows, as well as the Research Director.

No one so lowly as an intern at Biscayne

General was even allowed above the twentieth floor now. In fact, few of the staff had been there except by invitation of the Director during one of his biennial seminars, when Malone performed newly developed operative procedures before packed galleries of visitors. In the new addition, Dr. Theodore Malone ruled as a czar, a potentate who might be hated by his subjects but was given free rein because of his worldwide reputation.

The office of the Institute Director was furnished in keeping with the importance of the doctor who occupied it. Photos of famous and grateful former patients, from kings and sheiks to motion picture and television stars, as well as prominent politicians who saw that the Biscayne University Medical School received its share of government grants and more, occupied almost one entire wall of the office. Another was taken up by certificates of membership in learned societies and awards from others. Topping it all was a portrait of the great man himself, painted by Salvador Dali, hanging on the wall behind the massive desk.

By means of an array of buttons and switches on that desk, even the lowliest member of the Director's retinue could be summoned into the royal presence at will.

There he would stand before the anger of the surgeon because of a dropped instrument, an incorrect report of a laboratory test, or even the death of an experimental animal. Upon a bank of closed circuit television monitors, too, Dr. Malone could watch the activities going on at any time in the three operating rooms of the Institute, merely by flicking a switch.

During the three days of the biennial seminar, heart surgeons from countries throughout the world would hear described the latest miracles being performed at the world-famous Institute. If suitable patients could be found, they would actually see the operations and experimental procedures performed during the sessions. There, in turn, would be created tomorrow's newspaper and TV headlines in press releases prepared by Malone's personal publicity staff with photographs by the Institute photographer.

This morning, however, the Director wasn't particularly concerned with such details. He could be sure that under Lynn's capable direction, plans had long since been made and the schedule set up for operative procedures. They included a new technique of coronary artery by-pass he would demonstrate an hour from now as the seminar program proceeded. The same was true for the ward walks, lectures, and both motion picture and closed circuit television programs to be staged during the three days, including the opening reception this evening and the final luncheon for ex-residents and Fellows on Sunday.

Lifting the white telephone on his desk, Malone told his secretary: "Get me Dr. Sanchez, Essie. I want to give him some last minute instructions for the surgical clinic at ten o'clock."

"I'll page him, Dr. Malone. He was just by here so he can't be far away."

Dr. Ernesto Sanchez knew better than to try cashing in on the fact that his employer was now his brother-in-law. Two minutes after he heard his name over the paging system, he was standing before Malone's desk.

"Damn it, Ernesto!" said Theo Malone. "You've got to find me a case for the new operation before the seminar is over."

"I have tried, Doctor, but no suitable patient has come to the emergency room."

"We would have had one last night if Lynn hadn't been so damned efficient."

"It was a brilliant operation."

"There's no place for brilliance here except

in my own operations," Malone barked. "Understand?"

"Yes, sir."

"Tell Peter Shelbourne to find me a patient with a heart damaged beyond repair, or his application for a Fellowship may not be approved."

"I will do my best," Ernesto promised, then dared to add: "In any event, the procedure of patching a septal defect with two umbrellas you're going to perform tomorrow will be dramatic enough."

"That operation has already been done in New Orleans. I trained most of the surgeons who will be here at the seminar and they expect me to show them something new and dramatic. Something they can take back to their own clinics and get publicity with in the media. You don't do that by repeating someone else's discoveries, Ernesto."

Or by stealing other men's procedures and changing them just enough to call them yours, Sanchez thought as he left the office. He was careful not to put the conviction into words.

A buzzer on Malone's desk sounded softly and he picked up the telephone. "Yes. What is it?"

"Mr. Dexter Parnell would like to speak

to you for a moment."

"Put him on," Malone said resignedly.

"He's here, Doctor. Shall I send him in?"

"All right. Call O.R. Three and tell them I'll be a few minutes late in starting the by-pass."

Dexter Parnell was broad-shouldered and handsome, a solid, if unimaginative man in his early thirties. Moreover, he wasn't afraid of Malone but knew very well where his best interests lay.

"Good morning, Doctor."

"What is it, Dex?" Malone demanded testily. "I don't have much time."

"We may not have to go into court against old Jock LeMoyne to get title to that house he owns in the block where the partnership plans to build the rent-subsidy housing unit."

"Plans to, hell! We're going to! What's the hitch now?"

"I went by the place this morning to make Jock another offer. The neighbors told me he'd been taken to the satellite clinic but the new doctor there told me on the phone that he'd sent Jock to Biscayne Gen—"

"They'll only dry him out and send him back, as stubborn as ever."

"This doctor sounded as if he knew his

business. He says Jock's in bad shape and may not make it."

"The title would still be tied up in the bastard's estate."

"I don't think so," said Dexter Parnell. "I've been looking into old Jock's family background, trying to find a relative we could pay to have him declared incompetent so we could take over. As far as records in this country are concerned, though, he's a man without a relative and I'm sure the Duvaliers took over all his property after they booted him out of Haiti."

"Good work," said Theo Malone. "What next?"

"If Jock dies, we'll have the county judge's office file for probate and declare that he died intestate. We ought to have title in a few months, and at our own price. The County Housing Authority's anxious to get Liberty City cleaned up as fast as possible so we shouldn't have any trouble going right ahead with the project."

"You're a bright boy, Dex." Theo Malone stood up. "Let's pray that Jock doesn't make it."

"I've got still another card up my sleeve," said the lawyer. "From what I hear about Jock in Liberty City, he's sort of a Good

Samaritan. Through the years he's kept a fast boat moored down among the Keys and knows that area and the southern Bahamas like the back of his hand. Between drinking bouts, he's been running cocaine that he picks up off ships from Colombia and he's also been bringing in groups of refugees. First it was those Cuban dregs Castro emptied out of his jails and mental institutions but lately Jock's been picking up Haitians. Got a bunch of 'em living in the house in Liberty City."

"Then we've got him by the balls. Call the sheriff; he owes me a few favors."

"Putting old Jock in jail would only mean tying up the title to the property," Dex pointed out. "If he lives, I'd rather go to him and make a deal. We don't turn him in for running dope and he sells us the property at a fair price."

"At a *low* price," Theo Malone corrected him. "The son-of-a-bitch has held us up for six months already and I'm not in the habit of letting people push me around."

"Either way, it looks as if we're in the driver's seat. By the way, it's nice to have Laurel home again."

"I managed to get her a residency in Tropical Medicine, though why she'd want it, I can't see," said Theo Malone. "There's no money in that field."

In the lobby of the great hospital, Dexter Parnell met Laurel Malone as she was coming through the entrance. "I was going to have you paged," he told her. "What did you think of little Dex?"

"He's probably just coming down with a cold but I did a throat culture for strep and started him on Pentids anyway. Kelley looks fine, even if you do seem to be trying to turn her into a brood sow."

"We both enjoy it," the lawyer said with a chuckle, "so why not?"

"After the next one's born, get your gynecologist to slip a laparoscope through her abdominal wall and clamp off her tubes permanently. Then you can have your fun without turning her into a hag at thirty."

"We've talked about it," said Dex. "How does it feel to be home again?"

"Like heaven, after a year in the outlands of Zaire."

"You haven't seen Liberty City. Months after the riot it still looks almost like those pictures of Nagasaki after the first atomic bomb was dropped."

"What takes you out there? Harvard Law School graduate students don't have poor black people for clients."

"Some of my classmates do, running store-front clinics in slum areas. I felt a little guilty about accepting a cushy job as your father's legal adviser, until the Liberty City riots gave me a way to salve my conscience."

"How's that?"

"A dozen or more blocks of the area were practically destroyed by fire and vandalism in the May riots. Your father and a group of high-bracket doctors have formed a limited partnership, with me as the general partner, to build a large rent subsidy housing unit for low-income people."

"Low rent?" Laurel's eyebrows lifted. "I don't see Father doing that."

"The government will give a rent subsidy to the people who'll live there, if their income isn't up to a certain figure. On top of that, the IRS allows investors who built that kind of housing to write off something like one per cent per month for a hundred months, a bonanza for high-bracket people like your father."

"I knew there was a trick somewhere, if Father was involved."

"It's no trick! The poor come out ahead

with decent housing at a price they can afford."

"While Father gets a rake-off and you salve your conscience?"

Parnell flushed and Laurel put her hand on his sleeve in a soothing gesture. "Forget I said it, Dex. What brings you here so early in the morning?"

"The owner of the last three lots in one of the blocks we need is an old wino named Jacques LeMoyne. He won't sell, so it looks as if we'll have to declare him incompetent and put someone in as his guardian — unless he solves our problem by dying first."

"What makes you think he might?"

"When I went by Liberty City early this morning to make our final offer, they told me Jock had been taken to the satellite clinic but a new doctor out there sent him to Biscayne General as an emergency. Jock's been hospitalized with cirrhosis of the liver several times but this time the neighbors say he's worse off than before."

"Solving your problem neatly, I suppose?"

"I didn't poison him, if that's what you're hinting." Dexter Parnell had the grace to flush angrily, then calmed down. "But I suppose with Theo Malone for a father you can't help having a sharp mind

— and a sharp tongue."

"Forgive me, Dex," Laurel begged. "Kelley and you are the best friends I've got but that doesn't give me the right to criticize you."

"Your father just told me you're assigned to Tropical Medicine. With your training plus that year in Zaire, the hospital and the medical school are lucky to have you on the staff."

"There's not much tropical disease in Miami any more so I'm filling in on Internal Medicine, with an assignment to the Critical Care Unit. Lisa's giving the opening seminar hour there now so I'd better go and see what I can learn. Will you and Kelley be at the reception tonight?"

"Unless the baby-sitter fails to show. And sharp tongue or not, it's nice to have you back, Laurel."

IV

At Lynn Rogers' knock, Meg Downing opened the back door to the Hospitality Shop storeroom and let her in. "Mabel told me you'd been summoned by the Great One," she said. "Do you still have time

64

for a cup of coffee?"

"I'll make time. It will give me a chance to think."

"I saw Theo coming in the back way when I left the parking lot." Meg turned up the heat under the glass flask of water and put a jar of instant coffee on the small table. "He looks fine."

"He usually does when he's up to something."

"How old is he anyway?" Meg inquired.

"Fifty-nine, his next birthday. He and Mother were married while he was in medical school, like Paul and myself."

"Worked as a nurse to send him through, didn't she?"

"Yes."

"A lot of us did. I guess that's why so many doctors marry nurses."

"And shed them afterward. You'd never guess what Father wanted to talk to me about, Meg."

"Don't make me." Meg Downing poured hot water into the cups. "I've been dying to know since Mabel told me he'd sent for you."

"First, he chewed me out for upstaging him in that operation last night, although he knows damn well the *Herald* reporter who was watching coined the word, not me. What he really wanted, though, was for me to persuade Mother not to come to the reception tonight."

"That would be criminal! It's the only time Mildred gets to see all of her friends at once. She loves being there."

"This time Father's got a good reason — for him. He's going to announce his marriage to Elena Sanchez tonight."

"Marriage!" Meg Downing's consternation made her voice rise to a squeak. "When's it going to be?"

"They're already married — at St. Augustine two months ago during the convention of the FAMA. The Bishop of St. Augustine performed the ceremony."

"The Sanchezes are staunch Catholics so they'd have to get some kind of a special dispensation for Elena to marry a divorced man. But why would he marry her when — "

"He's been sleeping with her for years?"

Meg shrugged. "Harris says Theo's the horniest man he ever saw, even at his age, but Elena Sanchez must be something in bed herself, to keep him happy so long. It's no secret that he was unfaithful to Mildred at least once a month."

"Once a week was the way I heard it."

"So what are you going to do?"

"Tell Mother and let her decide for herself. She may choose not to come, figuring Father might be embarrassed if she was there."

"Embarrassed? He doesn't know the meaning of the word."

"I guess you're right, but for some reason she still loves him. That in itself could make her stay away."

"*I* wouldn't! I've been dying for three years to see what Elena Sanchez looks like close up and this is my chance. You'll be there, too, won't you?"

"I suppose so. Somebody has to represent the family and Lisa is sure to blow her top when I tell her."

"By the way, I saw Lisa getting out of a taxi this morning at the side entrance to the Critical Care Unit. She was still dressed for the evening so she must have really tied one on last night."

"Roberto Galvez is in town."

"'Nough said; that Roberto is all man. Wish I could have met him when I was Lisa's age." Meg stopped suddenly and her eyes popped with surprise. "How could I say that when I'd been married to Harris Downing for two years and was six months' pregnant with Harris, Jr. Oh well, we all have a right to our might-have-beens. Which reminds me. Did you know Paul's already here?"

"Mabel told me."

"He certainly didn't come to see Theo Malone, after the way your father railroaded him and sold you against him."

"I know now that heredity had nothing to do with little Paul's death, but there were other things — "

"Like Theo working Paul so hard that he couldn't perform to perfection in the sack?"

Lynn gave her friend a startled look. "Whatever gave you that idea?"

"Paul and Harris were — and are —friends. When Paul got to where he couldn't take Theo's hounding any more, he came to my husband for medical advice. Harris couldn't tell him anything to do, except to tell Theo to go to hell, and Paul couldn't do that as long as he wanted to head the Institute. Did you ever stop to wonder why so few young surgeons stay with your father after their Fellowships are finished?"

"They still come back in droves for the seminars."

"That's because cardiovascular surgery is

the most competitive field in the medical profession today; every major city has twice as many heart surgeons as it needs. To stay ahead, the Fellows who leave the Institute need to keep up on the very last word in the field. Your father may be the paranoid son-of-a-bitch all of us, including you, know him to be, but he's still ahead of the pack – DeBakey, Cooley, Diethrich, you name 'em. At the seminars, Theo shows visiting surgeons the last word while looking and acting like God, dispensing favors to the worshiping people so they'll come back two years from now for more."

"And go back home to curse him," said Lynn. "Still, I suppose you can't blame them, when his own daughters curse him, too."

"Except you."

"I'm enough like Father myself to understand the drive to succeed taking control of your whole life, if you let it."

"Maybe you do have some of Theodore's drive but that shouldn't make you turn yourself into a nun; you were a doctor's wife once and you should be again. Not like those I'll see trooping through the Hospitality Shop over the next few days, though, while their husbands are sitting at the feet of the master. They know most of the shop staff are doctors' wives, too, so they'll spend a lot of time and money to impress those of us whose husbands chose the academic — and low pay — life."

"Why have you worked here for so many years then?"

"This is the finest place around to learn who's about to divorce who; what prominent surgeon in Jacksonville or Tampa is sleeping with his secretary — in other words, the total medical scandal. I wouldn't give it up for anything." Meg looked at her watch. "It's almost time to let in the mob."

"You love it all, don't you?"

"I've been lucky, more lucky than most doctors' wives. Every morning when I wake up and hear Harris Downing snoring beside me, I thank the Lord: first, that he's close, and second, that he's still able to get it up — with a little help — whenever I need it." Meg chuckled. "Which is more often than you might think, even after forty-five, a birthday hysterectomy, and ovarian hormones."

"I'd better get to my office and warn Lisa about tonight." Lynn stood up and put her coffee cup in the sink. "She's guiding a tour of the new Critical Care Unit and the

Hyperbaric Laboratory and, if she's in the shape you saw her in a few minutes ago, she may need a backup."

"I'd better make sure the shop is ready for the thundering herd," said the diminutive faculty wife. "See you tonight?"

"I'll be there," Lynn promised, as she opened the back door of the Hospitality Shop and stepped through.

"I should hope so," said a familiar voice, and Lynn's heart took a sudden leap when she found herself looking into the smiling eyes of her former husband.

Chapter 3

When Mort Weyer came back into the satellite clinic, after seeing Jock LeMoyne off in the ambulance, he found Artemus Jones sitting on the table in one of the two examining rooms with his sleeve rolled up. The nurse was wiping the skin of a muscular arm with an alcohol sponge and an empty disposable plastic syringe lay on a small tray.

"Heard you talking to Dr. Shelbourne," said the man in purple. "Is old Jock really in that bad shape this time?"

"I'd bet on it – but why would another dead Whitey bother you?"

"Guess I was shooting off my mouth just now to impress a new doctor," Jones confessed. "Anybody can tell you're a considerable cut above the usual broken-down sawbones we find in a medical dumpyard like this. Half the time they've just finished taking the cure the government provides free in Lexington,

Kentucky, for those who shoot themselves full of their own morphine supply – "

"Sounds like a case of the pot calling the kettle black – and I don't mean skin. How much 'Horse' were you shooting before you got some sense and turned to methadone? And why do you take it by hypo instead of by mouth like the rest of the addicts?"

"I like it better with the needle and it does me more good," said Jones. "As to how much 'Horse' I was taking, it was more than I could afford without turning into a sneak thief, mugger, and murderer – in that order. Where I grew up in Harlem, that was the normal route.

"Did any of your family follow your example?"

"What family? I was found in a trash can where my addict mother – God rest her soul, wherever she is – tossed me after I insisted on being born. I don't even know my last name, Doctor. The sisters in the foundling home called me Baby Jones and I added the Artemus later because it sounded important."

Mort picked up the empty methadone syringe and looked at the record card upon which the nurse had noted the time and the dose.

"Twenty milligrams! That dose would put me into respiratory failure. You must have been shooting enough 'Horse' to kill a stableful, if it takes this much methadone to taper you off."

"Who's tapering? If the government wants to provide me with a permanent high just for coming in here every morning, I'm for it."

"Don't give anybody else that size dose," Mort warned the nurse. "An average man wouldn't even get out of the building before he collapsed. On your way, Jones. You've had your high for the day."

"One thing more." For all his bizarre getup and casual manner, the usually jeering voice of the black man was sober now. "Old Jock has helped a lot of poor people in Liberty City through the years. He ran that big old house he bought, after Papa Doc chased him out of Haiti, as a combination soup kitchen and halfway house for young addicts. If he needs any blood, a lot of people will be glad to volunteer."

"I'll tell Dr. Shelbourne that when I see him late this afternoon." Mort was examining the next patient, a small boy who'd cut his hand on a piece of wire and needed a shot of tetanus toxoid.

"Another thing," said Jones. "Could some sort of a poison besides alcohol have knocked old Jock out like he was?"

"It's a possibility but Biscayne General's also got the finest poison center in the city. If that's the agent, they'll find it and treat him accordingly." He shot Artemus Jones an appraising glance. "Any particular reason for asking?"

"I was just wondering," said the man in purple. "A group of doctors headed by the Great Malone wants to build a rent-subsidy housing unit covering the block where Jock's house is located and he's been fighting them."

"No law I know of forbids an IRS-approved tax shelter," Mort observed.

"Maybe. But if you can bribe a few building inspectors to look the other way, you can put up a structure that will blow down in the next hurricane or burn down if some wino smokes in bed. A lot of poor black folks could get crushed or burned to death, while the white owners cash in on an overinsured building that was jerry-built to be a deathtrap to the people living there."

"Your education is showing again," Mort warned him, and Jones laughed, slapping his thighs Uncle Tom fashion.

"Had you fooled for a minute there, didn't I? That's my MA from CCNY peeking through."

"What field?"

"Industrial Psychology – with a minor in Labor Relations."

"So why is an educated union organizer down here instead of up north where the unions are strong?"

"Maybe for the same reason you turned down a career in a Park Avenue clinic to play family doctor to a bunch of exploited black vegetable and fruit pickers, who can't afford to buy in the stores the same tomatoes they pick in the fields."

"Making any progress?" Mort inquired.

"A little – but come the revolution – 'scuse me, white man" – Jones was back in his Uncle Tom role – "I've got to go shoot me some crap before I take my lesson in five-string banjo picking at the Community College tonight." The tall black shambled from the examining room, giving the nurse a pat on the backside as he went. "Save that for me, honey. I'll be by here around five-thirty to pick you up for dinner."

The nurse pranced a little, then was suddenly professional again when she realized Mort was looking at her.

"Maybe you'd better do like the man says," he told her.

"Yes, Doctor," she said dutifully, but the way her lips curved in a smile told him she was already quite familiar with Artemus Jones's amatory proclivity.

"Dr. Weyer." The clinic clerk had appeared in the doorway. "A man just brought in a baby that looks real sick but he don't speak English. I think he's one of them Haitians that's been pouring into Miami lately."

A tall light-colored elderly Negro carrying an infant had pushed his way into the room behind the clerk.

"*Posez l'enfant ici,*" said Mort in his best high school French.

Fortunately, the distraught man understood well enough to lay the baby on the table and when the stocky doctor examined the small black body it took him only a minute to note one startling thing.

The clinical picture presented by the child was exactly like the one he'd seen only a few minutes before — in an old man named Jacques LeMoyne.

II

"Hi, Lynn!" said Paul Rogers. "You look wonderful, as usual."

"Paul!" Impulsively, she extended both hands to him in a warm gesture. "You're younger – and handsomer."

"No younger, but getting away from here *has* done wonders for me."

In those last few months when they'd been having their problems – largely, Lynn knew now, because of her father's harassment of an assistant so promising that he threatened to eclipse the Great Doctor himself – Paul had become thin, nervous, and harried. She suspected, too, that he'd been tortured by a sense of guilt that perhaps some defect in his own genetic mechanism really had been – as her father claimed – the cause of little Paul's failure to breathe properly. All of that appeared to be gone now, however. The man she found herself facing as she left the storeroom was tanned, handsome, relaxed. He appeared much more sure of himself, too, than she'd ever known him to be, since they'd come back to Miami from Baltimore. What was more, she couldn't deny a stirring of feeling she'd been afraid was gone forever.

"How's it been going for you in Tampa?" she asked, and then laughed. "As if you weren't living proof that it's been going very well indeed."

"We're shifting the department into high gear now."

"You're getting outdoors some, too. That's a nice tan."

Paul smiled and Lynn felt again the familiar tug at her heart. "There's a swimming pool at my apartment and it's on the bay, too, so I can keep a small sailboat. You know I've always wanted to sail."

"The first time we went sailing you turned the boat over and we had to swim it into shallow water to right it."

"Which you could have done alone, but didn't want to show me up." He released her hands. "Isn't there somewhere we can go and talk for a while?"

"I just had coffee with Meg Downing but I could stand another cup. The staff cafeteria is rarely crowded at this time of day."

"Fine! Come to think of it, I fell in love with you one morning a long time ago, when I saw you across the cafeteria at Hopkins drinking coffee."

The memory brought another surge of

feeling, this time stronger than before. To hide it, she looked at her watch and said, "Father's starting an operative clinic at ten, so we've got plenty of time for a chat."

"That must have been quite an experience you had last night, according to the *Herald*," he said as they were walking into the cafeteria.

"I was scared," Lynn admitted. "Usually, I operate with Father or in the Research Laboratory on animals."

"Last night proved what I already knew — that you're a fully qualified surgeon in your own right. Only neither your father nor I was ready to admit it until now."

"He still isn't."

"Or ever will be, I imagine."

"Let's just let bygones be bygones, Paul," Lynn said impulsively. "I know I wasn't the easiest person in the world to live with during those last few months."

"Neither was I, but fortunately Tampa has changed all that."

"Tell me about it," she said as they carried their coffee to an empty table in the staff dining room. Only a half dozen tables were occupied, most of them by nurses discussing the myriad problems they encountered at home, if married, or in their love life if single.

"It's a perfect setup. I guess I never thought I'd admit it, but I've organized the whole thing very much like your father's Institute here – "

"Why not? Isn't he the best – in his own estimation?"

"He's the best in *everybody's* estimation. I had to get away from here – from his shadow – to know that without resenting it."

"You're not alone there. I learned the same thing when he sent me to St. Louis for six months right after our divorce to learn microsurgical technique."

"It took me a few months after I left to realize – and admit – what your father had taught me, and I don't mean just about surgery. When young surgeons first come here, we're all so busy trying to emulate him that we forget the other things he does, like operating a clinic successfully, selling himself to the patients, keeping the staff happy – "

"My father's staff is never happy, else why would so many of them go away from here hating him – to say nothing of his own family?"

"Arrogance is Theo Malone's one

weakness, but also his strength. The more I study great doctors, and lawyers, the more I realize controlled arrogance is the greatest power they possess."

She looked at him suspiciously. "You haven't been in analysis, have you?"

Paul laughed and Lynn suddenly realized that he was handsomer than she'd ever known, even during their courtship and the early days of their marriage. This was a new Paul, enough like the old one to stir memories, but also new enough to be very exciting indeed.

"So you learned that my father is not quite the ogre most people around here think he is," she said a little tartly. "How else have you changed?"

"I don't know whether I should tell you this." For the first time he seemed hesitant, more like the old Paul, yet with a difference.

"Go on. We both seem to be letting our hair down."

"You're your father's daughter, even if you hate him a little, which means your sex drive is pretty strong."

Lynn gave him a startled look. "You never told me that before."

"I guess there were a lot of things I wouldn't admit — one of them being that you're a very lovely young woman whose husband was so busy trying to keep up with her father that he didn't have the energy left to give you the satisfaction you wanted — and deserved to have."

"You make me sound like a tramp." She was trying to be angry at his amazing analysis of her basic impulses, and not succeeding very well. Which only made her resent the new Paul Rogers more for understanding her better than she understood herself.

"You're not that, not by any means," Paul said warmly. "You're a lovely person whom, like so many doctors where their wives are concerned, I wasn't able to understand — or deserve. Besides, I guess I was too much the humble subject, trying to possess the king's daughter but all the while knowing I wasn't worthy and would probably be punished by being cast into the outer darkness."

"I never acted that way toward you," Lynn protested. "I loved you."

And still do, she could have added with the sudden burst of insight that had come to her that morning at the sight of Paul. But instinct held her back, the instinct that rebelled against the utter surrender demanded by such an admission.

"I know, darling. The whole fault was I didn't feel adequate enough to be the princely lover the king's daughter needed and was entitled to. Whether your father understood that and drove me out for that reason is something I'll never know, but he did me the greatest favor he could possibly have done."

"By breaking up our marriage?"

"No, that was my fault for not standing up to him and fighting him. What he really did was make it so tough for me that I couldn't settle into the comfortable slot as his second-in-command I seemed to be headed for, with a typically unstable medical marriage. By making me seize the first opportunity I had to take command myself, he gave me back the conviction of my own capabilities and importance. If you and I had stayed together a little while longer, my leaving the Malone Heart Institute might have saved our marriage. I just don't know."

"I suppose I'm enough like my father that I did expect too much − in bed − for you to deliver," Lynn confessed. "From what I read, that's the most common complaint of married women throughout the country, especially doctors' wives."

"Statistics do seem to prove that."

"I remember one afternoon when I came

home early from school and didn't know my father was already there." Lynn's gaze was far away and her voice, too, was distant. "I went looking for Mother and found them in an upstairs bedroom. Mother never was a sexpot, but I saw her face when I peeked through the door and it was transfigured, like those paintings you see of a saint who's being seized with something. I didn't know what it was then, and I guess I still don't know."

"She was being transported to another world."

"I only know that, more than anything I've ever experienced in my life, I wanted to be my mother that afternoon," Lynn confessed. "I hated her, too, for a moment at least. If I hadn't somehow found the will to close the door and run downstairs into the garden, I might have rushed in and insisted on taking her place, maybe even trying to kill her, though I love her very much indeed."

"That sort of ambivalence isn't really very unusual. What *did* you do?"

"Ran through the woods until I saw a boy who was in my high school class. I didn't even know him very well but I made him take me right there, expecting to feel what

Mother had obviously been experiencing. But it didn't work then and it hasn't worked since." She looked at Paul across the small table and smiled wryly. "Now you'll hate me and I don't want that."

"You're wrong," he assured her. "I still love you and I'm sure I always will. If I'd only had the strength to stand up to your father after the baby died, things might have been different."

"You couldn't have done it, Paul. Some of his daughters have tried, but all we've got for it are scars."

"You, too?"

She nodded. "Mine are deep where they don't show but they're as painful as yours must have been. After little Paul died, I wanted not to believe what Father said – about your genes being at fault – but I guess that would have meant admitting mine could have been the cause."

"That's impossible – on both counts," he protested. "There's absolutely no question of heredity in hyaline membrane disease."

"I know that now – too late. An article I read the other day described a substitute for the surfactant that's missing in HMD. If I could have convinced myself early and had stood beside you –" She broke off speaking for a moment. "But what good does it do now to talk about what might have been?"

"What's Theo up to these days — besides surgery."

"Dexter Parnell is putting together one of those rent-subsidy housing units for Father and a group of doctors practicing here at Biscayne General. Dex offered me a limited partnership but I turned it down when I learned that it's a tax dodge instead of a legitimate plan to provide low cost housing for the people in Liberty City."

"Good for you! So Theo Malone hasn't changed?"

"He'll never change." Lynn looked at her watch. "I've got to call Lisa about something. Will I see you at the reception tonight?"

"Yes — and afterward, I hope."

"If Laurel has a date, I might have to take Mother home, unless she decides not to go."

"I'd be happy to take you *both* home. Afterward, we might go somewhere like we used to in the old days."

"I'd like that," said Lynn. "See you at the reception."

III

Lisa Malone's entrance into the new Critical Care Unit was accompanied by some low-pitched whistles of appreciation from the half dozen doctors of varying ages gathered near the main entrance from the lobby. They were chatting as they munched Danish pastry and drank coffee.

"Welcome to the Fifth Malone Institute Seminar, gentlemen," she greeted the small audience. "I have a few things to say about the new setup before we tour the facilities."

"We may be using them soon, Dr. Malone." Peter Shelbourne had just hung up the telephone on the wall at the entrance. "A *real* emergency is on the way by Rescue Squad ambulance from the Liberty City satellite clinic. The doctor in charge says it's circulatory failure, possibly from toxic shock or some poisonous agent – and the patient's near death."

"A Liberty City clinic doctor diagnosing toxic shock?" Lisa's eyebrows rose quizzically. "I'll believe that when I see it."

"This one is new down there, but he seemed to know what he was talking about. Name's Weyer."

"Would that be Mort Weyer?" one of the visiting doctors asked.

Shelbourne glanced at the scratch pad sheet upon which he had been writing while talking on the phone. "Dr. Mortimer Weyer. He took charge of the clinic yesterday, I believe."

"If he's the Mort Weyer I know, he was a Senior Fellow on Sondheim's service at Bellevue last year," said the doctor who had raised the question. "You'd better listen to what he says; the guy's a diagnostic genius."

"We've had trouble getting any doctor who's worth his salt to work in the Liberty City satellite clinic so I doubt that he's the same one," said Lisa dryly. "Besides, I don't see one of Dr. Sondheim's protegées being employed at Biscayne General. Sondheim and my father don't see eye to eye when it comes to cardiovascular surgery."

There was a round of laughter because the animosity between the famous cardiologist and the famous heart surgeon was well known.

"We don't want to be caught napping, though, do we, Peter?" she added. "Especially after the fine job you did in keeping that stab wound of the heart alive last night until my sister could operate. Better have some plasma sent down from biological supply, just in case."

"It's already on the way, Dr. Malone," said the resident. "Weyer sounded very convincing."

"If you've finished your coffee, gentlemen, we'll start the seminar," said Lisa. "Even if you took your residency or were a Fellow here at Biscayne General, much of this department, both in equipment and procedure, will be new to you. As most of you know, hospital Emergency Rooms are more often than not scenes of bedlam cluttered by patients who can't find a doctor, as well as the accident cases who need immediate treatment. When I learned about the development of a Critical Care Unit in Jacksonville last year, I went up there to examine it. What I saw impressed me so much that I persuaded the Board of Trustees to build an entire new wing to house one here. Inside this building we have also placed the new Hyperbaric Laboratory the Navy helped us build and staff. It's much larger and more modern than the one those of you who served residencies here will remember."

"Would you start by telling us the difference between Critical Care and Intensive Care, Doctor?" one of the visitors asked.

"Certainly. In this and most other large hospitals, critically ill patients were formerly treated in Intensive Care Units related to the particular service involved. That means duplication, not only of expensive special equipment but also an even scarcer item, skilled personnel. If you will follow me on a brief tour of this unit, you will see that it occupies roughly two thirds of a rectangular building which has been added on beside the tower. The other third houses the Hyperbaric Laboratory, which we will visit later in the hour.

"Rooms for patients are placed along the perimeter on three sides in the form of a triangle, with twelve rooms on each side," Lisa continued. "The nursing station where the sophisticated monitoring instruments are located is at the center of the triangle formed by the patients' rooms."

"I noticed that all the rooms have glass doors," said an older doctor in the group. "Don't patients object to the lack of privacy?"

"If you're sick enough to be transferred to this unit, Doctor, you're not going to be worrying much about privacy. In fact, it will be a comfort to you to know someone is watching you at all times, and not simply with monitors, although each patient's vital functions are continually monitored by observers at the nurses' station."

"You must have a lot of confidence in the ability of your nurses to give them that much responsibility," one doctor observed.

"Every nurse assigned to Critical Care is a volunteer and must have had six months of special training," Lisa assured him. "In addition, a trained doctor called an 'Intensivist' – the name for this new specialty – is on duty here at all times. A striking example of their training was exhibited last night when Dr. Shelbourne refused to accept the diagnosis of the ambulance attendants that a stab wound patient was dead. Suspecting cardiac tamponade, he found here in Critical Care everything needed to aspirate the pericardium for retained blood. And when he found blood in the pericardial sac, confirming his presumptive diagnosis of cardiac tamponade, he called my sister, Dr. Lynn Rogers, who was on duty in the Unit. As you may have read in the newspaper this morning, the patient is alive today."

"How do you determine what patients will be transferred to the Critical Care Unit, Dr. Malone?" one of the onlookers asked.

"If the patient is already in the hospital, the

same criteria are used that would send him to Intensive Care, whether coronary, surgical, or otherwise. If he has been brought to the Emergency Service next door, the critical nature of the injury is determined by triage, just as was done in battlefield hospitals during wartime. As most of you know, I am sure, only fifteen per cent of Emergency Room visits to hospitals are related to trauma, which means that the main function of the average Emergency Service is to provide primary care to a large number of people whose illnesses are not of an urgent nature."

"Who determines the degree of urgency?" someone asked.

"A nurse-practitioner specially trained in triage."

"Why not a doctor?"

"In our experience, Emergency Rooms are usually understaffed, particularly on weekends when the daily accident rate is roughly double the figure for the rest of the week. Adding to the patient load are 'walk-ins' who can't find their own physicians, if they have them, and come here for treatment."

"Who takes care of them when your regular Emergency Room surgical staff is busy?"

"For that we use Family Practice residents.

Two of these are assigned to the Emergency Room at all times on weekends and one during the week, plus a staff physician on call from that service."

"I still don't like the idea of a nurse doing the triage," an older doctor objected.

"I said a nurse-practitioner, Doctor, which means she has had roughly two years of additional special training after receiving her RN, plus the extra training we give our triage nurses. She must be able to examine a patient briefly, sometimes even inside the ambulance, and classify him according to the Illinois Department of Transportation Injury Severity Scale."

"I'm not familiar with those classes. Would you explain?"

"Certainly. Class One covers minor injuries with a history of momentary unconsciousness or complaint of pain but no visible wound. Those are usually shuttled to the Family Practice residents. Class Two patients have moderate, but not severe injuries, such as bruises, abrasions, or swelling and limping. They are treated by Emergency Service doctors and usually sent home. Class Three patients have severe injuries, such as bleeding wounds, distorted limbs indicating fractures and the like, and have usually been carried from the scene of the accident by litter. It is the duty of the nurse-practitioner to triage these patients immediately into those who can be taken care of temporarily in the Emergency Room before hospital admission and those who need immediate critical care. If they are in the latter category, our service is next door and available at all times."

"You don't perform emergency surgical procedures in this department, do you?" a visitor asked.

"No. What we do emphasize, though, is the determination of just how urgent any surgical procedures may be. In emergencies, surgeons usually like to move fast — I suppose Hollywood has conditioned them to that. But even the best operation isn't worth much, if the patient dies from an imbalance in his chemicals or an arrhythmia of his heart brought on by too little potassium in his blood."

"Do you use many transfusions?"

"Probably more than is strictly necessary," Lisa admitted. "We'd rather keep the patient off the operating table for a half hour and send him to the O.R. with his hematocrit restored to normal, than to spend hectic hours after surgery treating him for shock that developed during the operative procedure."

"That makes sense," an older doctor agreed. "These young fellows are always too anxious to use the scalpel – "

"And earn bigger fees," Lisa added dryly. "One thing we emphasize here in Critical Care, too, is not waiting for a patient to go into shock before we act. If we can't put a needle into a good vein on the first try, we cut down on the one vein that can always be found, at the inner side of the ankle, just in front of the internal malleolus."

"Suppose the patient has a rare type of blood that isn't freely available?" a listener asked. "What's your procedure?"

"We don't waste time there, either. We use Fluosol."

"I never heard of it."

"Not too many people have," said Lisa. "Fluosol is a chemical compound that possesses oxygen-carrying properties. For that reason it can be used as a temporary substitute for blood in an emergency and is also valuable in the treatment of shock. The main drawback is that it lacks factors promoting clotting and many other properties of whole blood, but it is still lifesaving when it happens to fit the needs of a particular case."

96

"How long do the effects of injecting Fluosol last?" one doctor asked.

"About seventy-two hours, but during that period it can be lifesaving. I'm convinced that you're going to see more and more of it used as time goes on."

"Where did you get it?" another listener asked.

"The major use up to now has been in Japan, where the original compound was first prepared. I was in Japan a few months ago and brought a few cases home. The FDA has given us permission to use it here in strictly emergency situations."

"Such as?"

"Primarily, so far, in life and death situations involving Jehovah's Witnesses. As I'm sure you know, these people have a sincere belief that blood transfusions of any kind are contrary to the Scriptures and will automatically deprive the recipient of any chance of eternal life and salvation. A lot of them have died, purely from the lack of blood."

"In my experience," a listener observed, "they can be very stubborn and suspicious about anything you put into their veins."

"Once you convince them that Fluosol is not a human product but a chemical and therefore in the same class as glucose or any other intravenous medication, they don't usually object," said Lisa. "Actually, some experimental evidence shows that compounds of the Fluosol type can keep an almost bloodless animal living more or less indefinitely. In our own experience with two cases, it was able to maintain life until surgery could be carried out, so I persuaded the Miami Director of Public Safety to place it in Rescue Squad ambulances.

"Two things characterize our patient monitoring." Lisa guided the conversation skillfully into more pertinent channels. "One is a constant watch on the circulation with instruments that tell when a patient's heart is getting into dangerous territory and sound an alarm signal. The other is the use of a Mass Spectrometer to record the levels of exhaled carbon dioxide and oxygen every few minutes automatically. If a patient is heading for trouble, we want to know about it before it happens and take measures to prevent complications. The determination of blood gas levels quickly gives us an immediate clue."

"What about the cost, Dr. Malone?" an older doctor asked. "Isn't all this special equipment and personnel terribly expensive?"

"Measured in terms of the lives we hold

in our hands twenty-four hours a day, it really isn't," said Lisa. "Actually, too, it doesn't cost much more to operate a Unit like this than it does to have Intensive Care Units in every major department, as in the past. By preventing complications, too, we get patients out of the hospital earlier."

"I can see that you would save a lot of trauma patients who might die with the ordinary Emergency Room procedures," a young doctor in the group agreed. "But bringing all emergencies here means by-passing a lot of community hospitals that would be closer to the scene of an accident."

"Admitted," said Lisa. "On the other hand, a comparative study in San Francisco County showed recently that, in an area where all accident cases were being transported directly to a trauma center instead of the nearest receiving hospital, as had formerly been the case, almost two thirds of the deaths under the old system could have been prevented. Or put it another way: when you're having the coronary you're likely to have before you're sixty, Doctor, wouldn't you rather be brought here than put off under the care of an FMG from the University of Guadalajara Medical School for a couple of hours, while your cardiologist was being located on the golf course or on his yacht?"

"Touché," the questioner admitted.

The whine of an ambulance sounded outside and moments later the vehicle whirled into the unloading area serving the Emergency Room. Peter Shelbourne opened the door so the group could watch the patient being brought in.

"That must be the patient from the satellite clinic we're expecting," he said.

"Is the plasma ready?" Lisa asked as the paramedics whisked a stretcher-borne patient out of the ambulance.

"You won't get to use any plasma or Fluosol on this one, Dr. Malone," the paramedic at one end of the stretcher reported. "We put in an airway as soon as we left the clinic in South Miami and we've had him on the pacemaker but he shows no spontaneous heartbeat or respiration. I've brought the old fellow here a lot of times before, but I'm afraid this was Jock's last ride."

"Better check him again to make sure, Peter," Lisa told the resident and the young doctor put the tips of his stethoscope in his ears as he moved to obey.

"No need for CPR here," he reported a few moments later. "The paramedic's diagnosis is correct."

"Send the body to Pathology and notify the Medical Examiner's office," Lisa directed and turned back to the group. "If you will follow me, gentlemen, I will show you the new Hyperbaric Laboratory. It was built for us by the Navy and is still operated by Navy technical personnel but, for the moment at least, it is part of the Critical Care Unit."

As the group was filing out, Lisa spoke to Shelbourne. "You'd better come along, too, Peter, in case I need some filling in on what's new in the Hyperbaric Laboratory. I saw my sister Laurel come in just now; she can take over here until the hour is finished."

IV

A few minutes after Lisa Malone and her entourage disappeared through the door leading from the Critical Care Unit to the Hyperbaric Laboratory, the phone rang for Laurel. She was filling in the preliminary form necessary to send the body of Jacques LeMoyne to the Medical Examiner's office in the Pathology Department located in the basement of Biscayne General.

Picking up the telephone, she said: "This is Dr. Malone. Can I help you?"

"I'd like to speak to Dr. Shelbourne. This is Dr. Weyer."

"He's with Dr. Lisa Malone in the Hyperbaric Laboratory. She's giving the first hour of the seminar."

"Then you must be the one I read about in the *Herald* this morning. Nice going."

"I'm afraid I can't take credit there either. That was my sister Lynn."

"How many of you are there anyway?"

"Three." Laurel laughed. "Lisa and Lynn are twins. I'm Laurel, the youngest."

"Did an old fellow named Jacques LeMoyne get there yet?"

"He did but he was D.O.A. I was just writing up the case for the Medical Examiner before sending the body to the morgue. The Rescue Squad had him listed as a case of toxic shock. Is that right?"

"Your guess is as good as mine," said the brisk masculine voice at the other end of the line. "I think now that we're dealing with some sort of an epidemic."

"Like what, Doctor?" Laurel's interest was immediately aroused.

"I don't have the least idea. I've got another patient here with a clinical picture exactly like the one Jacques LeMoyne showed – except that this little fellow is only eight months old."

"That pretty well rules out cirrhosis. The Record Room computer reports that as the diagnosis in Mr. LeMoyne's previous admissions."

"It rules out anything I can think of at the moment, too," Mort Weyer admitted, "but I'm not a pediatrician. We've sent for an ambulance so the baby should be there soon. He's critical, too, so you'll probably want to keep him in your department for a while."

"I'll see to that," said Laurel. "Any other suggestions?"

"Touché. By the way, if I come to the opening reception of the seminar tonight and you're there, how would I know you?"

"I'm a redhead; my sisters are both blondes." Laurel's momentary pique at the other doctor's slightly tolerant tone was assuaged by his apology. "And I'll be pushing my mother's wheelchair. She's a paraplegic."

"I know. An aunt of mine was in college with your mother at Sweet Briar and told me to pay her a call. My boyhood days were spent in the Shenandoah Valley, although I was born right here in Miami."

"Mother will be glad to see you," Laurel assured him. "Be sure and look us up tonight."

"Will do. Let me know what you think of the baby, after you've seen him."

V

"Because of the transfer of much of the Navy's submarine activities to Key West recently, as well as the need to establish a diving laboratory nearby in connection with a medical center," Lisa told the seminar group who followed her through the door marked "Authorized Personnel Only," "a new hyperbaric chamber was recently built here at Biscayne General. I am told that it is the largest of its kind south of the one at Duke Hospital and I think you will find the new equipment interesting, especially to those who have some knowledge of the field."

The building was nearly filled by two huge steel cylinders joined in the middle by a third round tank and connected to a control panel, where two Navy technicians were sitting. The tanks were fitted with glass-covered portholes through which those at the control panel could see inside. What startled Lisa, however, was the identity of the tall Naval officer who moved to meet them. He was the same one into whose arms she had crashed about an hour earlier, when she'd raced from the taxi into the hospital.

"I'm Commander David Fuller, Dr. Malone." His voice was soft with a native southern accent and his tone gave no intimation of previous acquaintance. "I only took command of the Navy unit operating the Hyperbaric Laboratory last night, so this is my first chance to report to you as head of the department."

"Glad to have you aboard, Doctor," said Lisa. "I believe that's correct Navy parlance."

"Correct enough," said Fuller. "Can I be of assistance?"

"A visit to the new hyperbaric chamber is part of the schedule for this section of the seminar, Dr. Fuller. I must admit that I know very little about it, so would you mind filling us in?"

"My pleasure," said Fuller. "If you will follow me into one of the three chambers, I will try to explain how the laboratory operates and also answer any questions."

"We're at your command, Commander,"

said Lisa. "Please carry on."

"The present chamber is quite similar to one we have been using in underwater research at Duke Hospital and Medical School," Fuller explained as the group filed into one of the huge steel tanks which easily held the dozen visitors and Lisa. "During the past year I have been working with a research team using the Duke hyperbaric chamber. Prior to the construction of this one, it was the most advanced of its type in the world. You may have read in the news recently that a group of divers achieved a simulated depth there of over two thousand feet. Perhaps I'm overly proud of having been associated with that particular experiment; if so, please forgive me."

"As I remember the story, the divers in that experiment took a considerable risk." Lisa's voice had taken on a slightly acid note. "I wonder how you can justify the danger to human life, except as part of a stunt, Doctor?"

"I can assure you that no stunt was involved." Fuller showed no sign of offense at her tone.

"Then it wasn't just to establish a new record?"

"Not at all. The proof that men can survive, and even work, at depths several times what was believed possible earlier has created scientific and commercial possibilities which still remain to be explored."

"For instance?"

"The Continental Shelf several thousand feet below the surface of the ocean is thought to contain very large deposits of both oil and scarce minerals which, as yet, have not been explored." Fuller's voice took on a slightly sarcastic note. "Surely I don't have to remind you that any possible reserve of oil or scarce minerals could be of inestimable value to the country."

"You've made your point, Dr. Fuller," said Lisa, with a shrug. "Please go on."

"Thank you, Dr. Malone. All of you have studied physiology and are familiar with Boyle's Law, so I won't repeat it. Except to remind you that prior to the invention of hyperbaric chambers, the only way a person could be subjected to an increase in the pressure of the atmosphere around him — and therefore inside his lungs and hollow organs — was to dive beneath the surface of the water. Exposure to a depth beyond about thirty-three feet was hazardous, however, so cases of what is called the 'bends' were frequent, particularly in those working in caissons to dig tunnels."

"Then the hyperbaric chamber is essentially a refined form of the decompression tanks used to treat 'bends' in the old days, isn't it?" Lisa asked.

"Exactly," Fuller agreed. "What we have here is essentially a group of steel tanks in which the air pressure around those occupying them can be raised at will to many times that of the normal atmosphere – "

"Which is fifteen pounds to the square inch," Lisa observed. "We all know that, Doctor."

"Fourteen and seven-tenths, to be exact. Or, at sea level, a weight of two thousand, one hundred sixteen and eight-tenths pounds per square foot."

"Which would be unbearable for the human body if the pressure inside it were not the same as that outside, making the actual mathematical difierence zero," Lisa observed.

"Exactly!" Fuller conceded, then added, "So I'm forced to admit that, beyond the possible uses of pressurized oxygen in the treatment of early senility – which I believe will be covered in another hour of the seminar, plus the treatment of anaerobic infections where they show favorable possibilities – hyperbaric chambers are most interesting to those specializing – as I do – in Undersea Medicine. Are there any particular questions?"

There were only a few, which Fuller answered competently before Lisa dismissed the group to the next hour of the seminar, which was to be her father's operative exhibition of the famous Malone technique of coronary by-pass.

"Thank you, Dr. Fuller," she said as the group filed from the laboratory. "I hope you will find Miami as interesting as you did Duke."

"I already have, Dr. Malone; much more interesting indeed."

"Dr. Malone," a nurse called to Lisa as the seminar group filed back into the Critical Care Unit. "Telephone call for you. It's Dr. Lynn Rogers."

"Get ready for a shock," said Lynn when Lisa answered the phone. "I figured you'd be about finished with the seminar and waited to call you."

"We just visited the Hyperbaric Laboratory. Congratulations on the sewing job you did last night. I hope you thanked Peter Shelbourne for making sure the patient got as far as surgery."

"I went the second mile by telling the reporter that, if your department hadn't been on the ball as usual, the patient would never have gotten to the O.R. at all. Have you heard the news about Father?"

"No. I had a rather late date with Roberto Galvez. What's he up to now?"

"Father called me early this morning. He wanted me to persuade Mother not to go to the reception tonight."

"You'd be doing her a favor if you could. They're always a crashing bore but he insists on being seen with his family."

"Not tonight. He's announcing his marriage to Elena Sanchez."

"That socialite bitch from Little Havana he's been sleeping with?" Lisa exploded. "She's young enough to be his daughter."

"Perhaps about Laurel's age," Lynn agreed. "He called to give me hell for making the news with the heart operation – and to warn me about tonight. Said for me to tell you and Laurel, too."

"I'm *warned*," said Lisa on a grim note. "Warned not to be seen at his damned reception. I didn't want to go anyway, so now I've got a good excuse."

"I thought you'd feel that way."

"Don't make any excuses for me. I want

him to know why I'm not there."

"He will. I'll see to that."

"Is Paul here for the seminar?"

"Yes. We just had coffee together."

"Give him my love and, if you want my advice, have more than just coffee the first chance you get. I think I'll take Roberto to Key Largo for the weekend. We can do some scuba diving, if we stay sober enough. Is Paul going to stay over through Monday?"

"I – hope so."

"Tell him I'll see him then and don't be foolish enough to let him get away again."

"I'm working on it," said Lynn. "Have fun."

VI

In Operating Room Three, part of a suite reserved for the patients of Dr. Theodore Malone, the Great Man was putting in the last suture of a second coronary by-pass. The gallery, from which observers could look almost directly down at the operating table, was about half filled. On the closed circuit TV system, a more detailed picture of the operative field was being recorded on video tape and also shown on a monitor at one side of the gallery for the benefit of those who wished to study the technique in more detail. The Institute Director had recognized several of his former assistants and now spoke for their benefit, as well as for the medical students and visiting doctors who always appeared to watch when a Malone heart operation was scheduled.

"I see that some of you are former students of mine." Malone was speaking into the microphone placed against his neck, with the cord hanging down his back. It was plugged into a special loudspeaker circuit for the gallery and also the two surgical amphitheaters equipped with closed circuit television for teaching students and physicians.

"Some of you are not, however, so I will briefly describe what we have been doing," Malone continued. "This patient had an almost complete block from arteriosclerosis in two of the three coronary arteries that supply blood to the heart muscle. The third coronary is also somewhat constricted, as you will see from the cineradiographic picture on the viewbox against the wall."

All eyes in the gallery and on the floor below it — except for the first assistant who continued to watch the previously made suture lines for any sign of a leak — swiveled as one to the viewbox. There the radiologist, in constant attendance should the need for a film occur, indicated the offending vessel with a stick-pointer.

"What we have done so far," Malone continued, "is to remove a section of the saphenous vein from the patient's left leg. Because narrowing of the coronary arteries prevents an adequate flow of blood to the heart muscle, we have used part of the vein to make a by-pass and bring an ample supply. By connecting one end of a vein section to the aorta just above the heart and the other end to the obstructed coronary artery beyond the block, we've achieved our objective."

With a Kelly clamp, being careful not to intrude his hand into the field being surveyed by the TV camera located inside the large light above the operating table, the surgeon traced out the by-pass circuit and also each coronary artery coursing across the muscle of the heart itself.

"This patient has already had one heart attack, as you can see by the scar in the heart wall, but is still suffering from severe anginal pains because his heart muscle is not receiving enough blood — and oxygen. The rhythmic pulsations in the vein segments by which we have by-passed the obstructed heart vessels indicate that blood is now flowing freely through them to the heart muscle, so the pain incident to the obstruction of these two vessels should be alleviated.

"The question now is, having by-passed the obstruction in two of the three coronary arteries, should we not go ahead and by-pass the third at this time, thus relieving all of his coronary insufficiency both for the present and for the future." He paused momentarily, then added: "My decision is to go ahead and complete the operation."

In the gallery, a former Malone Fellow from Dallas turned to one from Chicago. "The bastard couldn't resist the temptation to do a triple by-pass for our benefit, even though I'd say the blood flow through the third coronary is adequate, wouldn't you?"

"Looks adequate to me, but we're going to be treated to another Malone Miracle just the same. Even so, you've got to admit that he's fast enough to do three while we'd be doing two."

"Make it more like three to one," the Dallas man admitted wryly. "Any way you cut it, the Great Malone is the fastest scalpel in the south."

"Probably in the world but a couple

of younger men are close on his heels, particularly Paul Rogers, who left him a couple of years ago and went to Tampa."

"Left – or was pushed out?"

"What's the difference? If you get to where you can give the Great Doctor competition when it comes to heart surgery, out you go."

"Don't forget that after a year or two as Fellows here, though, we usually jump into some of the finest clinics in the country. And at the top, too, where fees are only a little lower than what Malone himself gets."

"He can do two things better than almost anybody else: operate on hearts and beget beautiful daughters," the man from Chicago said. "Too bad he never had a son."

"He had his heart set on a grandson when Paul Rogers married Lynn. I was here when the baby died and the old man never forgave Paul – "

"For what? I heard the kid had hyaline membrane disease."

"It did, but Malone still blamed that on Paul Rogers' chromosomes and afterward rode him like he was a pariah. Paul's too good a surgeon for even the Malone isolation treatment to destroy him, but he did get jumpy and I guess he must have been hard to live with at home, too. Anyway, he and Lynn were divorced not long afterward."

"Everybody in our field is hard to live with at home," said another surgeon sitting beside them in the gallery. "I guess you could call it an occupational hazard with cardiac surgeons; plenty of our marriages end up in divorce. But when you hold human lives in your hands all week, knowing one wrong decision or one false cut can bring death to another human, it's hard to manage even a simple physiological feat like getting it up on Saturday night."

"Not Malone. I hear he's installed that Cuban mistress of his in the apartment next door, so she'll be ready to relieve his tensions, when he comes home after a hard day in the O.R."

"I saw her last year and she can relieve my tensions any time she feels like it," said the man from Dallas with a knowing grin. "I understand something like that did happen to Paul Rogers when Malone started riding him so hard. Which was a pity, for Lynn's a real woman and entitled to a real man. If there ever was a love match, that seemed to be it; yet it went *kaput,* like a lot of other doctor marriages."

"Doctors have one of the highest rates in

the country for psychiatric breakdowns and suicide, besides divorce," the Dallas man observed.

"Plus alcohol and narcotic addiction," said the Chicagoan. "I certainly wouldn't want my daughter to marry one."

Below them, Malone had now completed the third by-pass and stepped back from the table, leaving Ernesto Sanchez to complete the closure.

"All of you attending the seminar are invited to make rounds on our surgical wards tomorrow morning at eleven," he told the gallery. "We have been hoping to find a suitable patient for a new kind of heart operation I have developed. Also, my daughter, Dr. Lynn Rogers, will give a film demonstration of microsurgery tomorrow morning."

"Speaking of daughters," said the doctor from Dallas to the one from Chicago, "I seem to remember that you were carrying quite a torch for the other Malone twin while we were here."

"Only for a few months. Lisa dropped me for Roberto Galvez."

"Roberto was quite a Don Juan — still is from the way he was squiring Lisa Malone last night."

"Where did you see them?"

"They were whooping it up at Sloppy Joe's and, from the looks of things, vodka wasn't the only stimulant they were treating themselves to."

"Roberto always had a supply of prime Colombian hash and was liberal with it. I heard some pretty wild tales about skinny-dipping parties on Key Largo at the Malone family cottage."

"Lisa's still a stunner by anybody's standards, but she'll never pin down Roberto with a marriage license."

"The way I heard it, Lisa isn't after matrimony either," said the other doctor.

"Judging from our experimental studies" – Malone's voice on the loudspeaker in the gallery broke into their whispered conversation – "an operation I have perfected and hope to show you before the seminar ends will be considerably more successful than anything of the kind done before."

"So he's just waiting for a donor in order to stun his former students with something new," said the Chicago surgeon as they were leaving the gallery. "I'll lay you ten even that a subject for it will turn up between now and Sunday afternoon."

"If one doesn't," said the Dallas man,

"Malone will probably go out and run down a kid of the right size himself. How about helping me drink some lunch?"

"Good idea," said the Chicagoan. "You know, it does me good to come back every year. Makes me realize how lucky I was to get away from here with my sanity — and without the kind of drive that keeps Malone in high gear all the time."

"And will probably kill him one of these days. I hear his blood pressure is sky high, but he won't let up or take the medicine Harris Downing prescribed because he doesn't want people to think he's not immortal."

"Or stunt his power as far as keeping that Cuban mistress happy," the other surgeon agreed.

Chapter 4

When Dexter Parnell returned to his office in downtown Miami he was surprised to find Artemus Jones waiting for him. The two had become friendly enemies during the negotiation of a contract between South Dade Packers — another business enterprise Dex managed for the group of doctors in which Theo Malone was the largest partner — and the International Agricultural Workers' Union. The contract, hammered out in weeks of negotiation, assured the largely black agricultural workers of year round employment in the groves and fields of South Florida, as well as providing a source of labor for the owners.

"What is it this time, Art?" Dex inquired as the gangling union leader followed him into his office. "More complaints about the Haitian refugees?"

"They're no concern of mine, so long as South Dade doesn't start using them to pick mangoes for peanuts instead of paying the union wage."

"We're sticking to our part of the contract."

"But not without howls from the partners, I'll bet, particularly the Great God Malone," said Artemus with a grin. Then he sobered. "Not that I don't feel sorry for the poor devils, as long as they don't invade union territory."

"They can find all the work they want with nonunion growers."

"I guess when you were working for fifteen dollars a week in Haiti, the fifteen dollars a day the growers are paying inland around Lake Okeechobee makes you consider yourself lucky."

"Lucky to be alive, if what I hear about their home island is true."

"It's true enough," said Jones. "But American workers, who made two hundred and fifty a week packing lettuce last year and now can't find work, are sure raising hell."

"You can thank your stars the refugees didn't start arriving before South Dade Packers signed the contract with the union," Dex told him. "The only thing that keeps my employers from trying to break the one we have with you is the certainty that, if they did, the federal government would come down on them like a ton of bricks."

"Especially the IRS. Nothing scares a rich doctor as much as the thought of having his tax returns audited."

"So it's a standoff —"

"As long as the county authorities see that the Haitians are shunted away from Dade County into nonunion territory," Artemus Jones agreed. "Did you know Jock LeMoyne died about thirty minutes ago?"

"No." Dex was suddenly alert. "I stopped by his house in Liberty City on the way to the office. Somebody told me he'd been taken to the satellite clinic, but I thought he only needed drying out again."

"This time it was something else."

"How do you know that?"

"They've got a smart new doctor at the clinic — named Weyer. He took one look at old Jock and recognized that he was *in extremis*. I came straight here from Biscayne General, where the youngest Malone girl told me Jock was D.O.A. So what are you going to do?"

"Find out if Jock had a will."

"How?"

"One of the county judges will appoint me the Personal Representative — they used to be called Administrators – of Jock's estate."

"Why you?"

Dex shrugged. "Everybody at the courthouse owes me a favor for one thing or another."

"What next?"

"I search Jock's house in Liberty City tomorrow, right after I leave the courthouse with a writ. If I don't find a will or a receipt for renting a bank deposit box that I'll be empowered to open, he'll be declared to have died intestate."

"I know that one. You get to milk his estate for every penny you can charge before it's settled."

"So long as it's legal," said the lawyer with a shrug.

"So that's what they teach at Harvard – legal stealing?"

Dexter Parnell ignored the thrust. "Want to help me search old Jock's house?"

"Sure." Artemus Jones got to his feet. "They tell me that place is haunted."

"Come to think of it, you're right," Dex agreed. "I remember when I was in school at Dade High not far from there, nobody would rent the place because there'd been several murders in it. The house was supposed to be filled with secret passages and panels that moved when you pressed the right button."

"Ask anybody in Liberty City and they'll tell you the same thing, even now."

"While I was at the University of Miami, before I studied law at Harvard, I had to spend three hours out there after dark for a Sigma Chi initiation," said the lawyer.

"See anything?"

"Nothing but Old Jock. He came out of the bushes with the shotgun and told me to get the hell off his property. You can bet I skedaddled."

"Hope his ghost doesn't take a shot at you when you start looking for his will. Good hunting!"

"Good hunting hell! It's *no will* I'm hunting for."

"Just tear it up, then, and you've got it made," the labor leader advised. "When can we expect construction on the rent-subsidy housing unit to start?"

"Three months — if I'm lucky and my conscience doesn't sell me short."

"*That* I won't worry about, as long as you're representing Dr. Theodore Malone," Jones assured him. "Like master, like servant."

"Get the hell out of here so I can start petitioning the court," said the lawyer. "A union organizer is the nearest thing available nowadays to a scavenger, so who's the pot calling the kettle black."

"Better watch out!" Artemus Jones called back from the door. "You're threatening to deprive me of my civil rights."

II

Laurel Malone had barely finished writing the initial note on the top sheet of Jacques LeMoyne's bulky hospital record, when an ambulance whined to a stop at the loading platform. A stretcher on which lay a small black bundle, shaking perceptibly in a chill or a convulsion – she couldn't tell which – was wheeled in. A tall mulatto with gray hair and oddly aristocratic features walked behind the gurney.

"Are you the father?" Laurel asked him as the child was being transferred to one of several baby beds occupying one corner of the Critical Care Unit.

"Grand-père." His tone was cultured and his eyes, as he looked down at the small patient, were deeply concerned.

"I see Dr. Weyer obtained the admission information." Laurel was looking over the typed sheet from the satellite clinic containing details of residence, the fact that the baby was eight months old, and its name was Pierre DuVall. Below the heading, Weyer had scrawled in a bold, purposeful hand:

Eight month old black infant brought in by grandfather. Complaint: fever, convulsions intermittently for past five days. Healthy before onset of P.I. Brief examination: Temp. 104, pulse 120, resp. 30. Brief rigor while being examined. Only notable physical factor, spleen about twice normal size. Transfer to Critical Care, Biscayne General. Dr. Malone notified.

Mortimer J. Weyer, M.D.

While a nurse inserted a thermometer into the tiny rectum, Laurel made a brief physical examination, interrupted several times by a convulsive shaking of the entire small body. The child showed no sign of consciousness but, when she lifted its eyelids to test the pupils with a pencil flashlight, the reaction was normal.

"Can you tell me any —?" Laurel spoke over her shoulder to the grandfather, but stopped when she realized he was no longer there.

"Where's the man who came in with the baby?" she asked the nurse who was helping her.

"I don't know, Doctor. One minute he was standing by the bed, the next he just walked away."

"See if you can find him and bring him back. We need more of a history."

The nurse departed as Laurel continued the examination, studying the throat with the light before she shut it off, then feeling the neck for enlarged lymph glands that might give a clue to the nature of the obviously serious illness. Percussion of the lungs and listening for the breath sounds with her stethoscope yielded no positive information, nor did the heart sounds, except that they were rapid but, fortunately, quite strong. Movement of the limbs elicited some resistance from the convulsive tendency but was otherwise normal. She left for last the one abnormal finding Dr. Weyer had noted, the enlarged spleen. And when she pressed on the tiny abdomen beneath the ribs on the left side, her eyes widened.

Fever, convulsions, an enlarged spleen, and so far nothing else brought to mind a possible diagnosis, one she'd seen often enough during the past year. The trouble was that those cases had been on another continent altogether – Africa.

She was still considering the strange findings, mentally listing the causes of the clinical picture and rejecting each with computerlike accuracy, when the nurse she'd sent for the grandfather returned.

"The man who brought the baby in seems to have disappeared, Dr. Malone," she reported. "When he saw you start examining it, he just vanished."

"Never mind," said Laurel. "I want to examine an immediate blood smear."

"I'll order a CBC –"

"I'd rather do it myself. Is there a tray on the ward?"

"We have a small laboratory for emergencies."

"Bring me the blood count tray," said Laurel. "Then get an I.V. of five per cent glucose in normal saline ready and call the pediatric resident. He's probably more experienced at hitting small veins than I am."

"Yes, Dr. Malone." The nurse removed the fever thermometer and glanced at it, then took a second look. "His temperature is 106."

"Get some blankets over the patient. What we're seeing probably aren't simple convulsions from a high fever."

"What could they be then?"

"Bring me that tray and I should know one thing they *aren't* due to in a few minutes – if we're lucky."

Pricking the baby's finger with a needle, Laurel squeezed a drop of blood onto a slide and quickly made a thick smear and a thin one. In the small but compact laboratory, she stained the thin smear and dried it before placing it under the objective of a binocular microscope. When she spun the controls and brought the blood cells of the smear into focus, she saw a picture she'd seen many times in Africa, but not in the United States since her studies in New Orleans.

"The nurse said you wanted me to start an I.V., Dr. Malone." The nameplate of the tall young man in white duck standing in the doorway said "Dr. Aaron Rosenberg, Resident in Pediatrics" and his tone was slightly sarcastic. "What's the diagnosis?"

"Malaria!" Laurel turned to face him. "Malignant falciparum malaria."

"You've got to be kidding! That doesn't happen in the U.S. anymore – not even in

South Florida with the mosquitoes we have most of the year."

"It's happened now." Laurel leaned to one side so he could look into the microscope. "Take a look."

"The other doctor studied the slide under the microscope briefly and whistled softly. "They're there, all right. I haven't seen malaria parasites in a slide for so long I'd almost forgotten what they look like, but you couldn't mistake them with that many plasmodia in the blood." His tone was decidedly respectful. "What do you suggest doing?"

"That depends on whether we're dealing with a chloroquine-resistant strain of *plasmodium falciparum* or not. In Zaire we saw a lot of them."

"You've worked in Zaire?"

"Spent last year there with the WHO; that's why I suspected malaria when I felt a large speen. Get a nylon catheter into the largest vein you can find, even if you have to cut down. A big danger with malignant malaria is sudden circulatory collapse when the parasites and the red cells building with them block the capillaries. I hope the pharmacy has an intravenous solution of chloroquine on hand."

"What if they don't?"

"We'll have to get some, and fast. Meanwhile, you can start an I.V. of low-molecular weight dextran to dilute the blood once you get a catheter in his veins. I'd notify the service chief, too."

"I'll do that right away," said Rosenberg. "But I still can't figure out how this little fellow got it."

"That's what my mother likes to call the Sixty-Four-Thousand-Dollar Question," said Laurel. "Seems like there was a popular TV program with that name a long time ago."

III

At noon, Lisa Malone called Dr. Roberto Galvez at his downtown hotel, from which she had fled four hours earlier – and awakened him to a monumental hangover.

"How about going with me to the cottage at Key Largo this afternoon for some scuba diving?" she asked.

"I couldn't dive this afternoon if my life depended on it. I was stoned last night."

"So was I – in case you don't remember."

"How could I forget?" Galvez's voice had taken on some life. "But why today?"

131

"I have reasons for wanting to go down late this afternoon but, since you're so hung over, we'll put off the diving until tomorrow. Take your toothbrush, razor, and pajamas – if you need them."

"I'll need them," said Galvez. "After last night, my gonads won't be producing for a week."

"Let's hope not." Lisa laughed. "I'll be giving myself morning-after shots for at least that long."

"Why are you so anxious to leave Miami? Some other of your old flames are certain to be here for the seminar."

"One old flame is about all I can take for a weekend. Besides, Father is announcing his marriage to Elena Sanchez tonight."

"Marriage? Why? He'd been living with her for at least six months before I left Miami."

"She's pregnant, according to Lynn."

"So maybe the Great One is going to get himself a son at last? I can understand why you wouldn't want to be there – after the way he treated your lovely mother."

"I'll pick you up around four," said Lisa. "We'll spend a quiet weekend at the cottage on Key Largo."

"A man would have to be dead to be

quiet with you around. Or a eunuch."

"And you're neither, as I very well know."

IV

By the time Laurel finished studying the blood slide from the sick baby, Dr. Rosenberg had skillfully inserted a small nylon catheter into an arm vein and started the dextran solution flowing. The department head for many years, Dr. Joshua Michaelis, arrived as Laurel finished writing the admission note on the chart and greeted her with a kiss on the cheek.

"I hear you've been diagnosing malignant malaria practically in the ambulance, Laurel," he said with a smile. "When I used to give you tetanus toxoid shots for skinned knees in your teens, I never thought you'd be stealing a march on me in my old age."

"You're not so old, Uncle Josh; I read that last paper of yours on Burkett's lymphoma. Your conclusions were exactly the same as what I was seeing in Africa at the time."

"Your mother did tell me you were spending a year there with the WHO but didn't say where. A few strange tropical diseases have been discovered among the refugees pouring into Miami lately from various parts of the world. So far, though, we've had no cases of falciparum malaria but several cases of chills and fevers have been diagnosed in adults."

"Want to take a look at the smear to confirm my diagnosis?"

"I'd be lucky to recognize even a white blood cell; it's been so many years since I looked at a blood slide. What do you propose to do with this little fellow?"

"I'm assigned to Critical Care, not Pediatrics, Uncle Josh."

"As of now you're in charge of this *pediatric* patient *in* Critical Care," he told her. "Obviously you know more about malignant malaria than anybody else around Biscayne General."

"I was going to see whether the pharmacy has an I.V. solution of chloroquine we can let drip slowly in with the dextran. If this particular parasite isn't resistant to the drug, that ought to bring the patient around in a hurry."

"Anything else?"

"The health authorities should be notified so they can make an inspection of the area where the baby lives for malaria-carrying mosquitoes."

"My secretary can do that. What's the address?"

Laurel glanced at the top lines of the chart and a sudden bell rang in her mind. Holding the sheet, she read off the address to the other two, and asked, "Where would this be?"

"Not far away, in what's now called Liberty City, largely populated by blacks and practically destroyed by the riot," said the resident. "Why?"

Laurel picked up Jock LeMoyne's chart, which had been lying beneath the one from which she was reading. "The address is the same as that of the baby Dr. Weyer sent in from Liberty City. He said its illness looked exactly like that of Jock LeMoyne, too."

"Jock's dead," Dr. Rosenberg objected. "I met the stretcher taking him to the morgue on my way to Critical Care and recognized him from the times I'd seen him in the Emergency Room when I was an intern."

"What's this all about, Laurel?" Dr. Michaelis asked.

"I don't know, sir, but I'm certainly going to find out as soon as I get the chloroquine ready for the patient, sir. There has to be a connection."

"An alcoholic bum and an eight-months-old

baby with the same clinical picture?" The resident shook his head. "No way!"

"I agree with Dr. Rosenberg," said Michaelis.

"There could be one way," Laurel corrected him but gave no details because the idea that was forming rapidly in her mind seemed impossible, too. "When they bring down the chloroquine, please start it dripping very slowly into the dextran," she told the resident.

"I'll get it right away, but what are you going to do?"

"Solve a mystery," said Laurel cryptically. "Or maybe start a bigger one."

Fortunately the hospital pharmacy carried a stock of chloroquine, for treating the occasional case of malaria detected by the Health Department among patients arriving by air or boat from tropical countries where the disease was commonly prevalent. Ordering a dose for intravenous use sent down to Critical Care, Laurel took the elevator to the basement, where the morgue was located. It wasn't a particularly attractive place, half of it being occupied by the huge refrigerator in which the bodies of the dead were stored. The bodies were awaiting claim by relatives, after the autopsy required by law in emergency cases to establish the cause of death, plus a few problem cases.

On the way down, Laurel had picked up the blood count tray from Critical Care. At the window outside the Medical Examiner's office, she asked the technician in charge: "Has the body of Jacques LeMoyne been examined yet?"

"We just put him into the refrigerator, but Dr. Bradshaw won't even need to do an autopsy to determine the cause of death. Jock's been on the verge of dying from cirrhosis for years."

"Mind if I take some blood smears?" Laurel asked. "It's for a research project."

"Not at all, Doctor. I'll open the refrigerator for you." The technician had noticed the name Malone on the plastic identification plate pinned to Laurel's white uniform jacket.

The refrigeration room was cold, causing Laurel to shiver, though not entirely from the temperature. It reminded her of the dissecting room where she'd spent much of the time during her first year in medical school. Except that in the big cooler where the cadavers were stored in New Orleans, they'd been hung like clothing on a rack with the points of a pair of tongs resembling those used to carry blocks of ice stuck into the ear canals.

"Here's old Jock." The technician pulled out a long drawer. "He was a lot of fun when he was alive; always smuggling bottles of wine into the hospital and sharing them with the staff. What part do you want to examine?"

"A finger will do, unless I have to puncture a vein on the back of the hand to get some blood."

As Laurel had suspected, Jock LeMoyne's blood had already coagulated to where she wasn't able to get enough for a set of smears from a finger. With the attendant holding a pale, gnarled hand, she slit a bluish blood vessel visible on the back and took her smears from there.

"If the Medical Examiner asks about that wound, tell him I'm doing some blood studies," she told the morgue attendant. "And please call me in Critical Care when he does the autopsy."

"Like I said, there's no need to waste time opening Jock up. Everybody knows he's a chronic alcoholic so all we'll find is a shrunken liver. Besides, there's no indication of accident or foul play."

"Give me time to stain this smear and

examine it and I may give you a reason for a different diagnosis," said Laurel curtly.

"Certainly, Dr. Malone." The morgue attendant had suddenly remembered that her name was one to conjure with at Biscayne General. "Just let us know if you want a post done on him and I'm sure Dr. Bradshaw will be glad to co-operate."

In the laboratory upstairs, Laurel wasn't surprised to find a dead man's blood filled with *plasmodium falciparum*. Next she called Mort Weyer at the Liberty City satellite clinic to tell him her diagnosis in the case of both Jock LeMoyne and the baby. Told that he'd gone to lunch, she left word for him to call when he returned.

She was dialing the County Health Department, when the technician from the Pathology Laboratory came into the Critical Care Unit office where she was working and put a gauze sponge with a dead mosquito in the center of it on the blotter of the desk.

"I was looking through Jock LeMoyne's clothes before sending them to the incinerator when I found this," he explained. "I thought you'd like to see it."

Laurel took one look and the excitement of discovery – and mystery – started a conflagration in her brain.

"Does it mean anything?" the technician asked. "You can find a lot of mosquitoes around Miami this time of year."

"You won't find many of this particular breed — I hope. Take a look at a specimen of *Anopheles Gambiae.*"

The technician frowned. "Never heard of it."

"Neither have a lot of people in the Western Hemisphere," Laurel told him. "The last one in this part of the world was supposed to have been killed in Brazil around 1943 but not before thousands of people had died from malignant malaria caused by the *plasmodium falciparum* it carried. Incidentally, that's the same parasite I found in the blood of Jock LeMoyne and also a very sick baby here in Critical Care."

"Good God! This could be the start of a malaria epidemic —"

"Not just *a* malaria epidemic, but the worst malaria epidemic ever to hit the United States."

Chapter 5

Gathering her clothing of last evening from the locker in the Nurses' Lounge off the Emergency Room, Lisa Malone went to her apartment in Biscayne Towers shortly before three. From there she called the marina at Key Largo where the twenty-four-foot luxury speedboat owned by Theo Malone was kept. He had bought it for occasional fishing trips with distinguished guests offshore beyond the reef that paralleled the mainland and the hundred-mile-long chain of keys extending southwestward from the southern tip of Florida into the Gulf of Mexico.

The manager of the marina assured Lisa that the boat would be ready the next morning with scuba diving equipment also aboard. The chore finished, Lisa showered and changed into brief shorts and a blouse before packing a small case with swim suits, a nightgown, lingerie, and cosmetics. Finally she hung two summer dresses, for wearing in the restaurant where she and Roberto would take their meals, in a hang-up case. As she was finishing the packing, the telephone rang.

"Anything I can do for you while you're away with Roberto?" Lynn asked.

"Nothing except make sure Father knows I'm not at the reception."

"He could hardly fail to notice that for himself. You're always surrounded by a bunch of sex-starved males."

"You could be, too, if you wanted it that way."

"I'll settle for *one* this weekend. By the way, have you met the new member of your department, Commander Fuller?"

"We ran into each other – and I mean exactly that – as I was sneaking into the side entrance heading for the Nurses' Lounge this morning. I looked a mess but that didn't keep him from giving me a thorough feel when I almost fell into a Spanish bayonet shrub and he had to catch me. Of all the cheap –"

"Don't sell him short," Lynn advised. "From what I hear, he's the hottest man the Navy has in Undersea Medicine."

"They can have him. If there's anything I hate, it's a man who knows everything," said

Lisa with a snort of disdain. "By the way, your coronary suture case from last night is doing beautifully."

"Much to Father's disgust. He's been praying for the artery to be obstructed by a clot beyond my suture line so he'll have an excuse to operate on him again while the seminar's going on."

"Roberto's waiting downtown so I'd better run," said Lisa. "See you Sunday afternoon."

"Have a good weekend – and pray that I will, too."

"You want Paul back, don't you?"

"More than anything else in the world."

"Then take my advice and be aggressive. *I* always have been and when the truth is told, we're really two parts of the same person."

"Mi querida!" Galvez greeted Lisa when her sleek sports car stopped beneath the marquee of the DuPont Plaza. "You look wonderful."

"So do you," she said as she guided the El Dorado out into the traffic on Biscayne Boulevard. "I thought you were hung over."

"The headache is some better, thanks to two aspirins and a shot of, what do you call it here in the States?"

"'Hair of the dog.' That's the last one

you'll have before we get back from the reef tomorrow afternoon. I don't go scuba diving with somebody who's high. How long has it been since you've been down?"

"Two years; the last time was with you, *querida*. I've been too busy since I went back to Caracas for much in the way of recreation."

"Getting rich doing by-passes?"

"That, and making investments. I'm part owner of a real estate development that makes money faster than I can spend it. Come down and join me; I'm starting a clinic, too, and will be needing doctors."

"Is that a proposition — or a proposal?"

"A proposition, of course," Galvez said with a shrug. "We are both lone wolfs."

Lisa laughed. "In the U.S., only single males are 'wolfs,' darling. Thanks for the proposition, but my new Critical Care Unit keeps me busy by day and by night I can do as I please. In Caracas, I'd be labeled a hussy but here everybody's afraid to call me one to my face."

"So what is the program for the weekend?" Galvez asked.

"We ought to get to the cottage on Key Largo by six o'clock. You remember it, don't you?"

"How could I forget?" Galvez laughed. "It was the first time I ever went — what do you call it?"

"Skinny dipping?"

"That's the word. Do you have any idea how splendid you look nude in the moonlight?"

"I should; enough men have told me so. Back to the schedule: tonight we dine at the Reef, a fine restaurant on the Keys. With luck, the menu will be hearts-of-palm salad, Florida lobster, and key lime pie. Then we go to bed — in separate rooms."

"Christ! We could just as well have stayed in Miami."

"You won't feel that way when you're exploring the Key Largo coral reef tomorrow at a hundred feet. It's a fantastic world that's like nothing you're likely to see anywhere else."

"Why so deep?" Galvez looked a little apprehensive.

"A new Navy doctor who's in my department intimated this morning that I'd probably never dived in really deep water. He also admitted that he had never been down on the Key Largo reef, so naturally, I have to dive tomorrow and show him I'm ahead."

"If that's what we're going for, why didn't

you bring *him* instead of me?"

"I don't 'yield my favors' – as my mother's generation would have termed it – on the first contact, darling. Besides, we'll be on Key Largo *two* nights, which should make you happy."

"In that case, the sooner we get the diving over with, the sooner we can start enjoying ourselves. Is it not so, *querida?*"

Lisa didn't answer. She was too busy at the moment wondering why she'd let her pique at Commander David Fuller that morning lead her to embark on a weekend with Roberto Galvez in which she was rapidly losing interest.

II

The chief resident in Pathology, Dr. Sam Kleppermann, called Laurel Malone about three-thirty. She could tell by his voice that he was irritated by her official request that he perform an autopsy on Jacques LeMoyne late on a Friday afternoon. Nevertheless there was a note of respect in the pathologist's voice, the same one shown by everyone at Biscayne General when talking to a doctor named Malone.

146

"I understand that you requested an immediate P.M. on a case of what is obviously cirrhosis of the liver in a known alcoholic, Dr. Malone," said Kleppermann.

"I apologize in advance for the last minute request, Dr. Kleppermann but I need the findings for my report to the Health Department."

"The Health Department doesn't investigate cases of alcoholism, Dr. Malone." The pathologist's tone was one of amusement. "Of course I realize that you haven't been on the staff very long so you couldn't expect to be familiar with all the regula —"

"I have reason to believe the cause of death in this case was more than just cirrhosis, Dr. Kleppermann," Laurel interrupted firmly. "If my clinical diagnosis is correct, Dr. Washburn will be anxious to determine the facts as early as possible."

"The Medical Examiner isn't available but, as his deputy, I'll be glad to oblige — if that's what you want."

"Thank you, Doctor." Laurel kept her voice calm in spite of the other doctor's tone. "I don't think you'll be wasting your time, even on a Friday afternoon."

"If you'll give me some idea of what you're looking for —"

"The final diagnosis is usually your prerogative, Dr. Kleppermann." Laurel ignored the invitation to reveal what she already knew. "I'll be glad to let you have your usual moment of triumph first, though, and present the clinical picture afterward."

"Fair enough." As Laurel had hoped, Kleppermann fell for the bait. "Since the Malone Seminar is in progress, why don't I announce that this period will be added to the afternoon schedule as a Clinical Pathological Conference?"

"You're running the show, Doctor. Just give me a half hour to make some additional studies."

"Shall we say at four, then? I believe the last scheduled session of the seminar program will be over then."

"That should give me time enough to prepare the clinical presentation."

"Since the patient is already in my department," Kleppermann added, "may I ask what additional laboratory work you're doing that required taking blood?"

"I'm working on a patient with similar findings to LeMoyne's, Dr. Kleppermann. I'll be happy to fill you in on the details when I present the clinical part of the CPC."

"As you wish, Dr. Malone. After all, the name you bear comes pretty close to having the last word at Biscayne General."

Laurel chuckled to herself as she continued what she was doing, a meticulous dissection under the microscope of one salivary gland from the dead body of the insect vector presented to her by the technician from the Pathology Department. She had just finished making a slide from the material she'd found in the tiny gland, when the telephone rang again. It was Mort Weyer.

"I got your note to call you but I've been swamped," he said.

"That's all right," said Laurel. "I've been pretty busy, too."

"Have you made a diagnosis on the baby yet?"

"On both cases. The chief resident in Pathology has scheduled a CPC at four to humble another nonpathologist with his diagnosis of the cause of death in the case of Jacques LeMoyne. If you can possibly make it, I think you'll find it interesting."

"Not giving out any information in advance, eh? Don't say that I blame you. Pathologists have caught me napping more than once when it comes to a clinical diagnosis. I'll be there – and incidentally rooting for you."

"Thanks! This time the pathologist is going to eat crow."

"You sound pretty confident."

"I am."

"Did the baby I sent in die? It appeared to be pretty sick."

"He's holding his own under treatment and I'll let you in on one secret – the clinical diagnosis in the case of Jacques LeMoyne and the baby you sent in are the same."

"I'll be at the CPC if I have to treat my last satellite clinic patient in a Volkswagen Rabbit on the way," Mort Weyer assured her.

Laurel finished her examination of the slides she had made from the contents of the salivary gland carefully dissected from the mouth structures of the dead mosquito, then placed a call to the Health Department.

"This is Dr. Laurel Malone at Biscayne General," she said. "Could I speak to the Health Officer?"

"Dr. Wilson has already left for the day," she was told. "He's addressing a meeting of health officers in Jacksonville this afternoon."

"Could I speak to the next doctor in

the pecking order, then?"

"What? Oh yes! You must mean Dr. Prentiss. He's Assistant County Health Officer."

"This is Dr. Prentiss." An irritated voice came on the line. "I was about to leave for the day but if I can help you —"

"It's you I'd like to help, Doctor," said Laurel. "I'm taking part in a CPC at four o'clock on an important tropical disease that has suddenly developed here in Miami. It will be in the Pathology Auditorium at Biscayne General and I'd suggest that you be there."

"I didn't catch your name, Doctor —"

"Malone, Dr. Prentiss. Laurel Malone. I'd strongly advise your attending a CPC at Biscayne General starting at four o'clock. Can you make it?"

"I'll be there." Prentiss' voice had lost most of its confusion. "Can you tell me what it's all about, Doctor?"

"You'll find that out soon enough. See you there, Dr. Prentiss."

"Count on it, Dr. Malone. I live out there anyway."

"Better call your wife and tell her you may not get home for supper," said Laurel as she hung up.

Word had spread fast, thanks to Dr. Kleppermann's wish — common to all pathologists — to wreak a humiliating defeat upon a clinician. Clinical Pathological Conferences were the only time pathologists were able to prove publicly that their clinician compatriots — who had only the living patient to use for study — were wrong in diagnosing the cause of death. The amphitheater was almost filled with members of the house staff required to work over the weekend, and visitors there for the seminar.

Shortly before the start of the conference, Laurel saw a tall man with a gray beard and a camera hung by a strap around his neck come in and take a seat at the back of the auditorium. Even though she hadn't seen him in years, she recognized Jack Parker, the crack reporter for the Miami *Herald,* who'd written the story of Lynn's spectacular surgical feat last night and who, on the orders of her father, literally had the run of the hospital.

At the stroke of four, Dr. Kleppermann — a somewhat plump and very self-assured young doctor whose patients couldn't prove him wrong — called the session to order.

"This will not be the usual CPC, in which the clinical findings and the medical diagnosis are presented before the findings at autopsy," he announced. "Pathological findings will be presented first after which Dr. Laurel Malone will give the clinical picture. Dr. Malone, I might add, is a recent addition to the Critical Care Unit's staff to which this patient was brought this morning, dead on arrival."

A round of laughter greeted the announcement, but Laurel did not reply. A handsome, but stocky man who appeared to be in his early thirties came in just then and took the vacant seat beside her on the first row.

"Dr. Malone?" he asked.

"Yes."

"Mort Weyer," he said, holding out his hand. "That bastard Kleppermann deserves to be taken down. I knew him when we were both at Harvard. You can do it?"

"Watch me!" Laurel squeezed the hand he offered and smiled.

"Since Dr. Malone has requested that the autopsy report precede the presentation of the clinical findings," Kleppermann announced, "I will summarize the pathological picture as briefly as possible. We have here the body of a seventy-five-year-old male known to have been a heavy drinker. As would be expected, the liver is small, nodular, and heavily scarred, the typical picture of cirrhosis. The spleen is somewhat larger than would have been expected with this pathological picture, but no indication was found of any type of leukemia or other blood dyscrasia. The normal expectation of arteriosclerosis is found throughout the body, plus a somewhat enlarged heart, and moderate emphysema, no doubt from smoking. To summarize, this patient is a classical example of a man who drank too much, smoked too much, and otherwise failed to obey the principles of living known to produce normal health."

"In other words an alcoholic bum," said a doctor in the audience, to the accompaniment of a wave of laughter.

"You have made the diagnosis with admirable accuracy, sir," an older doctor in the audience said, as he rose to his feet. "Even that greatest of all pathologists, Popsy Welch of Johns Hopkins, where it was my privilege to study a half century ago, couldn't have done better."

"Thank you, Doctor," said Kleppermann modestly.

"I for one see no point in wasting my time with the clinical diagnosis," the older doctor added on a sarcastic note, heading for the door, "when it can be better spent over a glass of 'sipping whiskey' before dinner."

Again there was a wave of laughter from the audience, several of whom started to follow the eldrly speaker, until the voice of Laurel Malone, who had risen to her feet, stopped him.

"I, too, can appreciate 'sipping whiskey,' Doctor. If you can restrain your thirst a few minutes longer, however, I shall show you a case in which even the great Popsy Welch, under whom my father, too, is proud to have studied, could have made a mistake."

Without waiting for an answer, she turned to the broadly grinning pathologist. "You referred to the splenic enlargement just now but apparently considered it of little or no significance, Dr. Kleppermann. May I ask whether or not you took a blood smear from the cut surface of the organ?"

"There was no need," Kleppermann spluttered.

"Perhaps not — in your opinion. As it happens, though, I spent the past year in a WHO laboratory in Zaire where an enlarged spleen means only one thing. When a sick baby was admitted not more than an hour after Mr. LeMoyne's body arrived, with practically the same picture of fever, chills, and near circulatory collapse that Dr. Weyer described after examining Mr. LeMoyne, I became suspicious that we were dealing with something more than cirrhosis, even in a known alcoholic." She turned to the chief pathology technician. "May I have the first slide, please?"

At her request the chief technician, with a worried look at his superior, turned down the lights and switched on a projecting microscope, producing on a screen set up at the corner of the room, a highly magnified image of a field from the slide beneath the instrument.

"Good God!" The elderly doctor who had been on the point of departure was the first to recognize the picture, when the technician twirled the controls of the microscope to bring the slide beneath it into a clear focus.

"Plasmodium falciparum!" he exclaimed. "Look at those signet cells."

"Congratulations, Doctor!" Laurel addressed the speaker. "Your apprenticeship under the renowned Dr. Welch was not wasted."

"I can't believe it," said Kleppermann in a

tone of awe. "There hasn't been a case of malignant malaria in Miami since I came on this service."

"And not many in South and Central America since *Anopheles Gambiae* invaded the Amazon Valley around 1930, brought there from the African Gold Coast," said Laurel. "That epidemic caused thousands of deaths in Brazil before it was stemmed some ten years later, largely through the co-operation of scientists from the Rockefeller Foundation with the Brazilian health authorities."

"Are you saying malignant malaria is loose in Miami, Dr. Malone?" the Health Officer asked in a tone of horror.

"Not only malignant malaria, Dr. Prentiss, but also its principal carrier, largely limited until now to Africa. My second slide," Laurel added, as the technician placed another under the microscope, "is a blood smear from the cut surface of the spleen of the corpse just autopsied. The previous one was from a baby who was admitted to the Critical Care Unit, after having been sent in by Dr. Weyer, shortly after the patient whose findings Dr. Kleppermann has just presented, was sent to the morgue. As you can see, the blood cells of both the baby and the dead man have been heavily invaded with *plasmodium falciparum.*"

"Can you identify the carrier, Dr. Malone?" Prentiss was growing more disturbed by the moment.

"Fortunately, I can. It was *Anopheles Gambiae.*"

"I can't believe it!"

"Here's further proof," said Laurel. "A slide of material taken from the salivary gland of a specimen of *Anopheles Gambiae* found in the dead man's clothing."

"Alive?"

"No."

"Thank God for that!" said Prentiss fervently.

The third slide had been prepared less than ten minutes before by Laurel herself, working desperately against the 4 P.M. deadline set by Dr. Kleppermann.

"Here is indubitable proof that at least one mosquito in Miami was a carrier of malignant malaria," she announced. "The salivary gland from it that I dissected was teeming with gametocytes, the sexual and most rapidly reproducing form of the *plasmodium.*"

There had been no time to photograph the single mosquito the chief technician had found in Jock LeMoyne's clothing, so Laurel had placed the insect itself on a white sheet of paper. When, however, this was slid under the mirror of a special projector, the image of the mosquito appeared upon the screen with startling clarity.

In the hubbub that followed, the tall man with the beard who had quietly come into the auditorium when the CPC began, and had been transcribing the entire procedure with a small portable tape recorder, stood up and photographed the screen with its sinister picture. Nobody, however, noticed him except Dr. Prentiss, the Assistant County Health Officer.

"Mr. Parker," Prentiss called. "Will you wait a moment please?"

The tall reporter turned back. "Let me guess, Doctor," he said with a resigned look. "You want me to sit on the biggest story break I've had this year."

"Only for a day or two," said the Health Officer. "Until I can send that mosquito to Atlanta for a positive identification at the Center for Disease Control."

"How long would that be?"

"I'll have to ask Dr. Malone. She knows more about this situation than anybody in the United States at the moment."

"Fair enough. Let's ask her."

The two men worked their way through the

group of doctors leaving the seminar until they came to where Laurel was standing with Mort Weyer.

"Dr. Malone," said the Health Officer, "could Mr. Parker and I have a word with you?"

"Of course. This is Dr. Weyer, who discovered the two patients demonstrated at the CPC."

"But didn't make the diagnosis," said Mort Weyer.

"Neither did I, until I saw the blood smear." Laurel turned to the reporter. "Hello, Mr. Parker. I haven't seen you since I swam in the Olympic tryouts for the University of Miami."

"And set a new world's record for the butterfly, as I remember it," said the tall reporter. "Congratulations for setting the medical profession on its ear. I can see that you're every inch your father's daughter."

"I've asked Mr. Parker to delay printing the story of today's conference, Dr. Malone," the Health Officer explained.

"With a possible epidemic of malignant malaria breaking out any day now and its most important carrier in the city, I should think you'd *want* the public to be warned, Dr. Prentiss," said Laurel.

"We will warn the public of course." Prentiss looked embarrassed. "It's just that before releasing news that *Anopheles Gambiae* has invaded Miami, we need to be certain of our facts."

"In other words, you feel that you should double check my identification."

"Well, yes."

"Then I suggest that you send the mosquito to Atlanta tonight. Dr. Hugh Longaker at the Center is a world authority on *Anopheles Gambiae.* He visited our station in Zaire while I was in Africa last year."

"Is that all right with you?" Prentiss asked Parker.

"On two conditions: One, that I turn in my story tomorrow night in time for the Sunday morning edition. The other that I interview Dr. Malone about what all this means in time for the same edition, and that she provides me with a good picture of the species so I can use it in the story."

"That's no more than fair." Prentiss turned eagerly to Laurel. "Isn't it, Dr. Malone?"

Laurel looked at her watch. "I have no objection, except that the interview will have to wait, probably until tomorrow. I ordered a blood smear made on the baby who was the second patient to be discussed this afternoon

161

and it should be ready. If the *plasmodium falciparum* strain I just showed is chloroquine-resistant, I've got to start scouring around for another drug to use in treating him."

"Are you going to be at the reception tonight?" Parker asked.

"I expect so."

"Your father always invites me to them," said the reporter. "Why don't you and Dr. Weyer join me for a drink afterward? That way I can get both of your stories at the same time."

"Okay, if Dr. Weyer doesn't object," said Laurel. "I really must go now. That smear should be ready.."

"Mind if I take a look at the baby, too?" Mort asked. "I have sort of a vested interest in both cases."

"Of course. After all, you're the referring physician. I started the patient on chloroquine intravenously in a slow drip of dextran," she explained as they made their way from the basement to the Critical Care floor. "If there's no change in the rough plasmodium count on the second smear, we can assume that we're dealing with a chloroquine-resistant strain."

"What then?"

"I'll have to switch to another antimalarial drug, probably a new quinoline-methanol compound that we were using in Zaire. The only trouble is that it hasn't yet been released generally in the United States, even though it's been used in England for some time."

"Why?"

She shrugged. "For one thing, probably because the only malignant malaria seen in the United States these days is brought in by visitors from other countries, mostly Africa."

"How do you suppose this one got here?"

"Your guess is as good as mine."

They had reached the Critical Care Unit and one glance at the spiking temperature curve on the baby's chart told as much as did Laurel's brief examination. The disease course was definitely downhill, which meant that her fears about a chloroquine-resistant strain of the deadly plasmodium were being realized.

Mort Weyer had been studying the hospital record while Laurel was examining the small patient. "I've got something of a photographic memory," he said. "Jacques LeMoyne was listed as coming from this same address and you said just now that the dead mosquito was found in old Jock's clothes?"

"Yes, but —" She stopped suddenly. "Two patients with malignant malaria, plus the most frequent insect vector for spreading it — and both from the same address in Miami, where neither disease nor vector is supposed to be. It begins to add up, doesn't it? But to what?"

"A medical mystery, to start with."

"That's Dr. Prentiss's job," said Laurel. "I've got all I can do trying to find a drug that isn't supposed to be used in the United States."

"Leave the mystery to me," Mort told her. "I think I've got a clue back at the satellite clinic. See you tonight at the reception?"

"If I'm lucky enough to find the right person at the Center in Atlanta, I can have a supply of mefloquine on a plane for Miami in a few hours but I may have to go to the airport to pick it up."

"If the drug arrives tonight *we'll* go to the airport," Mort assured her. "Meanwhile the answer to our mystery may still be at the satellite clinic."

"Mind telling me what it could be?"

"A Purple People Eater. At least that's what he calls himself."

Chapter 6

Mort Weyer was lucky and found Artemus Jones snoozing in his purple sports car outside the Liberty City satellite clinic, waiting for Mrs. Bullock, the clinic nurse, to go off duty at five-thirty.

"Glad I found you here," he told the gangling labor leader. "Saved me the trouble of looking up your address in the clinic records."

"Anybody in Liberty City could've told you where I live, Doc. Got me a condo out in Buena Vista, near the river. What brought you back here, after leaving two hours early like any sensible city employee would?"

"I went to a seminar at Biscayne General. Did you know Jacques LeMoyne was D.O.A. when he got to the hospital?"

"I heard it before you did; keep my CB tuned to Channel Nine so I'll know when any of my people have to use the Rescue Squad."

"Did you know a sick black baby was admitted to Critical Care less than an hour after LeMoyne died – from the same address?"

Jones had been slumped in the car with his feet up on the steering wheel, but straightened up at once.

"Come again." He was all business now and fully alert.

"A baby, maybe seven or eight months old, was brought here *in extremis* this morning by a tall man, nearly white, with the features of a French aristocrat. The address he gave was the same as Jacques LeMoyne's –"

"Wait a minute, Doc. Old Jock lived alone; you could almost say he made a fetish of it. Valued his privacy and all that."

"The two addresses are the same. I checked them both at the hospital less than a half hour ago."

"So old Jock got charitable and took some-one in." Art Jones's tone was suddenly casual. "Did this dude you say brought the baby in give a name?"

"DuVall, I believe."

"Hell, Doc! There are DuValls all over Florida. The county Jacksonville is in is called that, with the second *l* missing. D'you say he was almost white?"

"Whiter than you are. When the clinic clerk asked him what relation he was to the baby, he only said *grand-père.*"

"A mulatto who spoke only a little English but was fluent in French." Art Jones's tone was thoughtful. "What does that add up to in your educated mind, Doc?"

"A Haitian, probably an aristocrat, who's on the run from the secret police," said Mort. "Which made me ask myself: if the Purple People Eater knows so damned much about what goes on in Liberty City, how could he miss knowing about him – and the baby?"

"What answer did yourself give you?"

"One, *grand-père,* whether DuVall is his name or not, hasn't been here long. Two, he's probably a well-to-do Haitian who had to flee the island, maybe with quite a lot of his money. Three, since Jacques LeMoyne was at one time a highly placed Haitian, too, he probably knew DuVall, and for a good price arranged to pick him and his group up somewhere down in the Keys where you said old Jock kept a boat. And four, the refugees could be hiding in Jock's house in Liberty City because, with practically the whole place burned out during the riot – except that house – they'd be safe there for a while."

"You're a regular Ian Fleming, Doc. Anything else?"

"Yes, but it's on the Q.T. — at least until midnight Saturday."

Art Jones held up his hand. "Scout's Honor — for what that's worth."

"Old Jock didn't die of alcoholism or cirrhosis and neither will the child, if it doesn't come through in spite of Dr. Laurel Malone's efforts."

"She's the youngest one, isn't she? Just came back from a year in Africa studying Tropical Medicine?"

Mort gave the tall man a startled look. "How would you know that?"

"I could claim to know about everything that goes on in Miami — with good reason — but I'll be honest with you. The Miami *Herald* carried a piece about her last Sunday, before you arrived. Doctors' daughters are always news in Miami — if their father is named Theodore Malone. One thing I don't understand; why would a specialist in Tropical Medicine be interested in an old wino?"

"Both patients have or had malignant malaria. Besides, the pathology service technician who prepared old Jock's body for autopsy found a dead mosquito in the old man's clothing."

"So what? Forget your Six-Twelve around here on a summer's night and you'll be eaten up."

"Not by a traveler from the Gold Coast of Africa – named *Anopheles Gambiae*. One that hasn't been seen in the Western Hemisphere since it took part in an invasion of the Amazon Valley in the thirties that caused thousands of deaths. It wasn't eradicated from there until about the time World War II began."

Art Jones whistled softly. "You're a smart guy, Dr. Weyer."

"I wouldn't know one mosquito from another but obviously any member of that particular family, especially when carrying a parasite called *plasmodium falciparum* that causes malignant malaria, spells trouble for the whole of South Florida, if more than one came over." Mort looked at Art Jones quizzically. "Would you have any idea how that sort of passenger could have gotten to Haiti, and then on to Miami with a special sort of refugee like the man who brought the sick baby to the clinic this morning?"

"Nothing but rumor. There's been talk among the Haitian refugees about a plane

headed for Brazil that was wrecked somewhere on the island. It's supposed to have
been loaded with diamonds, or maybe gold,
but that's all it was – a rumor."

"From Africa?"

"Naturally, for either diamonds or gold,
and the shortest distance would be to Brazil.
I'll search old Jock's house tomorrow morning and see what I can find."

"Don't go getting yourself arrested for
breaking and entering."

Art Jones grinned. "This time it'll be
legal. A fellow I know has probably already
been appointed administrator of Jock's estate.
Name's Dexter Parnell and he's Dr. Theo
Malone's lawyer. They've tried everything
but murder to get possession of the house so
they can build one of those rent-subsidy tax
shelters, but who would have thought a
mosquito from Africa would come along and
take care of the problem for them."

"I was wrong. You *do* know everything
that happens in Liberty City."

"Almost," said the tall black. "I suppose
you'll be going to the reception tonight?"

"I plan to, with Dr. Laurel Malone and
her mother."

"You'll probably meet Dexter Parnell then.
If you do, tell him I'll help search old Jock's

house tomorrow morning about eleven. He's probably leery about going into Liberty City alone."

"What'll Parnell be looking for?"

"A will — and hoping he doesn't find it."

"I can understand Mr. Parnell hoping Jacques LeMoyne didn't have a will," said Mort Weyer. "But just what would *you* hope to find?"

"Nothing, probably; you know how rumors are. But just say a plane from Africa really did crash in the mountains of Haiti and *Grand-père* DuVall discovered it. He'd have to get off the island with whatever was valuable in the cargo before the Haitian government arrested him. Jock LeMoyne not only had a boat that could make the run but also knew a lot of upper class Haitians who could have put DuVall in touch with him. Suppose something valuable — like diamonds or gold — *was* smuggled in, along with mosquitoes and malaria. Jock's dead and DuVall would be an illegal alien, so finders keepers."

"Making you a rich man?"

"What do I need with money when the government keeps me supplied with methadone for free. That treasure would be a lot more useful as the down payment on a low-rent housing unit for agricultural workers."

"I knew it the moment you picked up old Jock's legs this morning and helped me to carry him into the clinic. You're a People Lover, not a People Eater."

"Don't let it get around, Doc," said Artemus Jones with a chuckle. "I'll be negotiating a new contract for my union with the packers next spring. If Dex Parnell and his partners get the idea I'm really a bleeding heart, they'll take the shirt off my back."

II

About 6:30 P.M. Laurel came into the large bungalow on the bayfront in the northwest section of the Buena Vista area where she'd grown up. She found her mother manipulating her wheelchair expertly around the kitchen, as she prepared sandwiches for their dinner.

In the years since removal of a spinal cord tumor had made her a paraplegic, with no feeling or muscular control below her pelvis, Mildred Malone hadn't let her disability turn her into an invalid or a recluse. With the aid of a maid, who had been with the family since the girls were babies, she managed to perform practically all of the duties she had handled before the operation.

"What are you going to wear tonight?" Mildred asked her youngest daughter.

"A summer dress. I'm on call so I might have to leave."

"Goodness! I hope not. A woman isn't safe in Miami alone at night."

"That's exactly what Dr. Weyer told me less than an hour ago."

"Who's he?"

"The new doctor at the Liberty City satellite clinic. He's going to meet us in the lobby of the Terrace a little before eight."

"*Us?*" Mildred Malone smiled. "Or *you?*"

"*Me,* for starters. When I told him you'd be with me, he said he'd love to meet you. You'll like him, too, Mother."

"If you do, I know I will. Don't worry about me, either, if you have to leave. Lynn and Paul are going to meet us in the lobby of the Terrace. Did you know your father's going to announce his marriage to Elena Sanchez tonight?"

"The old bastard! When did you find out?"

"This morning. Lynn came over here after

173

your father asked her to tell me."

"So you wouldn't go?"

"That was the general idea, but it didn't work."

"You know why he asked you, don't you?"

"Out of consideration for my feelings, I suppose."

"Bushwah!" said Laurel. "He knows you'll outshine that young Sanchez bitch. Your Randolphs-of-Virginia blood will take care of that. What about Lisa?"

"Your sister inherited the Malone temper. Lynn said Lisa blew her top when she heard and swore she wouldn't show up but she did call me this afternoon. Said she was going to the cottage to do some skin diving with Roberto Galvez."

"Isn't he the Venezuelan surgeon she had that torrid affair with while he was a Fellow at the Institute?"

"Yes — and very handsome, too."

"Anything serious between them?"

"I don't think so. Roberto is a charmer but not the marrying kind."

"Neither is Lisa," said Laurel. "Which is a pity when she's so beautiful and has so much on the ball. The Critical Care Unit she wheedled the trustees of Biscayne General into building is fantastic."

"Even your father complimented her on it, so it must be."

Laurel gulped down a sandwich and drank her coffee, then took their dishes to the sink and rinsed them before putting them in the dishwasher. "I'd better run and get my shower so I can help you dress."

"Take your time. Margaret helped me with my bath before she left and everything I'm going to wear is laid out where I can get to it."

"You'll be the loveliest woman at the reception," Laurel promised. "That Cuban bitch will wish she'd stayed in Little Havana."

It was a quarter to eight when Laurel, in a blue linen sleeveless dress that set off her dark red hair, pushed her mother's wheelchair across the lobby of the Biscayne Terrace Condominiums toward the elevator leading to the Terrace Dining Room on the second floor, where the opening reception of the Malone Institute Seminar would be held. Mort Weyer was talking to two young doctors near the entrance to the crowded lobby but left them and came across to meet the two women.

"Mother, this is Dr. Weyer," said Laurel.

"You're even lovelier than your daughters, Mrs. Malone." Mort lifted the hand she extended to him and touched it to his lips in an Old World gesture of courtesy. "You and Laurel are more than gracious to let me join you."

"Your accent sounds Virginian, Dr. Weyer," said Mildred Malone.

"Virginian, but German in origin. The original Weyers came to America around 1732 and tried to settle in eastern Pennsylvania. Like a lot of Americans already there they were called Dutchmen, although many were Englishmen who had fled to the Palatinate States along the Rhine, to avoid persecution by the followers of Oliver Cromwell. When Pennsylvania became crowded, my ancestor moved with some others to the area south of Winchester, Virginia. A lot of my people still live in that part of the state, in a lovely area called Weyer's Cave."

"Some of my best friends, when I was younger, were of Pennsylvania Dutch extraction," said Mildred Malone. "Our home was only a little south and east of there. My maiden name was Randolph."

"It's a name to conjure with in Virginia," Mort assured her. "Or anywhere else for that matter."

People were approaching the wheelchair in a steady stream now to greet Mildred Malone and Laurel and be introduced to Mort Weyer. Among them were Lynn and Paul Rogers.

"If you're the Dr. Mortimer Weyer who co-authored a paper last year with Eric Sondheim accusing us cardiac surgeons of doing too many coronary by-passes, we should be enemies," Paul told Mort with a smile.

"I plead guilty to the charge, but I hope you're at least a friendly enemy," said Mort.

"I'm more than that," said Paul. "One of the reasons I got kicked out of the Malone Institute two years ago was because I dared to argue with the Director against surgery for some of the cases we were operating upon."

"I promise not to make that mistake with Dr. Malone tonight," said Mort. "They tell me his wrath is something to behold."

"As one who was the target for it, I can vouch for that."

"Don't believe him, Dr. Weyer." Lynn had stepped out of the queue of people around Mildred Malone's chair and came to stand beside Paul. "Paul was kicked out because he was becoming real competition for my father."

"Which — if you can believe the Miami *Herald* — you're about to become yourself," Mort complimented Lynn. "Are you liable to share the same fate as Dr. Rogers?"

"She will if I have anything to say about it," said Paul. "I need her badly in Tampa as a microsurgeon — and for other reasons."

Lynn changed the subject abruptly. "Mother says you're a fellow Virginian, Dr. Weyer, and that puts a stamp of approval on you. She just told me she wasn't sure whether the Dutch — or, rather, Germans, to give you the right origin — were in northern Virginia before the Randolphs or not."

"Some of them were but none could compete with John Randolph of Roanoke for the honor there or anywhere else. My immigrant ancestor was among those who settled in what was then called Frederick Town — later Winchester — as early as 1732, near a Shawnee Indian village. That was before John Randolph of Roanoke was born, but it certainly does nothing to decrease his glory in the history of early Virginia."

"I see that a line is beginning to form where my father is receiving," said Lynn.

"Shall we join it and get an unpleasant duty over with?"

III

The young woman standing beside Theodore Malone — she could hardly have been more than thirty — was a lush Spanish beauty in every sense of the word. Her skin — no darker than an Anglo-Saxon girl's would have been with a moderate suntan — was set off by a white gown cleverly designed to display her considerable physical charms, as was the necklace of diamonds she wore.

"You can say one thing for the Great One; he always knew how to pick 'em," said Paul Rogers as he, Lynn, Mort, Laurel, and Mildred Malone joined a queue that had formed near the door and was now passing before the guests of honor. "His list of conquests include the most beautiful women in Miami."

"No more so than the one he divorced," said Mort, and received a quick squeeze of his hand from Laurel in return.

"Good evening, Theo." Mildred Malone was the picture of aristocratic courtesy, as Laurel brought her wheelchair to a stop before Malone and Elena Sanchez. "You look well."

"Thank you, Mildred." Malone stooped to kiss the mother of his three daughters on the cheek, but Laurel managed to move the wheelchair just then, foiling him and, judging by his sudden flush of chagrin, succeeding in disturbing his composure.

"I hope you're going to be very happy, my dear," Mildred Malone told Elena.

"Thank you." The younger woman blushed with obvious pleasure and appreciation. "You're very, very kind."

"I'm Laurel; I believe we've never met." Laurel was moving her mother's chair along the receiving line.

"We did long ago, during a swimming meet," Elena said with a smile. "I was competing in the butterfly class and you left me so far behind, I just folded my wings and fled."

Behind them, Lynn Rogers was presenting Mortimer Weyer to her father.

"Weyer?" Theodore Malone frowned. "The name seems familiar."

"I'm the new doctor at the satellite clinic in Liberty City."

"Oh yes." Malone was turning toward the next guest, having dismissed Mort Weyer from consideration. Then he stopped suddenly and faced the younger doctor again. "Weren't you the co-author with Eric Sondheim of that article attacking me and other cardiac surgeons because of our by-pass operations?" he demanded.

"We didn't *attack* anyone," said Mort. "All we did was cite the record to prove that many patients selected for surgery could have done very well on a strict medical regimen."

"That," said Malone flatly and with obvious displeasure, "is a matter of opinion."

"Of course," said Mort. "But then, much of medicine belongs in that area."

"We are indeed fortunate to have such an authority on cardiac diagnosis and treatment in our midst during the Institute Seminar." Malone's voice had risen and his flush betrayed his irritation, while causing a sudden hush in the conversation of the other guests.

"Theo, don't you think —?" Malone's young wife put a restraining hand on his arm but the surgeon shrugged it off with an abrupt gesture.

"We must not overlook the opportunity to gain knowledge from an authority on Dr. Sondheim's theories, my dear," he said. "My daughter, Dr. Lynn Rogers, has an hour scheduled tomorrow morning for a demonstration of microsurgery but she already accomplished that last night. Dr. Weyer, would you be so kind as to favor us with a discussion of Dr. Sondheim's *theories* at that time?" The sarcastic emphasis was on the word "theories."

"I wouldn't want to usurp Dr. Rogers' place on the program," Mort objected.

"I'm sure my daughter would not mind. Would you, Lynn?"

"Not at all, Father. But is it quite fair to our guest to put him on the spot like that?"

"It's settled." Malone overlooked her objection with a grandiloquent gesture. "With Sondheim's — and your — theories so controversial, Dr. Weyer, we can assure you of a large audience. What time were you scheduled for, Lynn?"

"Ten o'clock, but — "

"Shall we say ten tomorrow morning, Dr. Weyer?" Theodore Malone asked.

"Ten will be fine." Mort's voice was tense in the face of the contemptuous challenge. "Fortunately, I have copies of the slides Dr. Sondheim and I prepared for the paper before the American Heart Association. I will bring them to the seminar for showing

182

tomorrow and I think those attending will find them very interesting indeed."

"Please don't stint on the evidence, Doctor." Malone's voice was still openly contemptuous. "We surgeons are always willing to learn from our wiser medical confrères."

"The son-of-a-bitch really trapped you there, Mort," Paul Rogers said *sotto voce*, as they moved away from the receiving line toward the champagne table.

"I asked for it by coming here tonight," Mort admitted wryly. "But I always heard that a good fight was better than a bad stand — even when you lose."

"Thank God, that ordeal is over," said Lynn.

"John Randolph of Roanoke would have been proud of the gracious way you handled the usurper, Mrs. Malone," Mort Weyer assured the older woman. "You proved yourself a true Virginia aristocrat and I'd like to toast you with a glass of champagne, if I may."

"So say we all of us," Paul Rogers echoed. "I'll help you bring it, Mort."

The evening passed like almost any such social occasion. Many former Fellows and faculty members of the medical school greeted Mildred Malone and the two Malone daughters. A few asked where Lisa was and to these Lynn gave the excuse that her twin sister was out of the city.

Meg and Harris Downing were at the hors d'oeuvre table when Mildred and her entourage approached. "You were superb, darling, a real aristocrat," Meg told Mildred, kissing her on the cheek. "This must be the marvelous Dr. Weyer I'm hearing so much about."

"Just the new doctor from the slums, ma'am," said Mort. "After tomorrow, I may not even be that."

"I'm Harris Downing." The internist extended his hand in greeting. "Eric Sondheim and I are old friends."

"Dr. Sondheim told me to look you up when I came down to Miami, sir." Mort shook hands with the portly internist. "I'm familiar with your work in nephrology, of course."

"I wish we could offer victims of kidney disease more hope than we do," said Downing. "Kidney transplants aren't turning out to be everything we'd hoped they'd be — except between siblings. I'll be very much interested to hear your presentation tomorrow on medical versus surgical treatment of coronary heart disease."

"I still don't think I should be given Dr. Rogers' place on the seminar program – especially after the job of microsurgery she did last night," said Mort.

"You needn't feel guilty; I was only going to show a film I made to teach microsurgical technique to the residents," Lynn assured him. "Actually, I'm being punished for the publicity the *Herald* gave me. At the Malone Institute, only one doctor is ever supposed to be featured in newspapers or on television."

Meg Downing glanced at the receiving line, which now extended out through the lobby of the apartment hotel to the entrance. "Theo's really hogging the publicity tonight with that girl," she observed. "It's indecent for an old man to marry a voluptuous creature like her."

"Not only indecent, but downright dangerous for somebody carrying Theo's blood pressure," said Harris Downing. "He could keep it under control with pro-pranolol, but he won't take the dose he needs because he's afraid it will diminish his libido. Says he needs all of that he can generate – and I guess he's right."

"Doctors are worse than women about

gossip," Meg Downing scolded her husband fondly. "Come on, Harris, it's time old folks were going to bed. Nice to meet you, Dr. Weyer. I hope you're going to stay in Miami."

"You couldn't drive me away." Mort looked at Laurel. "I came down here because I remembered the palm trees and the water from when I was a small boy but I've already found some other attractions that promise to make the future even more pleasant."

"I hope you'll come to see me sometime so we can talk more about Virginia," Mildred told him.

"You can be sure of that," said Mort. "In fact, I hope to be around quite a bit."

The small pager Laurel wore attached to her belt suddenly beeped sharply. "That must be the laboratory," she said. "Excuse me while I check with the operator by phone. The blood smear I ordered done by eight must be ready."

"The way Laurel slapped down a cocky pathologist this afternoon is the talk of the seminar group," Paul Rogers commented while the younger Malone daughter was away. "I wonder how much danger there really is of a malaria epidemic?"

"More than you might think," said Mort Weyer. "Laurel was telling me about *Anopheles Gambiae* after the CPC this afternoon. It's one of the most frequently found species of mosquito in central Africa carrying *plasmodium falciparum* and has the capacity to live at elevations up to six thousand feet with temperatures close to that of frost."

"You saw both cases, didn't you, Mort?" Lynn asked.

"Yes — though I didn't know what I was looking at."

"Does anybody have an idea how the carrier could have gotten from Africa to the United States?"

"Oddly enough, I may have found a clue. Do either of you know Artemus Jones?"

Lynn frowned. "Isn't he the shop steward for the agricultural workers' union? A tall black who always wears purple?"

"That's Art," said Mort. "I caught him at Liberty City after I left Laurel's CPC; he's got something going with my clinic nurse. According to Art, a rumor's been floating around Liberty City that a plane smuggling diamonds or gold from Africa to Brazil strayed off course and crashed in the mountains of Haiti —"

"It's not just a rumor," said Paul. "I read

in the Tampa *Times* that the Haitian police were combing the mountains for just such a plane but hadn't found any evidence of it."

"Health authorities often find dead mosquitoes in planes landing from Africa; I remember reading in a medical journal about some cases of malignant malaria discovered, I believe, in Minnesota," said Lynn. "Five members of one family had visited a son who was a missionary in Africa and came down with malaria a week or ten days after they got back home."

"So it's not beyond the bounds of reason that a plane used for smuggling diamonds or gold from Africa could have brought both the mosquito and *plasmodium falciparum*," Mort commented.

"To Haiti, yes," said Mildred. "But I still don't understand how it would have reached Miami."

"If infected anopheles started a small epidemic of malaria somewhere in the mountains of Haiti, the parasites could easily have been brought into Miami in the blood of anyone landing illegally," Mort explained. "Artemus Jones tells me that the man I sent in this morning with malaria, who died before he reached the hospital, owned a boat capable of making that run. He kept it somewhere in the Keys and it's common knowledge in Liberty City that he often brought in illegal refugees from Cuba and Haiti. He'd shelter them in a big house he owned in Liberty City until they could be moved inland and join the others working around Lake Okeechobee."

"It sounds like science fiction," said Mildred Malone.

"The science fiction of today is the science of tomorrow," said Mort.

Laurel came back from the telephone just then, her expression troubled. "The smear's ready but Baby DuVall's having almost continuous convulsions and his temperature's spiking. I've got to go to the hospital right away. Will you and Paul see that Mother gets safely home, Lynn?"

"Certainly."

"Mind if I go with you?" Mort Weyer asked as Laurel started toward the door leading outside.

"I wish you would." She reached for his hand gratefully. "I need all the backing up I can get and, after all, you *are* the referring physician."

On the way out, Laurel and Mort met a broad-shouldered man who reminded Mort oddly of Theo Malone, except that he was smiling. The newcomer was just entering the reception room with a bouncy and somewhat plump blonde. Laurel greeted them warmly.

"This is Dexter Parnell and his wife, Kelley," she told Mort. "Kelley and I were roommates in college. Dr. Mort Weyer, the Parnells. Dex is Father's lawyer but don't hold that against him."

The two shook hands with Mort. "Glad to meet you, Doctor," said Parnell. "I believe we have a mutual acquaintance in Artemus Jones."

"That reminds me," said Mort. "Jones asked me to tell you he'll meet you at Jacques LeMoyne's house in Liberty City at eleven."

"What are you going there for, Dex?" Laurel asked.

"To hunt for a will, and hope I don't find it."

"I'll go with you — to hunt for something else."

"What in the world would you be looking for out there?" Parnell asked.

"A mosquito." Laurel took Mort's arm. "We don't have time to explain now. I'll fill you in when I meet you in Liberty City tomorrow."

"Meet *us*," Mort corrected her. "I'm

curious about that mosquito, too."

IV

Paul and Lynn took Mildred Malone home shortly after Laurel and Mort Weyer departed hurriedly for the Critical Care Unit. Paul waited in the family room while Lynn put her mother to bed. When she returned, he was standing at the large window, watching the night traffic on Biscayne Bay and the lights of the hotels on the golden strand of Miami Beach — long since a little tarnished — across the water.

"I've just discovered how much I miss this," he told Lynn. "This — and you. Want to go somewhere and have a nightcap while we talk?"

"I can't, Paul — not that I wouldn't like to. Mother was more upset by tonight than I'd realized. I had to give her a sleeping pill, so I can't leave her, but I can make some coffee. And there's always a chocolate cake in the cake box."

"Sounds like heaven. I'm sorry Mildred was so upset."

"I guess the bursting vitality and sultry beauty of my new stepmother got to her."

Lynn started the coffeepot perking while Paul took the cake box and some plates out to the family room overlooking the bay.

"Bursting is certainly the word," he agreed.

"Mother still loves Father and doesn't really blame him for deserting her. In a way, she feels it's her fault, for getting that spinal cord tumor."

"Nobody can blame themselves for an act of God. Besides, Theo was already cheating on her long before the tumor, if what I've heard is true."

"It's true enough. Mother believes Dexter Parnell is Father's son."

"Along with a few others. It's strange that all of Theo's bastards — the ones we know of at least — are male."

"Mother blames herself for that, too — which doesn't make sense."

"One thing is certain," said Paul. "None of Theo's bastard sons can begin to stack up to his legitimate daughters. You three are about the finest specimens of womanhood anybody could look for."

"Maybe. But sometimes I wonder how much of our success comes from trying to be more successful women than any of Father's male offspring have turned out to be."

Paul gave her a startled look. "Surely you're not excusing him — for anything."

"No. He's wounded all three of us too deeply for that, by deserting Mother — and in other ways. But he still may have done his daughters a favor just the same."

"*You* maybe, but only because you had the potential to become the skilled surgeon you already are. Come to think of it, you'd already started to show that when we were doing experimental surgery our second year at Hopkins. You always finished your operations ahead of the rest of the class, and your dogs always lived."

"That was luck. Besides, I was only trying to keep up with you."

"We *were* a pair, weren't we?" Paul smiled. "I'll never forget how we always took the long way from our apartment to the hospital so you could enjoy the flowers growing in the median beds along Broadway. Those were happy days."

"Please, Paul — don't."

"Tell me something. Didn't you ask Theo to send you to St. Louis to learn microsurgery because it would give you a skill he didn't have?"

"Of course, but he still refuses to admit that it has put me ahead of him —"

"That surgical miracle you pulled off last night should convince him. How long do you think he'll keep you in the doghouse?"

"Until he finds a suitable case for a new operation he's planned; one I robbed him of last night."

"How is Lisa stacking up against Theo? From what I've seen of it, the new Critical Care Unit is a real accomplishment."

"It is, but she patterned it after the one in Jacksonville. Granting the truth of your theory about the success of the Malone doctor-daughters being a result of our drive to outdo Father, at that Lisa's certainly been concentrating on exceeding him as a lover."

"Has she succeeded?"

"I guess only Lisa knows that but she's quite a siren, judging by the swarm of males that are always buzzing around her."

"I'm sorry to hear that. Lisa's too fine a doctor to turn into a bed-hopper like so many of her masculine counterparts. What about Laurel?"

"The way she's been going after these malaria cases, she obviously inherited a lot of Father's drive. I've an idea she'll make her mark in the field of Tropical Medicine very quickly."

"If she doesn't marry Mort Weyer first. To

me, he looks like a fit mate for any Malone daughter – and that's saying a lot, as I very well know." He stood up. "Thanks for the coffee and cake, darling. Sure I can't seduce you into going back to my hotel with me?"

Lynn gave him a kiss and turned him so he pointed toward the front door. "Not tonight – tempted though I may be. I'm going to stay with Mother."

At the front door, he turned to face her. "Tomorrow afternoon the seminar schedule will be devoted to golf and nothing's slated for the evening. Could we go out to the ranch? You've still got it haven't you?"

"Actually, it's my surgical research laboratory now."

"Afterward, we might stop by that dinner theater we used to go to so often – the one that puts on the Toby Shows."

"I'd love it. Good night."

"Good night," he said, holding her and kissing her until she pushed him away. "Shall I see you tomorrow at Mort Weyer's lecture?"

"Wouldn't miss it for anything." Closing the door behind him, she stood leaning against it until she heard the taxi he'd called stop outside but she was smiling and her heart was singing.

Chapter 7

In the small laboratory serving the Critical Care Unit, Laurel moved away from the stool upon which she had been sitting while examining the eight o'clock blood smear from Baby DuVall under the binocular microscope.

"Take a look," she told Mort Weyer. "You won't see this picture very often."

The slide was a jumble of red blood cells. Many of them bulged to several times normal size, pregnant with the parasites of *plasmodium falciparum*. Others had ruptured, spilling out a host of variously shaped smaller cells, the lethal agents themselves.

"You're right," said Mort. "I've never seen anything like this before, not even in medical school. Those smaller crescents and banana-shaped cells are the parasites, aren't they?"

Laurel nodded. "Did you notice that they're shaped differently from those still inside red blood cells?"

"Yes."

"Those are the gametocytes, the reproductive forms, and they indicate a rapidly increasing infestation. We've been giving this baby a blood-thinning agent since this morning, but you can imagine how much danger still remains of the smaller capillaries in the brain being jammed with enlarged and broken red cells, plus the plasmodium itself."

"What's the prognosis?"

"Let's take a look at the baby first."

"He's been having convulsions for the past two hours, Dr. Malone," said the nurse who was specialing the baby in one of the cubicles of the Unit. "The cooling blanket Dr. Rosenberg ordered has only brought the temperature down a degree and a half."

While Mort Weyer and the nurse watched, Laurel examined the baby with great care, a procedure made somewhat difficult by the constant twitching movements of its entire body. When she looked up from listening over the tiny chest and took the tips of the stethoscope from her ears, her expression was grave.

"I don't find anything new, except that the spleen seems a little larger than when I examined him this morning," she said.

"Obviously, we're dealing with a chloroquine-resistant form of the disease."

"Does that occur very often?" Mort asked.

"More often than five years ago, since chloroquine is being so widely used in Africa."

"Then the prognosis isn't good?"

"Not unless I can get some mefloquine by morning."

"From the F.D.A. in Washington?"

"The best bet is to get some directly from the Center for Disease Control in Atlanta. With malignant malaria showing up so often now in travelers returning from Africa, they must keep a supply, even though the F.D.A. hasn't authorized its general use yet in the United States."

"Another example of government foot-dragging?"

"More like overcaution. Sometimes it's hard to find *plasmodium falciparum* in the blood, if you're not used to looking for them. And where a potentially toxic drug is concerned, you don't want doctors to start pouring it into every patient who's been to Africa lately and starts having chills and fever."

"So what can you do?"

"Shift to a dilute solution of quinine dihydrochloride and try to hold the production of those gametocytes you saw in check until I can get some mefloquine from Atlanta by special permission," said Laurel as they were moving through the Critical Care Unit to the office set aside for physicians to use when writing their notes for the charts.

In the office Laurel picked up the telephone and dialed the operator. "This is Dr. Laurel Malone," she said. "I need to speak to the duty officer at the Center for Disease Control in Atlanta."

"It's an 800 number, Dr. Malone. I can ring it direct."

Moments later, the voice of the switchboard operator in Atlanta sounded in Laurel's ear. "Center for Disease Control. Can I help you?"

"I'm Dr. Laurel Malone in Miami. Can I speak to the chief officer on duty? It's very urgent."

"Dr. Milne's on another line, Dr. Malone. Will you hold?"

"Yes." Laurel covered the mouthpiece with her hand and turned to Mort. "He'll be with me in a moment."

"I hope he makes it a short one. The monitor screen for the baby shows the temperature up another degree."

"Dr. Milne." A brisk voice sounded in Laurel's ear. "May I help you?"

"This is Dr. Laurel Malone at Biscayne General in Miami. I have a case of malignant malaria here in an eight-months-old infant."

"Falciparum malaria? Are you sure, Doctor?"

"Absolutely. It's chloroquine-resistant into the bargain and I need some mefloquine. Do you have it?"

"We have it but we really should examine a blood smear up here before releasing it, Dr. Malone."

"By that time the patient would be dead," said Laurel. "If you're worrying about my qualifications to make the diagnosis, don't. I spent last year at the WHO laboratory in Zaire where, incidentally, we saw quite a lot of chloroquine-resistant malaria."

"No offense, Dr. Malone." Milne's tone had changed from doubt to co-operation. "I can send you enough mefloquine to treat your patient by Air Express, first thing in the morning."

"I'd rather you sent it tonight, Dr. Milne. The patient is *in extremis*. We'll gladly pay the extra cost down here."

"I'll have it sent right away. You should

be able to pick it up at the Miami airport by nine o'clock tomorrow morning. May I ask what African country your patient came from recently?"

"We don't know, Doctor. Dr. Prentiss of the Health Department here is sending you a specimen of *Anopheles Gambiae* by Air Express for identification."

"*Anopheles Gambiae?* Are you sure?"

"I saw a lot of them in Zaire, Dr. Milne. Fortunately we've found only the one specimen yet and it was dead. Thank you for your co-operation."

"If you've identified *Anopheles Gambiae* before it has a chance to spread, the whole Western Hemisphere will owe you a debt of thanks, Dr. Malone. May I call you as soon as I've had a chance to examine the mosquito?"

"I wish you would," said Laurel. "Good night."

"You certainly put the fear of God into him," said Mort Weyer admiringly. "I could hear his voice change in the telephone when you mentioned Zaire. What next?"

"I've got to make up a dilute solution of quinine dihydrochloride and add it to the intravenous drip. Quinine can be pretty toxic when given intravenously but we have no

201

choice this time. I'll make it as dilute as possible, though, while containing an effective level of the drug to at least hold the parasites in check."

"How much can you give safely?" Mort asked.

"Five milligrams per kilogram of body weight is usually safe, but I'll have to stay with the baby for at least an hour or so after the intravenous drip is started. If you need to get ready for that joust with Father tomorrow morning, why don't you go on home? He can be a pretty dirty fighter."

"So can I. If you don't mind, I'll stay."

"I was hoping you'd say that," she told him with a smile. "I know my way around where malaria is concerned but you've had far more experience in treating heart failure. That's the thing we have to fear most for the next twelve hours, until I start the drug that's coming from Atlanta in the morning."

It was two hours later and past eleven, when Mort Weyer brought his Volkswagen Rabbit to a stop at the curb in front of the Malone cottage in Buena Vista.

"I could use a nightcap," Laurel told him. "Care to join me?"

"I thought you'd never ask."

Tired to the bone, she leaned on his arm

as they went up the walk and he opened the door with her key. Moving quietly so as not to disturb Mildred, who was asleep, they made their way to the kitchen. There Mort poured nightcaps of Bourbon and ginger ale for them, taking them back to the living room. The wide glass doors overlooked the bay with Miami Beach in the background and Laurel had curled up on a sofa there.

"This is Miami as I remember it from my boyhood," he said, sitting down beside her and putting his arm across her shoulders. "Next door to paradise."

"A somewhat flawed paradise but still pretty wonderful," she agreed, taking a deep pull at her drink. "New Orleans was an exciting place to study medicine and Zaire was fascinating, even if we were almost worked to death, but I'm glad to be back in Miami — this time for good."

"Me, too, and even more so since I met you. Unless you and your mother object, I'm going to be around here a lot from now on."

"I don't object, and if Mother does, I'll overrule it." Laurel finished her drink and put her glass on the coffee table beside his also empty one. When she leaned back on the sofa, it was the most natural thing in the world to find herself in his arms, and her lips on his. It was a long kiss and a warm one, becoming very warm indeed before she pushed herself away.

"I think you'd better go, Mort," she said, a little shakily. "I just discovered that I inherited something from my father I didn't know I had."

"What's that?"

"His libido."

II

At exactly five minutes before ten o'clock on Saturday morning, Mort Weyer came into the auditorium of the Malone Heart Institute. Seeing Lynn Rogers sitting with Paul, he took a seat beside them.

"I hope you're loaded for bear, Mort," said Paul. "Theo's sure to go after you with every trick he can muster — and he knows them all."

"I'm not worried, but I still don't think I should have taken Dr. Rogers' place on the program."

"Father and I have had a lot of arguments in the past about the indications for by-pass," Lynn told him. "I'd like to hear what you have to say."

The speaker at the podium ended his presentation and, gathering up his material, moved away from the platform. From a seat on the front row, Dr. Theo Malone got up and moved to the lectern.

"As some of you know," he began, "I heard last night during the reception that one of the authors of a recent paper attacking the surgical procedure of coronary by-pass is now in Miami. In a spirit of fair play I naturally invited him to give us the benefit of his wisdom."

Malone paused, while a ripple of laughter passed through the audience.

"I warned you," Paul Rogers told Mort.

"You don't spend two years at Bellevue without getting a tough skin. I'll survive."

"However," Malone continued, "it appears that the young man has failed to accept my invitation —"

Mort stood up. "I'm here, Dr. Malone."

"Good! I was afraid you'd decided against taking up my offer."

"Challenge would be a better word," Mort said as he descended the sloping aisle of the auditorium floor toward the stage and the lectern. "I do want to thank you, however, for letting me tell something about the work of Dr. Sondheim and the team of which I was a part at Bellevue for two years. Especially, since our findings have not been favorably received by many specialists in cardiac surgery."

"You can say that again," said Malone as Mort ascended to the stage and crossed to the lectern. "Unfortunately, I don't know enough about your medical background to introduce you —"

"I can sum it up for you in a few words," Mort assured him. "Harvard College and Harvard University School of Medicine. A residency in Cardiology at Massachusetts General plus a two-year Fellowship in Cardiology at Bellevue in New York on the service of Dr. Eric Sondheim, followed by a third year as Instructor in Cardiology, also at Bellevue."

"Perhaps I should add that you are presently employed as a physician at the Liberty City satellite clinic here in Dade County," said Malone. "Although the clinic would appear to be somewhat less than a worthy theater for the display of your talents."

"Nevertheless a lucrative one, while I put away enough money to open an office here as a cardiologist. Incidentally, since you haven't yet mentioned my name, it's

Mortimer Weyer, M.D."

"The floor is yours, Dr. Weyer," said Malone as he moved back to his seat.

"Thank you, Dr. Malone," said Mort. "I would also like to thank so many surgeons in the audience — whose every instinct, I am sure, is to regard me as an enemy for questioning the need for such a lucrative procedure as coronary by-pass — for coming to hear me. As a prelude to telling you some of the conclusions reached by the Sondheim team at Bellevue regarding heart disease in general and coronary heart disease in particular, I would remind you of some words spoken by a famous physician of other years. To wit: *It is much easier to write upon a disease than upon a remedy. The former is in the hands of nature and a faithful observer with an eye to tolerable judgment cannot fail to delineate a likeness; the latter — being the remedy, will ever be subject to the whim, the inaccuracy and the blunder of man.*'

"Those words," Mort explained, "were written almost two hundred years ago by Dr. William Withering in *Account of the Foxglove*, which was a description of his discovery of digitalis."

A wave of polite laughter greeted the quip, but Theodore Malone didn't join in it.

"The first successful operation in which a section of vein from the thigh was used to divert blood from the aorta just above the heart past the blocking by arteriosclerosis of a coronary artery supplying blood to the heart muscle itself – the operation known popularly now as aorto-coronary by-pass graft and sometimes shortened to ACBG was performed in 1964," Mort began his discourse. "Along with nitroglycerin and a few other drugs, digitalis was for many years the only weapon by which physicians were able to reduce the agonizing pain known as angina pectoris, caused, as you all know well, by an insufficient flow of blood to the heart muscle. Subsequently, the addition of propranolol, lidocaine, and other compounds to the medical armamentarium has aided considerably in treating that most painful symptom by medical means.

"The second operation in 1967 started a new specialty which has grown at an astounding rate, as effectively proved by the size of this audience. From that specialty has come a stream of literature on the nature and value of ACBG as a remedy for coronary heart disease, much of which, I'm sure Dr. William Withering would label, *'whim, inaccuracy and blunder.'*"

"Get on with your lecture, man!" Theo Malone growled in a tone loud enough to be heard everywhere in the auditorium. "If you're going to indulge in nothing but verbiage, we might as well go home."

There was a moment of silence, then Mort started putting the sheets of his manuscript back into the folder from which he had taken them. "I'll save *you* the trouble of going home, Dr. Malone." The utter contempt in his tone was like the slash of a sword. "In Dr. Withering's day medicine was practiced by gentlemen but it seems now that it is practiced – at least here – by boors."

As Mort was turning away from the microphone, Lynn Rogers' voice sounded from where she was sitting at the back of the auditorium.

"This hour was scheduled to be mine for a presentation on microsurgery, Dr. Weyer," she said. "I relinquished it gladly at the suggestion of my father to hear you discuss the work of one of the most respected cardiologists living today. If *he* does not wish to hear you, I would suggest that *he* leave but *I* wish to hear what you have to say and so do most of those gathered here. Please proceed as a favor to us."

"Yes, go on, man," Theodore Malone growled, "but give us more facts."

"You want facts, Dr. Malone? I'll give them to you." Mort kept his tone even. "I spent several hours earlier this morning studying statistical reports detailing the experience of the Malone Heart Institute in ACBG surgery. Your operative mortality for the last three years stands at about two per cent, yet in many major clinics over the country the mortality figure is less than one per cent. The conclusion is, therefore, inescapable that you're not only operating on patients who should not have surgery but are also performing too many by-passes."

The hush that seized the room at Mort's direct frontal attack against Malone was broken by the surgeon's angry words: "Damn you! Prove it!"

"Your computer could have told you that long ago," Mort assured him. "Unfortunately, you seem to have been too busy doing dramatic surgery and making headlines to consult it. Recently, a group at Duke studied their own results by storing a hundred and ten items of information in a follow-up of something over seven hundred patients with coronary artery disease, almost equally divided between those receiving medical and surgical treatment. They concluded that, while the lives of certain patients, classified as 'high risk,' may be prolonged by coronary by-pass surgery, the operation did not by any means always prolong life, when compared with skilled medical management over a period of two to five years."

Mort had his audience now and even Malone had lapsed into a steely-eyed attitude of watchful waiting.

"ACBG is rapidly becoming one of the most frequently performed major surgical procedures in America," Mort continued. "The number of operations each year has probably reached almost a hundred thousand, perhaps more. And that, I might remind you, in spite of a sharp decrease in the amount of coronary heart disease among the general population, probably due to better health measures like cutting down on fats and smoking, plus the great increase in exercise by the general population.

"The cost of an ACBG operation today is between fifteen and twenty-five thousand dollars, with a fourth of that amount probably representing the fee for the surgeon. Operations upon a heart case can command, roughly, a thousand dollars an hour. And since by-pass operations take an average of about five hours, it is hardly surprising that the number of procedures is increasing in spite of statistics showing that the index of the disease they are supposed to cure – but often do not – is still decreasing. One more figure makes the list complete. The cost of roughly a billion dollars a year for coronary by-pass surgery in the U.S. alone represents about two and a half times the entire budget of the National Heart, Lung and Blood Institute, from which funds for research in curing human illness and suffering are appropriated.

"The question conscientious physicians must face then is simply this: Can the vast amount of expensive surgery be justified by the results that follow its use? The answer, in light of the steadily increasing mass of data Dr. Eric Sondheim and the Bellevue team – of which I was a member – has been accumulating has to be a resounding 'No!'"

"What are *your* indications, Doctor?" a surgeon inquired.

"Coronary by-pass surgery is indicated without question for patients who suffer the agonizing pain of angina pectoris and are not relieved by medical treatment in the hands of competent and experienced cardiologists. It may also be indicated where properly conducted visualization of the coronary arteries by heart catheterization shows a single obstructive lesion in the left main coronary artery, supplying much of the left ventricle, the main pump of the heart."

"What about incipient myocardial infarcts?" another listener asked.

"The answer is 'No,'" said Mort. "A recent survey of ACBG operations over a period of ten years published in *Circulation* confirms our conclusions that the operation does not prevent heart attacks and may indeed bring them on."

"Isn't that a rather sweeping statement?" The listener who had asked the question objected.

"Not when the mortality following surgery in such cases can run as high as thirty-eight per cent, far above that of patients who reach the hospital after a heart attack and are treated medically," said Mort. "In fact, signs of small infarcts can be found in the EKG after ACBG for whatever cause in ten to fifteen per cent of the cases. Some cardiologists believe such what might be called small heart attacks after by-pass operations account for much of the dramatic relief of pain in many cases after surgery has been done."

"I don't believe it," Theo Malone growled. "Surgery relieves pain; we all know that."

"I never said it didn't," Mort countered. "If I had severe angina that was not relieved by the standard medical regime followed in the best cardiac clinics, I'd be the first to ask for surgery. But I would do it with the full knowledge that relief is not permanent and also not likely to lengthen my life. In fact, it would probably shorten it."

The statement brought a rash of objections and he waited patiently for them to subside before continuing.

"If patients are followed closely after an operation, the admittedly spectacular and desirable relief of pain is found to undergo a steady decline," he added when the room grew quiet. "This effect is due, in part at least, to the fact that by-pass surgery, however effective and dramatic in the initial relief of pain, appears to speed up the development of further coronary heart disease at a rate which may be as much as five times what would be normally expected under medical treatment."

A murmur of amazement − and con-siderable doubt − came from the audience, punctuated by a loud snort of "Poppycock!" from Theo Malone.

"Again your reaction is what I would expect from a surgeon who probably does more ACBGs than anyone else in the country," Mort retorted. "Yet the true facts can easily be verified from the article by Dr. Sondheim and the Bellevue team of which I was a member. Moreover, the truth that heart surgery is far from being the panacea most cardiac surgeons claim it to be is proved by the simple fact that seven and a half times more by-pass patients choose to retire from employment after the operation than would be expected in the general population under fifty-five. And with those above fifty-five, the incidence of retirement in one study was roughly eleven times what would be expected — even though practically all post by-pass patients remain under the care of a car-diologist and follow much the same regimen as nonoperative patients."

"What is the real value of ACBG surgery then?" Lynn asked.

"Very little beyond the immediate relief of pain," Mort answered. "But here again the dramatic effect is misleading in the light of cold hard facts. Our studies showed that pain relief lasted an average of thirty-six months, following which no advantage can be shown for surgery over medical treatment.

"To sum up the alleged benefits of this fantastically expensive – but enormously profitable to the surgeon – operation," he concluded, "it is a boon only to patients with the unbearable and medically unrelieved pain of angina pectoris – plus perhaps a few with only one coronary artery blocked.

"On the other hand, the drawbacks are an almost certain progression of disease after surgery to a more rapid degree than if an operation was not performed in the first place. And in addition, the patient quite often becomes a socio-economic casualty, with the only real profit in the majority of cases going to the surgeon and the hospital."

There was a spattering of applause but Theo Malone lumbered to his feet before it died away and began to speak.

"I will not dignify the presentation you have just heard by presenting arguments to show that it is what I designated it just now, namely, poppycock," he said heavily. "Those of us who have seen the startling relief of pain in angina as well as the hopeful life given to our patients will go on operating, regardless of such unfounded criticism.

"This afternoon," he continued, "will be without any scientific program, since that period is allowed for the Malone Cup Golf Tournament, whose winner will be honored at the annual luncheon for Fellows and guests on Sunday. Those of you who plan to take part in the golf tournament should be at the Doral Country Club by two P.M. The rest can no doubt find entertainment for themselves here in a city which has for so long been one of the major entertainment centers for the world."

A few of the listeners stopped to talk briefly to Mort as the others filed out of the auditorium. When he finally came up to the door, he was surprised to find Paul and Lynn Rogers waiting for him.

"I would like to apologize for the boorish behavior of my father, Dr. Weyer," said Lynn. "For nearly two years I've been trying to get him to let me make a study of our operative cases like the Duke project but he has steadily refused. I wasn't aware of the two per cent mortality so perhaps that is one of the reasons why he wouldn't let me send questionnaires to patients operated on here during the past five years."

"Our work at the new clinic in Tampa has not been going on long enough for us to have any really definitive results," said Paul, "but I am familiar with most of the figures you quoted and can verify their correctness."

"Please call me Mort. At least I have two friends in the enemy camp."

"Three, including Laurel," said Lynn. "But then I don't suppose you count her as being in the enemy camp."

"I hope not," said Mort fervently. "I certainly hope not."

Chapter 8

The center of South Florida, extending from the northern end of Lake Okeechobee almost to Marathon among the hundreds of Keys to the south, has rightly been called a vast "River of Grass." Better known as the Everglades, it is a wide, south-flowing stream of fresh water that becomes brackish only in its lower third where it mixes with water from the higher level of the Gulf of Mexico in what is known as Florida Bay. Over much of that distance the stream is contained to varying degrees, depending upon breaks made by both nature and man, between two banks that are like no other in the world.

Fresh water, flowing south from Lake Okeechobee for countless thousands of years, has worn a trough in the soft oolitic limestone that forms the base of the southern tongue of the River of Grass. Westward the rim is low and merges imperceptibly along the Mangrove Coast with the Gulf itself. Eastward, the rim is much more distinct. A narrow strand of beaches and peninsulas alternating with higher ridges along the rim of rock, it supports, though sometimes poorly, and gives both sustenance and water to the famed Gold Coast of Florida.

Miami is the central jewel in the pendant, and the Florida Keys the necklace, oddly enough with only one strand. The long chain of limestone ridges curves steadily southward and westward below the water as reefs and above it as islands called Keys. Starting from Key Largo south, the chain of island-Keys is connected to the mainland – if it can be called that when it is as much water as earth – by the asphalt ribbon called U.S. 1. From the Canadian border in northern Maine, the first transcontinental U.S. Highway extending to Key West at the end of the Florida island chain was for many years the only single traffic artery from north to south.

West of the Keys lies the vast shallow island-studded and marl-bottomed area of Florida Bay, with a vast number of small islands around which flows water from the Everglades on its way to join the Gulf. Eastward, the continuation of the rocky ridge of limestone keeps the water of the Everglades from overflowing the Gold Coast. Buried like some shallow Atlantis, it extends in the form of a maze of reefs almost to the edge of the Gulf Stream in what has been known since its discovery by Juan Ponce de Leon as the "Florida Straits." A major passageway for Spanish galleons bringing gold from South America and, by way of the Isthmus of Darien, from the far off Philippines, the reef-studded western border of the straits has been the graveyard of countless treasure ships and a lure for booty hunters since Ponce de Leon discovered it.

II

Saturday morning was bright and warm when Lisa Malone and Roberto Galvez left the marina dock for the Key Largo Coral Reef Preserve. They were not seeking the gold of the Spaniards but a newer and even more rewarding pleasure of discovery, the beauty of the undersea world lying east of that long Key which, until the building of the Florida Overseas Railroad, had been the end of the land route in Florida.

The day was perfect and the twin diesels

of the twenty-four-foot boat with its hull of Philippine mahogany and its luxurious accouterments an ideal platform from which divers – or just plain viewers – could explore a world of strange beauty where new discoveries awaited every dive.

They had breakfasted leisurely at the Reef restaurant where they'd had dinner Friday evening before returning to the Malone cottage and, at Lisa's decision, separate bedrooms. Since they planned to spend the day on the reef, they carried a luncheon prepared by the restaurant and an ice-filled cooler containing refreshments.

In obedience to Lisa's call from Miami the manager of the marina had provided everything they could need for a day of diving, arranged in orderly fashion on the floor of the cockpit of the boat.

Now, as Lisa steered the boat away from the dock itself and headed through the channel toward the passageway leading to deeper water, they could see glass-bottomed sight-seeing boats putting out from nearby John Pennekamp Coral Reef State Park. Many other small boats dotted the shoreward area from which tourists wearing snorkels and diving masks could study the coral formation bottom. Equaled in beauty nowhere else within the continental limits of the United States, it was judged by many to be superior to any of its kind in the world.

A helicopter carried visitors interested in a view of the Coral Reef Preserve and the upper Florida Keys from the air. In the bright sunlight the bottom of the sea was easily visible even from a height of several hundred feet. The passengers waved to the lovely young woman in a bright blue maillot that fitted her like her own skin and was, to only a small degree, less revealing, as well as the bronzed dark-haired and very handsome man in the bikini swim trunks. They waved back.

"Take the wheel, Roberto," Lisa called to her companion from the flying bridge where she was steering the boat through the narrow channel. "I need to inspect the diving gear."

"Didn't the marina manager do that?"

"The first rule in scuba diving is to make the final check yourself. That way, nobody else is to blame if anything goes wrong."

"Don't speak of things going wrong. I don't even like the thought of it."

"Neither do I, so I'll make sure it won't," said Lisa. "The channel is plainly marked by buoys so you can't miss it. Just don't run over any tourists floating around with snorkels and remember to slow down for sailboats."

Using a pressure gauge, Lisa started by testing the air content of the tanks from which they would breathe while under water. She noted first that the four with which they'd been provided, in case they made two dives that afternoon, contained more than the minimum safe 70 per cent. A reserve of air in the tanks could mean safety rather than a sudden trip to the surface if a diver's tank became empty. The immediate danger of air embolism in the bloodstream called the "bends" was a result of ascending quickly from depths beyond thirty-three feet. She therefore made certain that the lever which would release a final three-hundred pound air pressure reserve from the tank to the diver was in the closed, or "up," position where it should be.

Moving on, she checked the backpacks and harness assemblies that held the tanks, making sure the straps could be released at will if it became necessary to discard the tank itself because of its weight. Inhaling sharply through the mouthpiece of the breathing regulator while the protective cap sealed it from the high pressure tanks, she examined it for leaks before attaching each regulator to its air tank. Then she checked the seating by opening the air tank valve and listening for the whistle that would have revealed a leak.

Finally, inserting each mouthpiece and breathing from it, she checked the air flow, making sure it started easily and stopped completely after each exhalation. The last check was for weight belts, which would neutralize the natural buoyancy of the body in the water, allowing the diver to sink gently after exhaling and float slowly upward after inhaling.

"Everything's ready," she told Roberto as she moved back to the flying bridge beside him and looked eastward toward the open sea beyond.

"How far out are we going?"

"First, we'll anchor somewhere near the edge of the reef and look around at a reasonable depth. If we see anything particularly interesting, we'll go still deeper."

To the east, the vast area of the sea was a gleaming mirror with almost no waves on this largely windless morning. Off to the south, a steamer was passing through the Florida channel; its size and the gleaming whiteness of its silhouette identified it as one of the large fleet of passenger ships now making regular cruises from Miami to the Bahamas, the Caribbean, and beyond.

"If we had food and water, we could cruise down to Caracas," said Roberto.

"That's the way a lot of Spanish galleons came to rest on the bottom. When I was diving a few months ago, we found coins and even an old cannon lying on the bottom but couldn't identify the wreck from which it came."

"You love this, don't you?"

"It's one of the reasons why I think I'd never leave Florida. Slow down and I'll go forward and watch for a grassy bottom area where we can drop the anchor. The depth here looks like maybe fifty feet, so we should be able to stay down an hour without any problems before coming up for lunch."

With the boat moving slowly and Lisa lying flat on the deck at the bow, looking down at the sunlit bottom, she soon detected a patch of grass. Signaling Galvez to stop the engines, she waited until the boat drifted over it, then dropped the anchor.

"The equipment is okay." She came back to the cockpit from the front of the boat and handed him a life vest. Though flat now, it was equipped with a small capsule of carbon dioxide which, when crushed, would inflate the jacket immediately.

"Why do we need these? We're both good swimmers."

"I take no chances." Lisa was beginning to be a little irritated with her companion as she strapped on her diver's watch, pressure gauge, and attached a diver's knife to her right leg. "That's why I'm in charge of the Critical Care Unit at the hospital."

"Okay." Galvez slipped his arms through the openings in the vest and snapped it into place before picking up the face mask and spitting into it, spreading the saliva around to protect the glass against fogging from breathing. "Do you need any help?"

"I'm okay." Reaching across the gunwale, Lisa dipped her flippers into the water so they would go on easily. Then slipping her feet inside them, she pulled up the heel straps until they fitted snugly. Strapping on her weight belt, she made certain the buckle could easily be opened, dropping the weights if she needed to ascend quickly. This done, she opened the main tank valve, nodding approval when she heard the air rush into the regulator that was the very heart of the diving apparatus. Galvez, meanwhile, had been doing the same and, reaching down, lifted Lisa's air tank in its harness and set it upright on the gunwale beside her.

"Ready?" he asked.

She nodded and he steadied the tank while she thrust her arms through the shoulder straps and buckled the harness, making sure it, too, could be released easily, dropping the tank. Then, resting on the gunwale with the tank on her back, she steadied Galvez's tank upright beside her while he stepped into his harness and buckled his belt.

Pressing the purge button that cleared water from the breathing tube and mouthpiece before putting the latter into her mouth, Lisa took two breaths and found that the valve worked easily. Then slipping on the mask, she inhaled deeply and felt it set itself snugly against the planes of her face and around her nose and mouth.

Raising her thumb and forefinger together to form a circle indicating she was ready, she waited while Galvez brought his own face plate down over his nose and eyes and set his teeth into the mouthpiece. As he tumbled off the gunwale backward and sank beneath the surface, Lisa turned her head to watch his body moving through the water, waiting for him to exhale the first breath of air from the tank. Seeing the stream of bubbles proving that his valve was working properly, she tumbled backward from the gunwale into the warm water.

III

On the way out of Biscayne General, after his presentation to the seminar, Mort Weyer stopped in the Critical Care Unit to see how Baby DuVall was doing. He was studying the monitor screen recording the patient's clinical course, and finding nothing encouraging in the picture, when Laurel came into the office.

"Hello," he said. "Did you sleep well?"

"That shot of Bourbon you gave me was just what I needed," she said, sinking into a chair. "I died – until the alarm went off at seven-thirty."

"Why so early?"

"I had to be at the airport by nine to pick up a package at Air Express with the mefloquine – the new malaria drug I was telling you about – from Atlanta."

"From the looks of that monitor, it didn't come a moment too soon."

"Or maybe too late. With a baby that small, I was afraid to give a very large dose of quinine dihydrochloride intravenously and maybe I erred by giving too little. His temperature is still spiking and the chills are almost continuous."

"*Nolle nocere* — do no harm — has been the first principle in medicine since Hippocrates."

"I know, but the line is sometimes hard to draw. I just finished starting the mefloquine but with so many red blood cells destroyed already by the malaria parasite, the hemoglobin and red cell counts are going down rapidly. I could remedy the deficiency with a transfusion, but that would also increase the possibility of blocking small arteries in the brain and damaging it permanently ... "

"Leaving you between Scylla and Charybdis?"

"With a narrow choice either way," she agreed. "How did the seminar program go?"

"About as you'd expect, with an audience of cardiovascular surgeons. Maybe ten per cent believed me; with the others I was hitting too close to home in telling them that fifty per cent of the patients they do by-passes on don't need them."

"I can imagine how my father took that."

"I'm sure it destroyed any chance I might have when I ask for his approval as a son-in-law."

"You do move fast, don't you? But if you need any encouragement, and after last night I'm sure you don't, none of his daughters or their mother have asked his approval of anything for quite a while."

The pager attached to Laurel's jacket pocket beeped shrilly and she picked up the telephone. She talked for only a few minutes but when she hung up, her expression was grave.

"That was Dr. Milne at the Center for Disease Control," she said. "Their expert has positively identified the mosquito Dr. Prentiss sent to Atlanta yesterday afternoon by Air Express as *Anopheles Gambiae*. Dr. Milne called Dr. Prentiss first with the report and Prentiss asked him to draft me as a consultant with the authority of the U.S. Public Health Service behind me, at least until Monday when a mosquito control team can be sent down from Atlanta."

"Proving that somebody besides me thinks you're something special," Mort assured her. "Liberty City's in my area of responsibility as a clinic physician, too, you know. So where do we start?"

"At Jacques LeMoyne's house. Right now I'm probably the only person in Miami who can recognize *Anopheles Gambiae* on sight. I'd like to inspect the premises before some technician from the Health Department's mosquito control section can start spraying everything in sight with an insecticide."

"Or worse."

Laurel gave Mort a startled look. "What do you mean?"

"Dexter Parnell and Artemus Jones are probably out there right now searching the house for a will. If any mosquitoes like the one the technician found in old Jock's clothing are still alive, both of them could get a dose of malignant malaria."

"We'd better get going, then. *Gambiae* is a home-loving insect. It likes to stay — and bite — inside the house."

IV

Even though Lisa Malone was an experienced diver, the beauty of the undersea world, with the sun shining almost directly overhead, fairly took her breath away. The bottom was easily visible, with the grass around the anchor moving gently in the faint current.

Swimming beside her, Roberto Galvez pointed to the east and she saw a small barracuda, only about two feet long and therefore a baby, floating almost motionless in the water. It was regarding them with an inquiring look but, when she took a deep breath and, turning her head slightly, directed the stream of bubbles she expelled toward it, the fish fled like the frightened baby it was.

Below them, a school of grouper swam by in a formation of almost military precision but scattered when Roberto kicked with his fins and shot down into their midst. Moments later they re-formed and proceeded on their way as decorously as if nothing had happened. Kicking slowly, Lisa moved downward, swallowing every now and then or yawning to keep the pressure equal on her ears. At what she judged to be about the thirty-three-foot level – equivalent to one atmosphere of pressure – she turned on her back to watch Roberto Galvez, who was descending behind her. He veered off toward a coral outcrop on which he tried to sit, only to rise suddenly when the rough, spiny surface scraped his seat.

As they swam over its surface, the color of the coral upon the reef changed constantly in the bright afternoon sunlight filtering through the crystal clear water. For millions of years, these tiny creatures had lived out their brief lives, leaving behind their empty sarcophagi. Since they were themselves little more than masses of protoplasm, they quickly dissolved or were devoured by the teeming life around them.

Even more fascinating than the coral itself were the inhabitants of the water that ebbed and flowed over the reef in constant motion. Starfish, mollusks, zebra-like sheephead — with the blunt noses that gave them the name — lobster, shrimp, crabs — all were busily scuttling about engaged in the pursuit of food. In dark caves formed by the growing coral, deadly eels lurked, capable of paralyzing a victim with a jolt of electricity that could almost incapacitate a human. Here and there, too, the wily octopus, snug in its lair, waited to wrap its many arms around a prey, holding it fixed with suction cups that enabled it to draw the captured creature into its central stomach.

Kicking gently, the divers drifted through the alien world of aquatic life. Spying a cowrie crawling along in search of prey, Lisa sank down gently until she could touch the mantle it had thrown about itself as a protection, turning it almost into the same color as the rock across which it was moving. Instantly, the creature drew itself within the shell, slamming shut the door fitting into the open portion of the shell like a portcullis dropped as protection from an invader.

Everywhere the battle for life went on, the litter of empty shells on the bottom telling its story of the struggle that always ended in death for one of the contestants. Here and there clusters of anemones looked deceptively like dahlias or chrysanthemums as their tentacles waved in the gentle current. *No wonder the name "Flower of Death" had been given them by humans,* Lisa thought, remembering that at the tip of each flower was a stinger able to stun a victim before it was drawn into the open mouth of the creature and gradually absorbed in the neverending battle for food.

Moving along the bottom in search of prey, a large starfish ceased all motion suddenly when it became aware of human presence. Four of its five stars were perfect but the fifth was only a nub blunted at the tip, resulting from a wound sustained perhaps in battle with another of its kind. How that fifth star could grow to become a duplicate of the other four was still a mystery unsolved by man, who, in the process of evolution over billions of years, had long since lost the power of regeneration possessed by creatures like the starfish and certain grass lizards often called chameleons. Once Lisa spotted a ray lying on the bottom, its sting-barbed tail hidden. When she shuffled her feet in the flippers on the sandy bottom, it shot away, the tail with its venomous weapon waving menacingly as it searched for a possible target.

For almost an hour, they floated, chased fish, picked lovely cone shells from the bottom and even watched a sea anemone capture a small fish by wrapping its tentacles around it, then leisurely bring the prey into its mouth and devour it. A large squid floated by, lazily waving its tentacles but, spotting them, suddenly ejected a spurt of black dye as it shot away. Kelp beds here and there waved in the faint current but these they avoided, for venomous creatures like sea urchins and Portuguese men-of-war could often be found among the jellylike formations of the kelp.

When the diving watch she was wearing showed they had been in the water for almost an hour, although their tanks were not quite exhausted Lisa gave the signal to ascend by raising her arm and pointing up.

Roberto replied with thumb and forefinger raised in a circle to show that he understood, and they rose gradually to the surface near the boat by following the anchor line. Lisa had hung the boarding ladder over the side of the boat at the stern before they started the dive and they had no trouble climbing out of the water and shedding the heavy tanks on the floor of the cockpit.

"I'd forgotten how beautiful it can be down there." Roberto moved into the half-cabin, where the ice chest with the food was located. "Why don't we have lunch, take a nap, and then go out a little deeper. You said you wanted to dive near the outer edge of the reef, didn't you?"

"I'd like to; we've got extra tanks so we'll have plenty of air. The sun doesn't go down until after eight o'clock this time of year so there's time left for a deeper dive."

V

Driving through Liberty City was like exploring a bombed area in wartime. The senseless riot following the acquittal – in a city far away from Miami to which the trial had been transferred – of police officers accused of beating a black man to death had turned parts of the once teeming area into a picture like the aftermath of a holocaust. Here and there a few buildings that were still intact teemed with people who could find homes nowhere else. Around and between them, homes, stores, service stations, repair shops, and anything left standing had been gutted by vandalism and fire, the fury of the rioters still attested by smashed windows, splintered doors, and unremoved litter.

"I remember this area when I was in college; it was what you could call a happy slum," said Laurel as Mort guided the Rabbit through the streets, dodging children playing stickball among the puddles in the street from a shower during the night.

Mindful of Laurel's presence beside him, he studiously ignored shouted insults from groups of teen-agers prowling for another gang with which to start a fight. Or seeking an expensive-looking automobile left parked at the curb waiting to be stripped in a few busy minutes of everything that could be removed and sold to buy drugs or cheap wine.

"It's far from happy now," Mort agreed.

"It's like a cancer! Why doesn't the city do something about it?"

"I guess the City Fathers figure the blacks that live here made this mess so they can just exist in it for a while. Still, from what Art Jones tells me, your father, of all people, is trying to do something by making a tax shelter profit for himself and some other doctors here."

"That must be the project for low-income housing Dex is working on. Kelley mentioned it yesterday while I was examining little Dex for strep throat. She said only one man was holding the project up by refusing to sell his house."

"That was Jacques LeMoyne," said Mort. "Art Jones says that if your friend Parnell doesn't find a will, the court will let the property be sold to his group for a song. Maybe then the low-rent housing project will get going and clean up some of this mess."

"I suppose in a situation like this, the end does justify the means," said Laurel. "But I shudder to think what a lethal combination all these puddles, plus *Anopheles Gambiae*, could make. It's a perfect breeding ground for mosquitoes. How much farther?"

"We're practically there; I see Art Jones's car at the end of the next block. Do you know him?"

"No."

"Art calls himself the Purple People Eater and dresses the part, but it's only camouflage. Actually, he's a well-educated and intelligent Negro."

"That's Dex's car parked in front of the purple one so he's here, too," said Laurel as Mort brought the car to a stop behind the purple sports model. "I hope they haven't messed up anything containing water where I might find mosquito larvae."

The house stood on three lots, allowing a wide border of yard between it and the nearest building which the fire had gutted.

"I want to walk around the yard before we go inside," said Laurel. "It doesn't look as if anything has been disturbed outside."

"Not for years," Mort agreed. "Old Jock apparently didn't even cut the weeds or remove trash."

"Wish I'd worn boots this morning." Laurel was removing a can of aerosol-propelled insect spray from the car. "We'll look for larvae first."

"You can understand why the people around here say the place is haunted," Mort observed as he took her arm to help her over a pile of broken concrete blocks, where the owner had apparently started to build an added room but stopped halfway. "It looks exactly like the one on TV in a program that was popular a few years ago."

"I remember that series," said Laurel. "The house had all sorts of secret passages and hidden rooms – plus a benign Frankenstein."

"People around here say the same about this house, according to Art Jones. It was left standing even during the riot because Jacques LeMoyne was good to them. With old Jock's connections in Haiti, maybe we'll find *Grand-père* DuVall here. This is the address he gave for Baby DuVall."

"One of the nurses told me he came to see the baby after we left last night. Visiting hours were over but he sneaked in somehow. She found him looking at his grandson and told him we had some new medicine coming in by air this morning from Atlanta. He didn't say anything, but when she made the patient's bed this morning, she found a doll he'd left for the baby."

"What kind of doll?"

"Just a little one, obviously handmade, with an evil-looking face."

"It's probably an obeah doll, proving that DuVall must have come from Haiti. I saw some of them once at an exhibit of Haitian art in New York. If *Grand-père* DuVall was using witchcraft, I hope it works for the baby."

Laurel discovered what she was seeking — but hoping not to find — in a corner of the yard behind the house. A small pool there had probably once contained a few goldfish but only a bullfrog jumped in when they approached. The murky water had been diluted some by the shower during the night, however, and they could easily see a swarm of larvae hanging from the surface.

"Damn!" she said fervently. "This complicates the picture."

"Think they could be *Anopheles Gambiae?*"

"I'll have to study them under the microscope." She took a small bottle from her pocket. "It's hard to tell the difference between ordinary *Anopheles* and *Gambiae* except under magnification."

Stooping, she scooped some water containing several of the tiny wriggling creatures into the bottle, then handing it to Mort, took the insect spray can from her pocket.

"We'll get a quart of oil from the nearest filling station, when we finish searching the house, and cover this pool with it," she said. "Meanwhile, spraying the surface will give us a head start on killing a lot of potential mosquitoes, whether they're dangerous or not."

"As I remember it, oil keeps the larvae from breathing air and kills them. Right?"

"Go to the head of the class," Laurel told him. "Let's go inside and see what Dex and your friend, Mr. Jones, are doing."

The two they sought were coming down the rickety stairway to the upper floors when they entered the open front door.

"You're wasting your time, Laurel," said Dex. "We've been through the whole house with a fine-toothed comb, but didn't see a single mosquito. Didn't find a will or a bank safe deposit key either, so I can file a petition Monday morning with the court to declare that old Jock died intestate. If no heirs turn up in a few weeks, we can buy this property and start building."

"Are you sure you didn't find the diamonds, too?" Mort asked with a grin.

"What diamonds?" Dexter Parnell asked.

"A rumor's been going around about an airplane from Africa to Brazil that crashed with a load of stolen diamonds or gold in the mountains of Haiti," Art Jones explained. "If the rumor happens to be true and someone in Haiti found the wreckage, he might have taken whatever was in the plane and escaped to the United States. He could have been picked up anywhere between here and Haiti by Jock with that boat he kept moored somewhere in the Keys."

"It's still there," said Dex. "I found the registration at the Coast Guard base but we didn't find any evidence of diamonds – or gold."

"It was just a rumor," said Art Jones.

Laurel glanced at the man in purple as he spoke and suddenly went rigid. "Don't move, Mr. Jones," she said, reaching for the aerosol can in her pocket.

"What's wrong?" Jones asked.

"That mosquito on your arm looks like it might be a *Gambiae.*"

"What th −" The word was cut off by the sudden jet of aerosol-propelled pyrethrins Laurel sprayed on the arm where she'd seen the insect, its body at the forty-five-degree angle assumed by Anopheles when biting.

"Got him!" she exclaimed triumphantly, catching the dead mosquito in her hand as it fell and lifting it to the light. "It's a *Gambiae,* too."

"Why so much fuss over ˆone mosquito, Laurel?" Dexter Parnell asked.

"Because where there are two, plus a fish-pond full of larvae, you've got the makings for a real epidemic of malignant malaria.

Gambiae likes closed places so any number of them could be in the house." She went on to explain what had happened in the case of Jacques LeMoyne and Baby DuVall, describing the malaria parasites she'd found in their blood.

"Are you sure about this particular mosquito?" Art Jones asked, when she'd finished the account.

"Absolutely. My identification was verified early this morning by a telephone call from the Center for Disease Control in Atlanta. But even if he bit you, a course of a new drug I've got could protect you."

"I wasn't thinking of myself, but if Jacques LeMoyne and the baby both had the bad kind of malaria and the mosquito that carries it in Africa is loose in Miami, a lot of my people could get it, too."

"Your concern is justified, Mr. Jones," Laurel told him, "but from here on the Health Service authorities will have to handle the problem."

"Go on and hunt mosquitoes as long as you want to, Laurel; as the court appointed executor of old Jock's estate I give you permission," said Parnell. "I've just got time to grab some lunch and change at the club. Your father and I are playing a foursome with a couple of doctors from California this afternoon – "

"That means Father is counting on you to bring up the total score. You'd better get going or he'll be hiring a new lawyer Monday morning."

"Do you and Dr. Weyer mind if I tag along while you're making your search, Dr. Malone?" Art Jones asked. "Dex and I weren't looking for mosquitoes and may have missed some."

"Not at all," Laurel assured him. "Since you've been through the house already, you can help us a lot."

The second search proved as fruitless as the first, however. No more mosquitoes were found but the presence of larvae in the abandoned fishpond, plus the dead insect that had been on Jacques LeMoyne's body and the very live one inside the house, were sufficient evidence of possible invasion of *Anopheles Gambiae* to justify a neighborhood-wide campaign, as well as a search throughout South Florida.

They left the kitchen for the last but that, too, yielded nothing, until Mort opened the door to a large pantry adjoining it. Packed on the shelves were hundreds of cans of food, all unopened, as were cardboard and plastic packages containing a large amount of staple groceries.

"What do you think of this?" Mort asked.

"Mr. LeMoyne kept his larder well stocked – for somebody who lived alone," Laurel observed. "I wonder why nobody stole it."

"Most of the people around here think this place is haunted," said Art Jones. "They wouldn't risk stealing this stuff, even if they were on welfare and eating dogfood."

"So what does it mean?" Laurel asked.

"That he often had guests, for one thing," said Mort. "Didn't you mention once that Jock was supposed to keep Haitian refugees here, Art?"

"The neighbors say so, but I never saw them."

"*Grand-père* DuVall must have been living here with the baby!" Laurel exclaimed.

"And probably still is," Mort agreed. "Check the pots and pans again, Art. You may find some evidence of their being used recently to prepare food."

The union agent examined the contents of the cabinets in the kitchen again but reported the cooking utensils as spotlessly clean.

"Wait a minute!" he exclaimed as they were leaving the house by the back door. "If the sick baby's grandfather has been living here and using canned goods from old Jock's pantry, we'll probably find evidence in the garbage can. It's Saturday, so no garbage would have been picked up this morning."

They found what they were seeking without difficulty. Several freshly opened cans from which the food had been removed and an empty wine bottle were in the bottom of the single garbage can beside the back stoop.

"Somebody certainly spent last night here and had a breakfast of canned beans," said Mort, dropping a can he'd picked up back into the garbage. "You can smell them inside the can."

"And he's probably still here since he visited his grandson in the hospital last night," Laurel added.

"But where?"

"Probably in one of those secret passages that are supposed to be in the house," said Art Jones. "I know most of the people living in this block and I'll ask them to keep watch on it. As long as that baby is sick, the grandfather will probably be coming and going, usually at night."

"If we find him, maybe he can clear up the mystery of how *Anopheles Gambiae* and malignant malaria got to Miami," said

Laurel. "I'll get the Health Department to print some flyers with a picture of the mosquito and distribute them to the people in this area too. If any more are found, we'll know the city's in danger of a serious epidemic."

"If you catch the grandfather, you can check his blood for *plasmodium falciparum,*" said Mort. "And if he's a carrier, the police can put him in a locked hospital room until you can kill the parasites in his blood with mefloquine."

"Let's go, then," said Laurel, but at the street they were stopped by a black woman who looked very agitated.

"You got a minute, Mr. Jones?" she asked.

"Sure. What's troubling you, Mrs. Cason?"

"My son was playing with some rough kids this morning. They dared him to go into Mr. LeMoyne's house and he went, but he didn't take nothing except this." She held out a small doll.

"That's just like the one *Grand-père* DuVall left with the baby last night," Laurel exclaimed.

"It's an obeah doll all right," Art Jones confirmed. "Probably came from Haiti."

"Obeah's witchcraft!" Mrs. Cason squealed. "Ain't nothin' but trouble can come from that thing. Burn it! Burn it before the devil gets us all. Burn the house, too, while you're at it, even though folks are sayin' Mr. LeMoyne had gold hid in there."

"Where does that leave us, Art?" Mort asked while Mrs. Cason hurried up the street, as if the demon she feared was already in pursuit. "At a dead end?"

"Maybe not," said the union agent. "I know the Haitian consul pretty well. Perhaps he can clear up some of this mystery for us."

"Could you get him on Saturday?" Laurel asked.

"I've got a mobile telephone in my car; let me see if I can raise him at home."

Art Jones went to the purple sports car and spoke briefly into the telephone before returning to where Mort and Laurel were waiting.

"The consul's at home but he can't see us until four o'clock," he reported. "Why don't you two meet me there at that time?"

"After we get the oil and kill those larvae in the fishpond, I'll take you to lunch," Mort told Laurel. "That way we can stop by the hospital and check on Baby DuVall before going to the consul."

"Suits me," she said. "I only had time at

the airport this morning for a Danish and coffee. I'm famished."

"Here's the address." Jones had been scribbling on a note pad and handed the sheet to Mort. "See you there at four."

Chapter 9

A few minutes after three Lisa was awakened from her nap by the closing of the door to the head. When she turned over on the comfortably upholstered cushion of the seat inside the half-cabin that served as an emergency bed, she saw that the bunk on which Roberto Galvez had been sleeping was empty. A few minutes later, however, he came out of the head, looking refreshed from the food, and the nap.

"Ready for that deeper dive you promised me?" he asked.

"If you are." Lisa swung her legs off the cushioned seat and yawned. "Though I'd rather go back to sleep."

"My flight back to Caracas leaves Sunday after the luncheon, so I won't have time for any more diving on this trip."

"Give me a couple of minutes. Why don't you change the tanks while I powder my nose?"

"I'll attach the regulators, too. When you come out, we'll be ready to head east toward the edge of the reef. I'm looking forward to seeing what deep water looks like."

"Maybe a hundred feet," said Lisa. "The pressure doubles every thirty-three feet and we have to allow time for decompression as we ascend afterward."

"Let's get going then."

When Lisa came out, Roberto had finished changing the tanks and was pulling up the anchor, coiling the rope on the foredeck atop the coils they hadn't used on the first dive. This done, he pulled in the small float with the "divers-down" flag on it warning that people were underwater and put it on the deck. Meanwhile, Lisa started the engines and headed the boat eastward toward the distant line of somewhat more turbulent water marking the edge of the reef. Though now some five miles away, the coast of Key Largo was still easily visible to the west in the warm afternoon sunlight.

Less than half an hour was required to reach a spot where they could still see grass growing on the bottom at what Lisa estimated to be about a hundred feet, with the darker depths of the water beyond the outline of the reef a lure of mysteries yet to discover. When the anchor was tossed over, the line kept snaking down until it was almost fully extended before it touched the bottom.

No other boats were out this far that afternoon but Lisa tossed the float containing the "divers-down" flag with its own line overboard anyway. Back in the cockpit, Roberto was finishing the inspection of the diving gear and held out the flotation vest for her to put on. He looked eager and not the least afraid of the dark water extending beyond the reef.

It took ony a few moments for them to don the diving gear and when Roberto tumbled backward off the gunwale of the boat Lisa did the same, moving to the anchor line so she could follow it down. Strapped to her wrist were both the watch by which to measure time in order to allow for the decompression necessary upon ascent and also the Navy depth gauge, as well as the diving knife in its sheath attached to her leg. Since the light would be much less at deeper levels, Lisa would have difficulty in determining directions so she also wore an aqualung compass strapped to her wrist above the depth gauge.

At a level of about fifty feet, she signaled

to Roberto, who was following her closely. When he came up beside her, Lisa tapped the pressure gauge on her wrist and held it up so he could see the depth of the fifty-odd feet they had reached. He nodded his understanding so she kicked out with her flippers and started downward. The light was less intense the deeper they went but they could still see the coral bottom clearly, with schools of varied colored fish swimming about.

At about seventy-five feet, a sea turtle with a shell perhaps three feet across passed them, its flippers moving languidly and its head extended looking for food. The depth gauge showed slightly over a hundred feet when Lisa's flippers touched bottom but she was breathing easily with no feeling of pressure on either lungs or ears. Roberto came up beside her and, when she held up the compass and pointed eastward toward where she knew from the charts the edge of the reef lay, though still invisible, he gave the okay sign as she began to swim in the direction the compass had indicated as east.

The reef edge didn't end abruptly, as Lisa had thought it would, but sloped steadily downward instead. When she took her eyes away from the amazing beauty of the craggy slope, she was startled to see that the depth gauge reported almost a hundred and fifty feet. Turning to see where Roberto was, she ducked instinctively when he shot by her, almost striking her as he passed.

Lisa realized immediately what must have happened. Unaccustomed to diving in deep water, Roberto had been stricken by what divers called "nitrogen narcosis," one of the most serious complications that could happen to a scuba diver. Inhaled under pressure at depths of a hundred feet or more, the 80 per cent of nitrogen in the air from a scuba tank could have a narcotic effect upon a diver, giving him much the feeling of being drunk from alcohol or from drugs. Most important of all, "nitrogen narcosis" tended to rob the diver of good judgment and those seized by it sometimes plunged steadily downward, not realizing the danger until their supply of air was exhausted.

Realizing she must somehow turn Roberto around and start him back to the surface, Lisa felt a second shock of apprehension when she saw a stream of bubbles flowing from the connection between his regulator valve and the tank. Those bubbles, however beautiful in the pellucid depths, could mean only one thing, she knew. When Roberto had changed the tanks before their second dive, he had failed to make a secure connection and now had barely enough air to get him safely to the surface — if indeed the leaking tank held even that much. And wasting no time now, she shot downward in pursuit of the other diver into ever deeper deeper and darker water as they passed beyond the outer edge of the reef.

By the time Lisa caught up with Roberto in his downward plunge, the depth gauge on her wrist showed a hundred and seventy-five feet. Wasting no time in trying to communicate with him by signs, she seized his tank harness, yanking him upward while kicking as hard as she could with the powerful flippers. He resisted momentarily; then as she tugged harder, while still kicking as fast as she could and sending them both toward the surface, the "nitrogen narcosis" befuddling his senses began to fade. It ended at roughly a hundred feet and, swimming close to him as she was, Lisa saw his face within the diving mask suddenly contract with fear when the struggle to inhale brought no air into his lungs.

Realizing that his leaking tank was now empty, except for the three hundred pounds of the reserve, Lisa reached over and pulled the lever releasing those extra pounds of air. Under normal circumstances the three-hundred-pound reserve would have meant fifteen minutes of air within Roberto's tank, possibly enough to save him, but the situation now was considerably different. When she released the reserve, Lisa saw bubbles start leaking again from the faultily placed valve atop the tank and knew the brief time available made an emergency – and rapid – ascent unavoidable.

Glancing at her own pressure gauge, visible at the end of a tube attached to the tank and clipped to the harness so it could be seen easily, Lisa saw that she still had nearly half a tank, quite enough to put them safely to the surface with her equipment alone, using what was known as "buddy breathing." A simple maneuver taught during any scuba diving course, "buddy breathing" consisted of passing the mouthpiece from the diver whose tank contained air to the one whose tank was now empty, each taking a few breaths before passing the mouthpiece back.

She wished for some way to tell Roberto his tank had been almost emptied by the leak, but it was more important to ascend as rapidly as possible, considering the amount of air available to both of them. That he realized what had happened was suddenly apparent seconds later when, as the stream of bubbles from the leak suddenly ceased, Roberto drew his hand across his neck in the universal gesture that spelled "No Air."

Breathing quickly several times, Lisa removed the mouthpiece from her own mouth and placed it against his lips until he opened his teeth and gripped it, clearing the water from the mouthpiece by exhaling. Meanwhile, she was expelling her breath slowly as they ascended, making it last as long as she could without risking a dangerous change of pressure in her lungs. The size of the bubble stream Roberto Galvez was exhaling told her he was gasping for breath in panic and she let him take several extra breaths before reaching for the mouthpiece when her own lungs began to demand air.

When Lisa's hand closed on the mouthpiece, however, Roberto set his teeth and reached up with his right hand to push her away. Only then did she realize that he did not intend to let her have any of the precious reserve of air still retained in her tank. And when she tried to tug the mouthpiece from him once again, he shoved her away, obviously not realizing in the panic induced by the sudden absence of air that he was now breathing from her tank.

Chapter 10

"I hope you left your beeper at home," Paul Rogers said as he got into Lynn's car in front of the DuPont Plaza Hotel at a quarter to four.

"I did better than that; I locked it in my office." She guided the sleek Porsche out into the traffic on Biscayne Boulevard and headed north toward the East-West Expressway interchange. "For the first time in months, nobody can find me until I'm ready to be found."

"Good. That means I have you all to myself."

"You did say you'd like to go out to the ranch, didn't you?"

"For starters, yes. We'll play it by ear after that, if it suits you."

"I'm at your command," she assured him.

Three-L Ranch, named long ago for Theo Malone's three daughters, was a few miles off the Tamiami Trail in a hammock-studded area. The land was traversed by a creek that drained a lake of some ten acres by way of one of the maze of canals leading eastward from the Everglades into the Miami River. At the long, low ranch house, Lynn parked the car.

"I don't remember that concrete block building being here before," said Paul.

"It houses my laboratory. Father built it right after — when I took charge of Institute research."

"Let's go down to the lake first," he suggested. "Does Old Joe still rule the roost down there?"

"Joe's still king of everything he surveys. I sometimes stay out here and at night you can hear him bellowing all the way to the ranch house. We'll probably have to shoot him one of these days, though. Even though we fenced in the lake and put a gate at the entrance, he still manages to get out and eat small calves."

They were following a path that circled the lake. When they walked out on the short dock where several rowboats were moored, a dark object — that could easily have been mistaken for a log, except that it had two eyes protruding near the end — regarded them curiously.

"That's not Joe," said Lynn. "His back is so broad now you could walk on it, if you wanted to commit suicide."

"Remember that night he chased us out of the water when we were skinny dipping? Those were wonderful days, weren't they?"

"Don't please. You'll have me weeping."

"I suppose there's no point in calling back might-have-beens," he agreed. "They only cause more pain."

A piebald yearling calf bounded up to Lynn while Paul was closing the gate to the fence around the lake after they finished their hike. Reaching into her pocket, she took out some lumps of sugar and held them while the calf nuzzled her hand.

"Looks as if you've found a friend," he said.

"A very special friend." She gave the calf an affectionate slap on the rump that made it turn around and Paul saw the operation scar, a white stripe on the left side of its chest where no hair grew.

"Your father's done it, hasn't he?"

"*We* did it over six months ago, shortly after I came back from studying micro-surgery in St. Louis."

"I knew he'd been working on an artificial heart for years and there've been rumors of something new even as far away as Tampa. But I thought all he'd accomplished was some modification of what's already been done, like Christiaan Barnard's side-by-side transplant —"

"This calf's heart is made of stainless steel and driven by nuclear power," said Lynn. "You can see the lump where we buried the power pack under the skin covering the left shoulder near the end of the incision."

"Are you sure you ought to be telling me this? Obviously, your father has been keeping it a secret."

"I wanted to publish our results in the *Journal of Experimental Surgery,* but he wouldn't listen. So far, we've put the new heart into three calves and they're all alive. The fellow you just saw is the oldest. Father was hoping a patient suitable for the operation would turn up during the seminar."

"If he'd had his way night before last, he would probably have used that severed coronary artery you repaired as an excuse to try the artificial heart."

"No doubt about that," Lynn agreed as they came up on the porch of the ranch house, a cool oasis shaded by a large banyan tree. "I'm sure he's been hoping a clot will block the artery at the suture line while the seminar's going on, so he can still put an artificial heart in and make the headlines."

"It would do that all right. I know they've been working on one such project in Bethesda at the National Institutes of Health. And a few days ago, there was a newspaper report that a committee at one large medical school had approved the use of an artificial heart when a patient was found."

"Let's have a rum collins while I tell you about the experimental work that went into the new heart," she suggested.

"Isn't Theo likely to punish you for telling me?"

"I'm being punished already. Besides, you had a part in some of the early work while you were Father's second-in-command, so you're entitled to know what has happened since you left. Take a rocking chair on the porch; I'll be back in a few moments with the drinks."

Paul was sitting in a comfortable rocker with his feet on a bamboo hassock when Lynn came out again, carrying a tray containing two tall, frosty rum collinses and pretzels. She put the tray down on a small table beside him, then pulled a rocker up close for herself.

"As you know, Father's been hoping for years to develop an artificial heart, the ultimate in cardiac surgery. While I was in St. Louis learning microsurgery technique, he constructed one that's mechanically perfect."

"What about the valves? That's always been a hang-up."

"Father figured a way to put valves from a pig's heart, as many cardiac surgeons have been using lately, into the pump. He used that new cement orthopedists are using in artificial hips."

"He certainly hasn't lost any of his genius in the mechanical field."

"It was quite a feat. Unfortunately, he couldn't connect the openings of the pump to the arteries and veins without leaks."

"That was the problem with the first heart transplants, remember? The California group that's been so successful solved it in transplant operations by leaving a cuff of heart tissue at the ends of the arteries and veins in both the heart they were removing and the donor one. That way, they were able to suture heart tissue to heart tissue, which is a lot easier than trying to fit the end of the aorta from the donor exactly to the aortic opening in the transplanted heart."

"That was Father's trouble, too, until I figured out a way to do it."

"What did you do?"

"Father gave me the idea by using that new cement for the valves. Dacron is being used a lot now for putting patches on cerebral arteries after they've been opened to remove the plaques that cause small strokes."

"And as tubes to replace arteries that must be removed because of aneurysms," said Paul. "I did a big one in the abdomen last week."

"It's the nearest to a perfect material produced so far for replacing arterial tissue," Lynn agreed. "Knowing that, and with Father's experience using the new adhesive compound, I cemented a cuff of Dacron around each opening on the artificial heart. I was careful to leave artery and vein cuffs on the pump large enough so that the patient's tissues could be sutured to them regardless of any difference between the size of their openings and those of the metal openings into the artificial heart itself. Once I had the Dacron cuffs in place, suturing them in an experimental heart replacement was easy. By using the microscope, I was able to make sure I had a leakproof suture line."

"Ingenious!" Paul exclaimed. "Did Theo

give you the credit you deserved?"

"Not so far. We haven't been able to use the pump in a human case and he doesn't want to publish the experimental results —"

"Because somebody might beat him to the feat of putting in the first artificial heart?"

"I guess that's why."

"You *know* that's why. Meanwhile, you're being denied the recognition for a major breakthrough in experimental surgery. And patients who might be saved by another surgeon, using your suture technique and your father's pump, are being denied a procedure that could save their lives, at least for a while."

"Are you going to try the operation?" she asked.

"No."

"Why? I've just told you how it's done."

He caught the meaning of her statement in a flash, and shook his head gently. "Would you let me have the glory, so your father could be denied it? Even though you'd be left out in the cold at the same time?"

"I know now that Father cheated you by using little Paul's death as an excuse to break up our marriage and drive you away from Miami. To that extent, I'd like to get revenge, but I don't like the idea either of his sitting on a major accomplishment and keeping it from people who might have good luck with it, just so he can have the satisfaction of putting in the first artificial heart."

"A totally unselfish Malone? Who could that be except you? I've known it, of course, since before we were married in medical school. Leave Miami and come to Tampa with me, darling," he pleaded, taking her hands. "Together, we'd make the most successful cardiovascular surgery team in history."

"I can't, Paul."

"Why? You certainly don't owe your father anything."

"Someone has to look after Mother, now that Father has married again."

"She looked fine last night at the reception."

"That was just the Randolph spirit putting on a front for her friends. In spite of the way Father treated her, Mother still loves him; some women are like that."

"She still has Laurel."

"Laurel and Mort Weyer are very much attracted to each other. They might decide to marry."

"What about Lisa?"

"Right now she's scuba diving off Key Largo with Roberto Galvez; tonight, if history repeats itself, they'll be out on a real binge. Lisa's enough like Father that she'll probably play the field most of her life, where sex is concerned, just to prove she's his equal at it."

"You're twins. Why the difference?"

Lynn smiled and reached over to kiss him on the cheek. "I was lucky enough to find a man years ago who was everything I wanted. I doubt that I'll ever marry again."

"So what's going to happen — to us?"

"Let's not worry about that now, Paul. Just enjoy the time we have together." She looked at her watch. "We'd better be starting for the theater."

"One more question, please. With a stainless steel heart, you obviously shouldn't have any problem with rejection. But even after simple heart valve surgery, we always need to give something to keep the blood from clotting around the artificial valve and spilling off clots to the brain or the extremities. How do you manage to avoid that with the calves you've operated on here so successfully?"

"I wondered when you'd ask about that. Remember when we studied about Vitamin

K and prothrombin time in blood-clotting at medical school in Baltimore?"

"Yes, but —" His frown cleared suddenly. "Clover! One of the first things that gave a clue to preventing the clotting of blood was the hemorrhagic condition animals sometimes develop after eating too much sweet clover. Didn't we see a field of it by the road as we were driving up to the ranch house?"

"That was my idea, too," Lynn told him. "All we have to do now is harvest the clover and feed some every day to the calves I've operated on. It works like a charm; we've never had an embolism."

II

Laurel and Mort Weyer had stopped by the Dade County Health Department laboratory before going to lunch. Under the microscope she'd had no trouble identifying the larvae they'd found in the abandoned goldfish pool at the LeMoyne house as those of *Anopheles Gambiae.* She had called Dr. Prentiss from the laboratory but, told that he was in Liberty City supervising the work of a mosquito control team in a preliminary spraying of the area around the house, she had left a message for him. The pager she wore, so as to be in touch with Critical Care because of Baby DuVall, sounded when she and Mort were almost through lunch and she went to a public telephone in the lobby of the restaurant.

"This is Dr. Prentiss," the Health Officer said when she dialed the number given her by the paging operator. "After Dr. Milne called from Atlanta this morning and confirmed your identification of the mosquito you found on Jacques LeMoyne's body, I decided to take a spray team out there so as to be ahead of any other *Anopheles Gambiae.*"

"That sounds like a wise move."

"Artemus Jones was in the area trying to quiet the fears of the residents. He told me you'd found another *Gambiae* in the LeMoyne house. Were you able to identify it?"

"Both it and some larvae I discovered in an old fishpond are *Gambiae* all right," said Laurel. "I suggested to the laboratory technician on duty at the Health Department that the rest of what I collected be sent to Atlanta."

"They'll be on their way by Air Express before the day's over."

"Did you find any more mosquitoes or larvae near the house?" she asked.

"No, but we sprayed the whole area and I put the house and yard around it under a strict quarantine to discourage anyone from trying to go inside. I understand that this particular mosquito likes closed places."

"More than anywhere else," Laurel confirmed. "I suppose the only thing we can do now is wait to see if anyone else develops malignant malaria. Art Jones has warned the people to be on the lookout for the sick baby's grandfather, who may be hiding in the house. If we find him and he proves to be a carrier of *plasmodium falciparum,* I can treat him with mefloquine and remove that possible source of danger."

"By the way," said Prentiss, "I learned something else interesting while I was at the LeMoyne house. Did you know the local Historical Society has been interested in the building for some time?"

"No. I can't imagine why they would be."

"Apparently, it's one of the oldest structures in that part of Miami, if not the oldest. The society tried to buy it from Jacques LeMoyne several years ago. According to what the minister of one of the black churches out there tells me, LeMoyne refused to sell but did write a letter to the president of the society saying they could have the first option to buy the property from his estate when he died."

"Oh! Oh!" said Laurel. "That would certainly gum up the plans of a local group of businessmen to build a low-rental housing unit there. The LeMoyne property was the last barrier to their being able to go ahead."

"I know," said Prentiss. "The minister I talked to was worried that, if the society exercises their option, the housing project could be held up."

"That area needs the project far more than it needs a run-down old building."

"I agree," said Prentiss. "When the original option was granted by LeMoyne, the area was a bustling slum but now it's a desert. Maybe the Historical Society wouldn't be interested any more."

"Dexter Parnell certainly *is*," said Laurel. "He's playing golf right now with my father but I'll call him later and tell him about this new development."

"Thanks again for your help," said the Health Officer. "When I talked to Dr. Milne this morning I recommended that he ask Washington to consider appointing you to the commission that obviously should go to Haiti to see if many *Gambiae* are still there."

"Trouble?" Mort asked when Laurel came back to their table.

"Not with the baby. That was Dr. Prentiss. He saw your friend, Art Jones, in Liberty City when he was out there directing a spraying team and Art told him what we found."

"Prentiss is probably beginning to hate you for staying ahead of him all the time."

"Maybe not. He asked Dr. Milne at the Center in Atlanta to suggest appointing me to a commission to see whether there's a nest of *Anopheles Gambiae* wherever *Grand-père* DuVall came from in Haiti."

"Would you like to go?"

"It would be an honor, but there are plenty of people in the U.S. Public Health Service and the WHO who know more than I do about malaria."

"I doubt that," said Mort. "But now that I've just found the girl I've been dreaming about all my life, I'd hate to lose her even for only a month or two."

III

Mr. Armand Latour, the Haitian consul, was a plump man with shrewd eyes and perfect manners. He was dressed in tropical white and ushered Laurel, Mort, and Artemus Jones to a table in the enclosed garden back of his home in Coconut Grove with a view of the bay. A tall banyan tree furnished shade and a cooling breeze came from the water.

"I agreed to talk to you this afternoon because my people owe you a special gift of thanks, Dr. Malone," he said in greeting.

"I've done nothing," she protested.

"On the contrary. Dr. Prentiss called me this morning with news of your findings yesterday and their confirmation by Dr. Milne at the Center for Disease Control in Atlanta. I talked with the Chargé d'Affaires at our embassy in Washington immediately and he has been in touch with the government in Port-au-Prince. An official request will be made to the World Health Organization Monday morning, asking that a commission be sent to Haiti at once to search the area where the plane crashed, looking for this deadly mosquito you have identified."

"Then there really was a plane crash?" Art Jones exclaimed.

"There was, but before I tell you more, I must insist that everything I say be held in strictest confidence."

"Okay by me," said Art, but Laurel

hesitated before answering and glanced at Mort questioningly.

"Is there some reason why you cannot agree to my request, Dr. Malone?" the consul asked.

"I promised Jack Parker of the Miami *Herald* that I would let him know what I discovered about the presence of *Anopheles Gambiae* and malignant malaria in time for him to finish his story for the Sunday edition."

"Dr. Prentiss informed me this morning that he is releasing all the information he has to Mr. Parker," said the consul.

"Prentiss knows everything we know about the danger then," Mort assured Laurel. "Which means you're under no obligation to tell Parker anything of a confidential nature Mr. Latour cares to tell us."

"All right," she said. "You have my word, Mr. Latour."

"Good!" said the consul briskly. "A large private plane did crash in the mountains of Haiti about three months ago but both the pilot and co-pilot were killed."

"Was the cargo diamonds?" Art Jones asked, and the consul smiled.

"I've heard that rumor, too, Mr. Jones, but it isn't true, although the real cargo was almost equally valuable."

"What was it?"

"From what the Haitian government was able to learn about the incident, a large-scale robbery took place in South Africa around March 1. A fortune in Krugerrand coins was taken and flown out of the country for transfer eventually to the United States. The plane flew to a small airport on the Gold Coast, intending to refuel before crossing the narrowest part of the Atlantic, between the bulges of Africa and Brazil. Unfortunately for the thieves, they were forced to remain at the airport in Africa for two days and nights while an engine was being repaired."

"Time enough for a few *Anopheles Gambiae* to become stowaways," said Laurel.

"From Africa they made the flight to Natal in Brazil without difficulty, even carrying a large cargo of gold coins," Latour continued. "They stopped at Natal only long enough to refuel before flying northward, evidently bound for the United States."

"A direct course to Florida would have taken them right over Haiti and planes bearing cocaine and marijuana land secretly in the Florida Keys all the time," Mort observed.

"That must have been their intention," the

consul agreed. "Unfortunately for them, the engine trouble must have returned, causing the crash in the mountains of my country."

"Then the plane was found?" Laurel asked.

"The day after the crash, Doctor, but not before a band of guerrillas, who call themselves Freedom Fighters, got to it first and removed about half the cargo. Haitian police killed most of the band and recovered much of what they had stolen, but a few escaped, particularly a former government official who was their leader."

"Was his name DuVall?"

"Yes. How could you know?"

"We have reason to believe DuVall escaped to Miami with the help of a man named Jacques LeMoyne, the same one who died yesterday of malignant malaria. In his clothing a morgue attendant found one of the two specimens of *Anopheles Gambiae* that we can be certain reached Miami."

"We have known for some time that Mr. LeMoyne was giving refuge to émigrés from Haiti." Latour didn't appear to be disturbed by her statement. "Frankly, we haven't troubled him, since most of those he helped to escape were malcontents whom we were glad to see leave."

"What about DuVall? Don't you want him, too?"

Latour shook his head. "My government would be happy to see Henri DuVall stay in the United States indefinitely."

"Could your country's willingness to prosecute DuVall be influenced by the fact that, as a former government official, he probably knows things you'd just as soon not be made public?" Mort asked, but Latour only shrugged.

"Right now our main concern is Dr. Malone's discovery that malignant malaria and its most important African carrier were probably introduced into Haiti when the plane carrying the gold crashed there," he said.

"What about the gold?" Art Jones asked.

"What Henri DuVall may have carried away is of little significance, compared to the bulk of the cargo recovered by my government."

"The commission from the WHO shouldn't have much trouble finding out how many cases of malignant malaria are present in the crash area," said Laurel. "A 'spleen count' would accomplish that."

"Spleen count?" Latour asked. "I don't understand."

"Wherever malaria is endemic, many children have enlarged spleens from a chronic form of the disease. You can feel a spleen in much less time than it takes to make a blood smear and study it, so the spleen count is a quick way of establishing the incidence of malaria. If the count is high, you look for sick children and examine their blood. The final diagnosis can be made in the laboratory as easily as I made it in the cases of Jacques LeMoyne and Baby DuVall."

"Baby DuVall?" said the consul. "I don't understand."

"A tall, light-skinned man brought a desperately sick baby to my clinic in Liberty City yesterday morning and I sent him to the hospital," Mort explained. "He gave the child's name only as Baby DuVall but the address was the same as Jacques LeMoyne's house. We just finished searching it but found no sign of Henri DuVall."

"As I said, we are not concerned about him."

"Or the baby?" Laurel asked on a caustic note.

Latour shrugged. "It's the babies of *Haiti* we're concerned about, Doctor. We heard that DuVall escaped with his daughter and a child, among others, plus a small amount of Krugerrands. In your expert hands, the baby is no doubt receiving far better treatment than would be the case for children in the mountain villages of my country who are our immediate concern at the moment." He got to his feet. "I have another appointment this afternoon. My secretary will show you out."

"What do you think?" Mort asked Laurel as they walked to his car.

"I guess he's right," she admitted. "The welfare of children in the mountains of Haiti whose blood may now be teeming with the gametocytes of *plasmodium falciparum* is more important than the life of one baby, who may be dead before morning from the destruction of its red blood cells by the parasite."

"And Henri DuVall?"

"He loves the baby enough to visit it daily so we'll probably catch him sometime. All I'll do is ask him for a blood smear and, if he's a carrier of the disease, I'll treat him."

"Shall we go back to the hospital then?"

"Yes, but stop by the Miami *Herald* so I can give Jack Parker the interview I promised him, plus a picture of *Anopheles Gambiae* from a tropical medicine textbook I brought from home this morning. When people read the paper tomorrow morning, they'll at least know what kind of mosquito to look for and be warned."

"Aren't you going to warn your friend Dexter Parnell about the interest of the historical society in the LeMoyne house?"

"Thanks for reminding me," she said. "Dex ought to be home from the golf tournament by the time I finish with Jack Parker. I'll give him a ring while we're at the *Herald* building."

IV

When Roberto Galvez, his eyes visible within the face mask still dilated from the terror of finding himself with an empty tank, refused to yield the mouthpiece, Lisa wasted no time trying to get it away from him. Her own lungs were clamoring for air and only one source was available – the surface. Realizing that his only source of air was from the tank strapped to Lisa's back, however, Roberto was holding her against him so tightly that she couldn't pull away.

The empty tank attached to Roberto's back by the harness was just so much extra weight now, slowing their ascent. Reaching down along his body, Lisa seized the buckle of the strap around his waist and gave it a sharp jerk. It came loose easily and, sliding her hand upward, she pushed aside the now-useless air hose dangling in the water above his head.

Kicking strongly all the while to send them upward toward the surface, she slid the harness off his shoulders with a quick jerk and pushed on the empty tank. Roberto instinctively tried with one hand to grab for the harness but it slid off his shoulder and the tank with everything connected to it sank from their view. By now Lisa's own need for air had increased to where she felt on the verge of blacking out from lack of oxygen. Working swiftly, however, she managed to find the carbon dioxide cartridge in Roberto's flotation vest and crush it between her fingers.

As the vest suddenly filled with the flow of gas from the cartridge, it pushed her body momentarily away from Roberto's frantic clutch, far enough for her to reach the cartridge in her own flotation vest and crush it, too. With the power of both vests pulling them upward, they shot toward the surface at a far more rapid rate than was good for either of them. But fast enough, Lisa dared hope, to get them there before she blacked out and opened her mouth, letting water into her lungs.

When they did surface, the propulsive force of the vests actually lifted them half out of the water. Gulping great breaths of air, Lisa loosened the buckle at her own waist and, pushing the harness off her shoulders, allowed the tank and its attachments to sink, jerking the mouthpiece out of Roberto's mouth easily. Too easily, she realized, when she saw him bobbing on the surface unconscious, supported by the inflated life vest.

Kicking rapidly with her flippers, Lisa seized Roberto's chin, towing him toward the boat that was mercifully floating only a few yards away. When she touched the boarding ladder at the stern, she jerked off her flippers and climbed up, tugging Roberto with her. The sky, the water, and the boat swayed in a crazy-quilt pattern through her field of vision, as the dizziness of oxygen-lack during that perilous ascent threatened to bring on unconsciousness.

Driven by the desperate urgency of their situation produced by the preponderance of the nitrogen dissolved in both their bloodstreams, she finally managed to drag Roberto's limp form over the stern and stretch him out on the floor of the cockpit. A finger on his pulse told her his heart was beating, though hurriedly and irregularly. Meanwhile, his breathing, though stertorous, was drawing vital air into his lungs, adding the oxygen he needed badly, as proved by the bluish pallor of cyanosis in his lips, ear lobes, and face.

Leaving Roberto on the floor of the boat, Lisa ran forward and, taking the diving knife from the scabbard strapped to her leg, began to saw at the anchor rope. The fiber was tough and her strength almost exhausted from the effort of dragging Roberto's inert body up the ladder and into the boat. Thanks to the saw-toothed edge on the back of the blade, however, she managed to cut the rope, dropping the anchor in the depths along with their diving gear and the empty tanks.

When the boat floated free, she started the engines, steering in a wide circle before opening the throttles and heading at full speed toward the distant shore and the marina where help would be available. Fortunately, the boat was equipped with an automatic pilot and, locking it into place once she had the swift craft on course, she moved back to check Roberto.

His hurried irregular pulse and labored breathing told her he had probably held his breath instinctively with his lungs filled as they ascended, a mistake that had no doubt saturated his bloodstream with dangerous nitrogen. In fact, everything about Roberto's condition warned her that he was in the early stages of a dangerous case of the "bends."

At the moment, Lisa didn't concern herself with the danger to her own life from the amount of nitrogen dissolved in her own bloodstream. Returning to the wheel she disconnected the automatic pilot and opened the siren wide to warn those at the marina of an emergency as the boat sped shoreward. All her senses, still not as clear as she would have liked them to be, were concentrated on keeping the speeding boat within the steadily narrowing channel through the coral-studded reef as they came nearer the shore and the bottom became shallower. Jagged as they were, she knew those same reefs could crush the bottom of the boat if she missed the channel, exposing them to a new danger from without almost as life-threatening as the nitrogen dissolved in their bloodstreams imposed a danger within.

As Lisa had hoped, the manager of the marina — an experienced scuba diver himself — had correctly interpreted the significance of the screaming siren, as she steered the boat through the channel at a highly dangerous speed. A crowd had gathered on the dock at the marina and willing hands reached down to seize the side of the boat when she guided it into an empty slip and cut the motor.

"We were diving at close to a hundred and fifty feet, when Dr. Galvez ran out of air," Lisa told the manager.

"Did you try buddy breathing?" he asked as she shrugged herself out of the flotation vest, leaving her body clothed only in the blue maillot.

"Yes, but he panicked and kept the mouthpiece. I inflated both vests and they brought us up in a few seconds but we've got to get to a hyperbaric chamber as quickly as possible. Is the pilot of the sight-seeing helicopter still around?"

"Yes."

"I'm chartering it to take us both to Biscayne General. Tell him to get ready — fast."

"Hey, Ramon!" the manager called as Roberto Galvez was being lifted from the boat. "Dr. Malone needs the helicopter to take her and a patient to Biscayne General. Do you have enough gas?"

"I've already filled it for tomorrow." The pilot was among the crowd. "But I can't land on that heliport at the hospital with pontoons."

"Call Biscayne General as soon as we're aloft." Lisa dropped into a chair on the dock, breathing deeply to overcome the waves of nausea and dizziness that assailed her. "Tell them Dr. Lisa Malone is coming with a patient and to have the hyperbaric tanks ready – plus a Rescue Squad ambulance to meet us at the Miami Yacht Club on the Miami causeway. The helicopter can set down near there."

"You'd better wear this, Doctor." The manager handed her a raincoat. "It can get pretty cool aloft."

While Lisa put on the coat the pilot used the mooring rope to pull the helicopter floating on its pontoons over to the pier, where it loaded passengers for the several-times-daily sight-seeing flights over the coral reef.

"I've got a small oxygen tank and breathing mask here at the marina for emergencies," the manager told Lisa. "I'll put it in the helicopter in case you need it."

"Right now, I could use some oxygen myself."

"Speaking as a diver, I would say you need a decompression tank more than he does, after bringing him up from over a hundred feet without any air."

The helicopter cabin was fitted out with a half dozen seats placed close together to accommodate the maximum number of sightseers. While she administered oxygen from the small tank and mask, Lisa had to steady Roberto in one of the seats and hold up his head to keep his chin from dropping and his tongue from falling back and blocking the airway. It was hard work, exhausted as she was and in serious danger herself, but she had no other choice.

Less than a half hour later, the pilot set the helicopter down on Biscayne Bay opposite the Miami Yacht Club and taxied to the shore. Lisa drew in a deep breath of relief when she saw the bright red cross on top of a Rescue Squad ambulance waiting at a landing where a ramp went down into the water for loading and unloading boats.

The pilot taxied the helicopter up to the ramp and when the ends of the pontoons touched the cement, several men waded out to steady it while a Rescue Squad technician opened the door. They took Roberto out and placed him on a litter but Lisa stepped from the helicopter under her own power, wearing the raincoat the marina manager had given her over her bathing suit. As she waded ashore, she was almost blinded by a sudden burst of light and looked up to find herself staring into the lens of a television mini-camera.

"Can you tell us what happened, Dr. Malone?" a reporter standing on shore beside the cameraman asked.

"Diving accident," Lisa said cryptically as she climbed into the ambulance beside the stretcher. "Let's go, fellows. A decompression tank is waiting for us at Biscayne General."

Minutes later the ambulance came to a stop at the loading dock for the Emergency Room at Biscayne General. Lisa staggered as she followed the stretcher through the door into the Emergency Room, but a tall man in white put his arm around her when she started to collapse. Gratefully, she looked up to see the red hair and familiar, but not now smiling, face of Commander David Fuller.

"We meet a —" she tried to say, but somehow her tongue twisted upon itself.

Just then, too, a blinding pain struck her

above the left eye and she had only enough time to wonder why her right arm and leg seemed to support her no longer – although the pain was on the left side of the head – before she felt the tall doctor lift her in his arms as blackness engulfed her.

V

Dexter Parnell himself answered the telephone when Laurel dialed his home number from a public phone in the Miami *Herald* building, after talking to Jack Parker and giving him a textbook on tropical medicine with a cut of *Anopheles Gambiae* in color.

"Brace yourself, Dex," she said. "I've got bad news for you."

"Spare me," he begged. "First Art Jones tells me that cock-and-bull story about gold and diamonds in the LeMoyne house. Then your father blows his top when I tell him about your finding more mosquitoes there and the probability that the house will be quarantined for a while. Theo drove into the rough on every hole and I wound up losing a hundred bucks to a couple of doctors who pull down two hundred thousand a year at least."

"He'll blow it again when he hears what I've got to tell you," Laurel assured the lawyer. "Did you know the Historical Society has a letter from Jacques LeMoyne amounting to an option to buy the house from his estate?"

"The hell you say! What would the Historical Society want with a run-down old house in a half burned out slum?"

"Dr. Prentiss talked to the black minister of a church in Liberty City when he went out with a spraying crew after we left. Apparently the LeMoyne house is the oldest one in that part of Miami."

"I can believe that."

"The society became interested a few years ago, before the riot, according to the man who talked to Dr. Prentiss. LeMoyne wouldn't sell but he did write a letter to the president of the society giving them the first option to buy it at his death."

"Where's the letter?"

"In the society's files, I imagine. Do you think they would want it now, when everything around it is burned over?"

"Who can tell what a bunch of old fuds who put history before progress will want," said Dex. "Even if the historians didn't buy it, they could petition for a rezoning to save the house and hold us up for months with hearings before the zoning commission and the rest of the bureaucracy down at City Hall. And God knows how many palms we'd have to grease down there to get our zoning back."

"So what can you do?"

"Call Theo and tell him about it. He'll blow his top again but when he simmers down, he'll know what to do. He's got a lot of influence with the politicians at City Hall and he'll certainly remind them that the Malone Institute is almost as well known as the city of Miami itself. If anybody can bring enough influence to bear on the Historical Society to make them decide not to exercise the option, that father of yours can do it. Maybe you'd better tell him."

"Oh no," said Laurel. "You're not going to put the bite on me to do that. My esteemed father and I don't see eye to eye on a lot of things. You'll have to pull your own chestnuts out of the fire, Dex."

"The fire will be hotter than hell and my tail will be on a spit over it; you can depend on Theo for that," said the lawyer. "But thanks at least for warning me before somebody else found out about the option and was able to spring it on me unawares."

"Good luck. Is little Dex okay?"

"He must be. He's out in the swimming pool trying to drown a couple of neighborhood kids. Good-by."

Chapter 11

"Why don't you check with Critical Care by telephone and order additional laboratory work on Baby DuVall, if you want it?" Mort asked as he and Laurel were leaving the Miami *Herald* building. "Then if there's no significant change, we'll go somewhere and have dinner before we go back to the hospital."

"I could use some food," Laurel said as she dialed the hospital number. "It's been a long day."

Informed by the nurse specialing Baby DuVall that the little patient was no worse, though no better, Laurel ordered a hemoglobin level and red blood count for seven o'clock and came back to the car where Mort was waiting.

"No change," she answered his questioning look. "I ordered bloodwork for seven."

"That gives us a couple of hours to unwind. If anything happens, they can always

296

call you on the beeper."

"Where are we going?"

"To a Spanish restaurant in Little Havana, if you don't mind spicy food."

"I love it."

"A friend in New York told me about this place. The family ran the best restaurant in Havana before Castro arrived and my friend says it's the best in Miami now."

"Sounds heavenly."

They had finished the savory bean soup, when the small pager clipped to Laurel's blouse pocket beeped stridently.

"Oh no!" she exclaimed. "Something must have happened to Baby DuVall. I'll have to call the hospital."

"Teléfono, por favor," Mort called to the hovering waiter.

The instrument was brought quickly and plugged into a receptacle in the wall behind their banquette. But when Laurel dialed the hospital operator, she was surprised to learn that the summons did not concern Baby DuVall.

"Just a second for Commander Fuller, Dr. Malone," said the operator.

"Who's Commander Fuller?" she asked Mort Weyer while waiting for the connection to be made.

"The new naval officer in command of the Hyperbaric Laboratory. Peter Shelbourne introduced me to him at the reception last evening."

"This is Commander Fuller, Dr. Malone," an unfamiliar voice sounded in the receiver. "I'm in one of the hyperbaric chambers with your sister, Lisa. She was diving off Key Largo and –"

"I know – with Dr. Galvez."

"I only have a moment. Your sister has a severe case of the bends and we're raising the pressure in the chamber as quickly as we can."

"You're in the tank with her?"

"Yes. A bubble of nitrogen seems to have formed in one of the more important arteries in your sister's brain about the time she reached Miami by helicopter. She walked into the Emergency Room but collapsed into a coma with a hemiplegia that is sometimes seen with the bends."

"Are you saying Lisa's paralyzed?"

"The left side of her face and the right side of her body are involved, but her respiration is good and so is her pulse. I'm giving her oxygen under pressure but it isn't without certain hazards and I didn't want to go that far without letting someone in the family know. The danger of brain damage from the bubble seems to justify the risk."

"Have you called the rest of the family, Commander?"

"All except your mother are not available and I hesitated to call her."

"You did right; at the moment she's under a severe emotional strain. I'll take the responsibility of authorizing you to do whatever is necessary."

"Thank you."

"Is Dr. Galvez —?"

"I believe he ran out of air and she had to bring him to the surface quickly."

"No doubt risking her own life by doing it! You may not know it yet, but in spite of being the most sophisticated of the three Malone daughters, Lisa is a Good Samaritan to boot — the kind who salvages sick kittens."

"I say all three of you are," the voice at the other end of the wire said with a chuckle. "I have to go now."

"I'll be there as soon as I can, but Lisa's in your hands. Good-by."

"What's up?" Mort asked when she hung up the phone.

"I'll tell you on the way to Biscayne General. It's Lisa, not the baby, who's in trouble. Commander Fuller has her in the tank."

"You can be sure she's in the best possible hands," Mort told her as they were leaving the restaurant. "Peter Shelbourne told me last night that Fuller is considered to be the best man in the country in Undersea Medicine — and that's what your sister's case comes down to."

II

When he hung up the telephone on its hook attached to the inner wall of the hyperbaric chamber, David Fuller carefully checked Lisa's condition once again. Everything appeared to be satisfactory, except that she showed no signs of returning consciousness, proof in itself that the shock to her brain had been severe when nitrogen started bubbling out of her bloodstream and blocked a major cerebral artery. Her breathing was still regular but when he tested her reflexes on the right side at knee and elbow, he found them definitely overactive, a sign that the paralysis had not yet begun to be reversed. All of which meant that the nitrogen bubble was still exerting its particularly deadly effect of blocking the flow of heavily oxygenated blood to the brain cells in the area supplied by the artery involved.

The mask Fuller had placed over Lisa's nose and mouth to administer oxygen was small, enabling him to note that the left side of her face was still twisted as the normal pull of the muscles on the right side drew her mouth in that direction with no opposition from the paralyzed left side. The breathing bag attached to the oxygen system and the mask was filling and emptying regularly, however, telling him that, just as the regulator valve of a scuba apparatus kept the pressure in the lungs equal to that of the surrounding water when diving, the oxygen she was breathing was at the same pressure as that of the air in the hyperbaric chamber.

"Tank pressure is three atmospheres, sir." The voice of the technician at the controls crackled over a small loudspeaker inside the tank. "Shall we go higher?"

David Fuller knew what was troubling the technician. The level at which the oxygen tension in the blood would cause convulsions varied from person to person. The odds in favor of its happening, however, increased steadily as the pressure in the hyperbaric tank — and therefore in the breathing bag — was raised.

"Dr. Galvez in the other tank is coming out of the coma," the technician added.

"Ask the nurse with him to see whether he remembers how deep they were when they got into trouble."

Through the glass porthole, David Fuller could see the technician talking on the telephone. Moments later the answer came back over the loudspeaker in the chamber.

"He says they were past the outer edge of the reef, sir, but he doesn't know just how deep."

"Break out a chart of the Key Largo reef area, Chief," David Fuller ordered. "I seem to remember that beyond the edge of the reef itself the depths out there increase pretty rapidly."

"Right, sir. Just a moment."

"You're correct, sir." The answer came back a few moments later. "The nurse who's in the tank with Dr. Galvez says she's been to the Malone cottage on Key Largo. It's just south of the John Pennekamp Coral Reef State Park and the chart shows the depth in that area at roughly a hundred feet when the bottom starts shelving."

"That means they could have been down

perhaps a hundred and fifty feet or more." David Fuller's voice was concerned. "If they came up as fast as Dr. Malone told the helicopter pilot they did, they would fit in with the severity of the bends in her case. But why would she have a more severe case than Dr. Galvez?" His voice suddenly changed. "Ask Galvez if they were buddy breathing, Chief."

The technician took only a moment to get the answer from the nurse in the second tank with Galvez.

"He says he was breathing all the way up," he reported.

"Which means that Dr. Malone held her breath during the entire ascent of roughly a hundred and fifty feet."

"Close to five atmospheres." The technician translated the observation into numerals.

"Or more. Take us up to five, Chief — but slowly."

"At that pressure, she could have an oxygen convulsion at any moment." The technician's voice was tense with concern.

"I'm counting on it, Chief, but don't ask me to explain why at the moment."

As the huge pump that controlled the pressure inside the tank sent more air through the entry vents, David Fuller began to sweat and his breathing quickened noticeably, as did Lisa's. The explanation was simple: when the amount of air in the huge metal tank increased, so did the amount of heat it contained. In fact, a glance at the thermometer on the wall recording the air temperature in the chamber told David Fuller how fast the tank pressure was increasing almost as accurately as if he had been watching the pressure gauge itself.

"Four atmospheres, sir," the technician reported. "If our estimates of depth are anywhere near correct, she ought to be coming out of it at any moment now."

"Her fingers are moving." Releasing Lisa's wrist, David Fuller gently lifted her eyelid to check the size of the pupil but she suddenly opened both eyes and used her left hand to push his own away.

"Wha —?" Her tongue twisted and her mouth jerked as she tried to speak.

"It's all right," he told her quickly. "You've had a bad case of the bends, but we're taking care of that."

"My right hand!" The words tumbled out, though barely intelligibly. "I can't move it."

"It's only a nitrogen bubble blocking a blood vessel in your brain."

"I'm paralyz —" The word ended almost in a scream and he saw her pupils dilate with horror as the realization of what had happened finally penetrated into her understanding.

"We're giving you oxygen; the paralysis should only be temporary," he assured her. "Just lie quietly."

The convulsion he'd been expecting still struck with a suddenness that startled him, with a sudden jerking of her hand and a flailing movement of her left leg and arm.

"I'm dy —" It was a scream of pain and fear. "Help me!"

Instinctively, David Fuller knelt beside the low-cushioned couch upon which Lisa lay and took her into his arms. She clung to him with her good left arm while the muscle spasms of the convulsion made her body writhe uncontrollably. Unwilling to subject her any longer to the convulsive attacks — although he had hoped they'd be a cure by breaking up the nitrogen bubbles inside the artery in her brain — he reached up and pushed the oxygen mask away, twisting the valve and shutting off the flow.

When a second convulsion seized Lisa's body, she screamed again with fear and the certainty of death. But as the level of oxygen in her bloodstream was lowered by the rapidity of her panting, the movements slowed and she clung to David Fuller as if she were a frightened child.

Reaching for the syringe of diazepam solution he had been keeping ready, he jabbed the needle into her arm with one hand and pressed down upon the plunger, injecting the powerful sedative into her tissues from which it would be quickly absorbed into her body and carried to her brain.

"Hold me!" The words were more distinct, even though she was gripped by a third convulsion, and David realized with a sudden rush of happiness, that the degree of paralysis must be lessening rapidly.

"Hold me, please," she begged, and still kneeling beside the couch, he cradled her in his arms murmuring over and over, "You're all right now."

After a few moments, the convulsive movements were no longer wracking her body, and she reached up sleepily to put her arm around his neck, as a child might have done just before falling asleep. And when she used the right arm, he knew with a sudden feeling of awe and pleasure that the terrible risk to which he had subjected her had been worth it all.

Sleepily, she smiled up at him but did not release her hold upon his neck with her right arm, even as her eyelids drooped and a soft snore told him the wrenching spasms that had helped destroy the nitrogen bubble in her brain – as he had hoped – were over.

III

Laurel and Mort Weyer parked the Rabbit in the hospital garage and hurried into the building through the side entrance to the Emergency Room and the Critical Care Unit. Crossing the latter, they opened the door to the Hyperbaric Laboratory and moved quickly to where the Navy technician controlling the huge pump was watching through a porthole. They were just in time to see Lisa's body suddenly arch in a convulsion.

"How long has she been in convulsions?" Laurel asked the technician without taking her eyes from the dramatic scene taking place inside the huge metal tank, as David Fuller skillfully injected the powerful dose of diazepam.

"It just started, Dr. Malone. Dr. Fuller is

trying to dislodge a nitrogen bubble that has paralyzed her face and her right side."

"By deliberately causing a convul –?" She stopped, for Lisa had suddenly quieted. And when she saw her sister reach up and put her right arm – the one that had been paralyzed – around the neck of the tall Navy underwater expert, she realized that the desperate measure had apparently succeeded.

"I told you Fuller knows what he's doing," Mort said beside her.

"You can say that again," the technician echoed.

"Have you seen this treatment used before?" Laurel asked.

The technician shook his head. "No, but it worked, so it must have been what she needed."

"I guess we can agree to that." Laurel turned to Mort, releasing the hand she had been squeezing in her concern for her sister. "I'd better call Mother and tell her Lisa's all right, in case somebody heard about the accident and called her."

"I've never seen a worse case of the bends than she had when she was brought in here," the technician told Mort while Laurel was telephoning, "but Dr. Fuller knew what to do. He's one hell of a fine doctor."

"Have you been with him long?" Mort asked.

"He trained me at Duke, sir," said the petty officer. "We helped organize the National Diving Accident Network, known as 'DAN,' there."

"What's the purpose of the network?" Mort asked.

"To make expert advice in Undersea Medicine available day and night by telephone. That way, divers with the bends can be referred to the nearest facility for treating them, as well as getting advice about complications, like the one that happened to Dr. Malone."

Mort was studying Baby DuVall's chart in the Critical Care Unit when Laurel came back from telephoning Mildred Malone.

"Mother hadn't heard about the accident," she reported. "I told her Lisa's going to be okay. Anything new happening here?"

"Take a look at the last note made by the nurse specialing the baby." Mort handed her the chart. "There's blood in the urine."

"Blood — or hemoglobin?"

Mort gave her a startled look. "It would make a difference, wouldn't it?"

"A big difference. If it's blood, the kidneys

have been damaged by ruptured blood cells and plasmodia jamming the capillaries, so he could be in deep trouble. The presence of hemoglobin would only mean that enough of it has been spilled into the bloodstream from red cells ruptured by the growing plasmodia to be filtered out in the kidneys."

"Looks like we'd better find out which, doesn't it?" he said. "I'll check a specimen of urine under the microscope."

"The blood gas report shows the oxygen level still falling. I'll do another red count while you're checking the urine."

Working together, they completed the two tests in about thirty minutes. "You were right." Mort reported first. "Quite a lot of hemoglobin is being excreted in the urine but no cells."

"The red count is down sharply from red cell destruction, but I'm pretty certain the plasmodium count is falling, too, so the mefloquine must be killing them. Do you agree that a transfusion is in order?"

"A *slow* transfusion," said Mort. "Even though the falling plasmodium count means he's getting better, we still don't want to clog up any of the small arterioles or capillaries in his brain and damage that, perhaps permanently."

Laurel ordered a plastic bag of blood from the hospital blood bank and when it came, they connected the tubing from it to the nylon catheter in the baby's arm vein. The flow was started at the rate of only a drop per second until they could see how the injection of another person's blood into the tiny black body would be accepted by it.

"It's going to be a long night," Mort said when the blood was flowing well. "I'll take the first shift and call you if there's any reaction. Why don't you take a nap in the Nurses' Lounge?"

Laurel shook her head. "With Lisa in the tank and still under hyperbaric pressure, plus the baby out here in the midst of a crisis, I could never go to sleep. Mind if I sit close to you? I think I'm losing some of my independence."

"Why don't we lose it together? That's the best way of all."

IV

The dinner theater was crowded on Saturday night and the food delicious. The play was known as a "Toby Show" because the comic character — who somehow managed to untangle the intricacies of the plot at the last moment and save the heroine from the clutches of the villain and a fate worse than death — always had flaming red hair, freckles — and was named Toby.

When the performance was over about ten-thirty, Lynn and Paul drove back to the city almost reluctantly. Crossing over to Miami Beach, they stopped at a famous ice cream parlor and gorged themselves on a small tub of the product for which the establishment was famous.

"Promise me you'll come to Tampa when the State Medical meets there next spring," Paul begged as they headed down Collins Avenue toward the General Douglas Mac-Arthur Causeway that would take them back to downtown Miami and his hotel.

"Father usually goes to that meeting. Someone has to stay here and mind the store."

"The Institute has enough surgeons on the staff to take care of emergencies."

"I'll try," she promised.

Each of them was silent, conscious that their lovely evening was almost finished. Then, as they came off the causeway and approached the exit to Biscayne Boulevard, Lynn suddenly said: "Would you like to go to the Terrace, Paul, to our – my – apartment?"

"You must have ESP, darling; I've been thinking of nothing else since we left Miami Beach. But you'd better stop at an all-night store on the Boulevard so I can get a toothbrush and a razor."

"We won't need to stop," Lynn told him. "Right after you went to Tampa, I was cleaning the apartment and found one of your shaving kits that you'd left behind. I put it away on a shelf in the closet and I can lend you a toothbrush."

"In that case, why don't we go home?"

V

Cradled in David Fuller's arms, Lisa slept almost four hours. When she awakened, she stared up at him groggily. "How long has this been going on?" she asked with a smile.

"Four hours; I froze after the first one. Anyway, I'm sure we've set the long distance record for a continuous embrace."

"You deserve a better reward." Raising herself on her right elbow, she kissed him, her lips soft and warm against his before she took them away and removed the arm that was still about his neck.

"Move around a little and loosen up," she told him. "I remember your giving me an injection. What was it?"

"Diazepam. You had three convulsions from oxygen."

"I had the bends before that, didn't I?"

"Plus, a nitrogen embolus. For a while, you even had a full hemiplegia."

"For which you used a desperate remedy? Right?"

"A convulsion was the only thing I could think of that might shake that nitrogen bubble loose."

"Then you saved my life."

"I can't claim credit for that; the decompression chamber would have cured the bends. The embolism struck just as you came through the Emergency Room door but I caught you —"

"That's getting to be a habit of yours, isn't it?"

"I hope so," he said, with a smile. "I certainly hope so."

"We'll talk about that later, when I get out of here. Tell me the rest of the medical side."

"Decompression might have cured the embolism in time — by dissolving the nitrogen gradually – but I was afraid to take the chance. From the extent of the hemiplegia, I knew the brain cells involved must have taken a beating, so giving you oxygen under pressure would accomplish two things. It would support the brain cells and was also the quickest way I could think of to shake out that nitrogen bubble. So I took the chance."

"Thank God you chose the dangerous route. What about Roberto?"

"He's fine. The nurse in the other tank with him reports that he's asking to come out. Want to tell me what happened? When I talked to your sister –"

"Lynn? Or Laurel?"

"Laurel. We haven't been able to get in touch with Dr. Rogers."

"What time is it anyway?"

"About midnight. Why?"

"If she's where she ought to be, she's with Paul – in bed."

"I haven't had time to call since."

"Don't. I'm okay."

"We couldn't get your father, either."

"I'd just as soon he didn't know I made a fool mistake that could have left me a cripple for life – but for you."

"You still haven't told me what happened."

"We took a shallow dive Saturday morning, only about fifty feet. Then we had a picnic lunch on the boat and a nap. I was planning that afternoon to see what it was like at the edge of the reef."

"A few hundred feet?" he inquired with an innocent look. "I seem to remember hearing somewhere that it's your favorite depth."

"You were so damn cocky Friday morning spouting Boyle's Law that I wanted to impress you. I'd never been that deep before and had lost my enthusiasm for the dive that late in the afternoon anyway, but Roberto was high on it."

"That apparently wasn't the only thing he was high on."

"You're wrong. I read the riot act to him on the way down to Key Largo. No alcohol, no drugs, not even a little grass while we were diving."

"The manager of the marina where you keep the boat called before you got here. He said he found some cocaine crystals and a sniffing spoon in the head —"

"That bastard! I remember now that his eyes were pretty bright when he came out of the head but it was getting late and we didn't have much time left for the deeper dive. I didn't smell any grass in the head, though, and Roberto didn't have any alcohol on his breath, so I had no reason to think he'd been sniffing. My big mistake was letting him change the air tanks before we started the dive near the outer edge of the reef. We were at about a hundred feet, when he suddenly shot past me —"

"Nitrogen narcosis! The cocaine he'd sniffed before the dive probably helped bring it on quicker than would ordinarily have happened."

"As he went by me, I saw a string of bubbles coming from where the regulator valve was attached to his air tank and knew he'd soon be in trouble," Lisa continued. "Around a hundred and fifty feet, I caught him and turned him around but he ran out of air when we were still over a hundred feet down."

"Why didn't you try buddy breathing?"

"You can't buddy breathe when your buddy won't share," said Lisa bitterly. "*I* had the tank but *he* had the mouthpiece and wouldn't give it up. The only thing I could do then was inflate the life vests and take us to the surface fast."

David Fuller grinned. "When I told your sister you were in here, she said you were a chronic Good Samaritan and I guess she was right. Before you and I take that deep dive over the reef you promised me Friday morning at the seminar we'll *both* check the scuba gear."

"How do you know I'll ever dive again?"

"Because you're not one to break a promise."

"You'd hold me to that?"

"Of course. I took charge of your life temporarily when you collapsed just as you and Dr. Galvez reached the Emergency Room, but at the same time I took an option on taking charge of it for good. Actually, I had already made that decision Friday morning."

"There you go being cocky again," she said, but her voice and her eyes were warm.

"Look where it got us – in the longest continuous embrace in history."

VI

As the night wore on and Laurel watched beside Baby DuVall with Mort Weyer, signs of improvement slowly developed, indicating, they hoped, that the crisis had passed. With fresh blood cells and their extra oxygen-carrying capacity moving slowly into the small veins, the complicated computer-operated instrument that kept a continual watch on the patient's blood gases reported a steady increase in the blood oxygen level, a sure indication that the malignant parasites in the small body were losing their hold upon his life. The pulse slowed perceptibly, too, and the temperature chart steadily declined.

By three o'clock in the morning, when the slow transfusion was finally ended, a blood smear told them the plasmodium count, too, had decreased sharply. Hardly any of the deadly gametocyte forms could be found either, indicating that the massive attack upon the patient's body by falciparum malaria was now being decisively repulsed. Mort looked up from the microscope where he was confirming Laurel's count, and smiled.

"You've licked it, darling," he told her. "The fight's nearly over."

"I'm glad." She staggered a little from sheer weariness when she slid off the laboratory stool and he caught her arm to steady her, holding her close to him as they left the Critical Care Unit.

"We'd better check on Lisa," said Laurel. "She was asleep in Commander Fuller's arms the last time I looked through the port."

"Too bad she's unconscious," said Mort as they made their way through the narrow passage in the Hyperbaric Laboratory between the tank and the pump. "I've an idea Fuller's the kind of man your sister should become interested in."

"If you'd heard what I heard about an hour ago," the technician watching through the thick glass window in the tank said with a chuckle, "you'd say she's already interested."

"Then she's out of danger?"

"Must be. Commander Fuller has given the order to lower the pressure gradually."

"How long will that take?" Laurel asked.

"Several hours at least."

"There's no need for us to stay, then," she said. "Let's go, Mort."

Outside the hospital, the breeze from Biscayne Bay was cool and refreshing but Laurel was still leaning on Mort's arm as they walked to where the car was parked.

"I wish there was some way I could get word to *Grand-père* DuVall," she said. "He must love that baby very much to have risked capture and return to Haiti by bringing it to your clinic."

"You could assure him that the Haitian authorities don't want him back, too," said Mort, "but as long as he chooses to hide in Jock LeMoyne's house, I guess there's no way to communicate with him. By the way, if you hadn't thought to order the drug from Atlanta and hadn't decided to risk giving the transfusion last night, the baby would have been a candidate for the morgue. You should give yourself a pat on the back."

"I'm too tired to reach around."

"I'll do it for you." Mort carried out the maneuver, which managed to end up with her in his arms and a long kiss.

"Let's go home, darling," he said when they broke away.

"Suits me," she said sleepily. "My place or yours?"

"Yours," he said firmly.

"Are you sure?" She giggled. "Tired as I am I couldn't put up much of a fight."

"At three A.M. I'm not taking advantage of a girl, who got up at six and just finished saving a patient's life twenty-one hours later," Mort said as they got into the car. "Especially when she's the girl I plan to marry."

Laurel didn't answer. She was already asleep with her head on his shoulder.

Chapter 12

The sun shining through the wide glass window of the bedroom facing Biscayne Bay awakened Lynn. She looked at the other side of the queen-sized bed but saw that it was empty. Then hearing a cheery whistle from the kitchen and inhaling the aroma of frying bacon, she sat up and called, "Is that you, Paul?"

"It had better not be anybody else." He appeared in the doorway of the bedroom, shaved and fully dressed but wearing an apron. "You'll just have time for a shower before break —" He broke off for she'd forgotten to pull up the sheet. "Wait a minute while I turn off the bacon before it burns."

"No you don't; we've had enough of that since midnight." Lynn clutched the sheet around her quickly. "Father's holding Grand Rounds at ten and I have to go to the hospital a little before that to make sure the cases are all lined up."

"But —"

"You'll have to wait till I come up to Tampa for the State Medical next spring."

"Come with me now, darling," he urged, leaning down to kiss her. "I never realized how much I need you until I awoke at six-thirty and saw you lying there beside me, the loveliest thing in the world."

"I can't, Paul. Maybe next year."

"I read a play with that title once — about two people who loved each other but were kept apart by circumstances beyond their control, except for a day or two every year."

"I remember it, too."

"Then you know that at the end they both went back to what they had away from each other — and after a while stopped coming back. That happened to us two years ago and I don't want it to happen again."

"Neither do I, but we'll just have to wait."

"How long?" It was a cry of pain and frustration.

"No longer than is absolutely necessary, I promise you. Now get back to the kitchen before the bacon burns so I can shower and dress. We'll eat out on the little balcony overlooking the bay where we always ate on Sunday mornings."

"I've got one just like it outside my apartment in Tampa. Chose it because it was so much like this one. But, God, what I would give to move it some two hundred miles to join this one."

When Lynn came out on the small balcony wearing a light robe, Paul had already set the table for two with orange juice in small glasses and plates with crisp bacon. A small fleet of sailboats setting out from the Miami Yacht Club for a regatta dotted the sunlit water with white. Farther down the bay, a party boat was heading out toward Government Cut and the open water beyond.

As Lynn drank the cool orange juice, the beauty of the scene and the sound of Paul moving about in the kitchen, plus the memory of the hours they'd spent in each other's arms last night, filled her with a deep sense of content. It was broken only by the thought that this time tomorrow morning, Paul would have gone back to Tampa and she would be alone once more.

"Still like your eggs over light?" he called from the kitchen.

"Always. Do you need any help?"

"I'm fine. They'll be ready in a minute."

Lynn was munching a piece of bacon

when he came out, carrying a skillet in which the eggs were crackling.

"You're spoiling me," she protested, as with a spatula he slid two eggs out of the skillet onto her plate and moved on to his own.

"Turnabout is fair play after the way you spoiled me last night. Toast will be out in a minute.

"What's on the program for today besides Grand Rounds?" he asked when he came back carrying a plate piled high with crisp toast.

"I'm scheduled to give an hour on microsurgery at eleven today. The one I gave up yesterday for Mort Weyer."

"I'll be interested to see how you do it; we're shopping for a microsurgeon to join the staff of my department in Tampa. Could we go down to your cottage at Key Largo this afternoon after you've finished your lecture?"

"Lisa's down there with Roberto Galvez. Besides, the luncheon for former Fellows and staff is at one o'clock."

"I hope you're going with me to it," he said.

"If you want me."

"If I want you!" He stood up quickly and

came around the table to take her in his arms. "Now that we've been apart for two years, until last night, I realize that I want you more than anything else in the world."

Enough to come back to Miami? She found herself wondering but put the thought from her. Theo Malone would never take Paul back on the staff of the Institute and he might even be able to carry enough weight with the administration of Biscayne General to deny him a place on the visiting staff of the hospital and a teaching position in the medical school.

"I'd better finish dressing so I can stop by to see my coronary anastomosis patient before Grand Rounds," said Lynn.

"Does the paper boy still leave the *Herald* outside your door?"

"Yes. Why?"

"I'll get it and see what's happened since we escaped into a new world yesterday afternoon."

"Let me get it," said Lynn. "I'm supposed to be in charge of publicity for the seminar, so I'd better check on how well yesterday morning's presentations were covered. The *Herald* reporter that father allows free access to the hospital, was listening when Mort Weyer dropped his broadside about coronary by-pass, so there are sure to be headlines about that."

Lynn came back into the living room a few moments later and opened the paper to the second section dealing with local news. From the kitchen Paul heard her cry out with alarm.

"What is it?" he called.

"Lisa and Roberto had a diving accident yesterday at Key Largo. They're both in the hyperbaric chamber at Biscayne General."

Paul came into the room and looked at the paper with her. A photograph of Lisa as she prepared to get into the ambulance was in the middle of the page. The raincoat she wore had flared open to reveal her slender body in the maillot but it was her face, twisted by pain that had made Lynn cry out.

"At least she was able to navigate under her own power," Paul reminded Lynn. "That must be Roberto on the stretcher."

"I'm going to call Biscayne General." Lynn reached for the telephone and started dialing the hospital switchboard.

"This is Dr. Lynn Rogers," she told the operator. "Please connect me with the Hyperbaric Laboratory."

"This is Dr. Rogers," she said when a

man's voice answered. "Are my sister and Dr. Galvez still in the tank?"

"Dr. Malone is still inside with Dr. Fuller but Dr. Galvez came out about an hour ago. There's a telephone in the tank and I can ring directly through, if you wish."

"Please do."

"Dr. Fuller," a masculine voice answered. "This is Lynn Rogers. Is my sister okay?"

"She had a nitrogen embolism in the brain, Dr. Rogers, but I managed to dissolve it."

"Oh, thank God! Will she be okay?"

"She had a hemiplegia for a short time but the signs of paralysis are about gone," David Fuller told her. "She's awake now if you'd like to speak to her."

"Please."

Moments later, Lisa's voice sounded on the phone. "I'm all right, Lynn, thanks to Dav – Commander Fuller. Are you with Paul?"

"Yes."

"Your place or his?"

"Mine."

"I hope you slept well."

"We did – later."

"So did I – in the arms of a perfectly beautiful man. But I was unconscious – worse luck."

"The hemiplegia –"

328

"It's gone and David says I shouldn't have any sequelae. I'm sure I would have had though, if he hadn't rushed me into the tank and started oxygen under pressure. He says I can come out around noon but wants me to stay in the hospital for a few days under observation."

"I hope you'll obey."

"I don't have any choice." Lisa's chuckle came over the phone. "After all, he's a commander and I'm only a lieutenant — in the Navy Reserve."

II

When Lynn dialed her mother's home, Laurel answered.

"I was just talking to Lisa in the hyperbaric chamber," Lynn told her younger sister.

"That must have been why your phone was busy. I tried to get through just now."

"Lisa's fine —"

"So the hospital operator told me when I called over there. How about you?"

"I haven't been so happy since the divorce. Paul and I are going to be married again — when we can get around to it."

"Wonderful! Mother will be happy to hear it."

"By the way, you made the headlines, too. Congratulations!"

"Are you talking about the malignant malaria business?"

"Yes. You certainly made a name for yourself in the field of Tropical Medicine."

"We still almost lost the baby yesterday before I got some mefloquine from Atlanta. Mort and I were up until three this morning, getting the little fellow through the crisis."

"Is he all right now?"

"The drug we used finally started killing the plasmodia, but then we had to combat a fall in blood oxygenation with a slow transfusion."

"Even the little I remember about malignant malaria from med school labels that a desperate measure," Lynn commented.

"We didn't have any choice," Laurel explained. "If Mort hadn't been there to back me up, though, I might not have had the courage to do it."

"I doubt that," said Lynn. "We Malone daughters are too much like our male parent to waffle much on an important decision."

"Anyway, when I called the hospital just

now, the temperature was normal and the chills have stopped. We're trying to locate the grandfather but he's hiding because he still thinks the Haitian government wants him extradited. It seems he's one of the leaders of a dissident group that's opposing the government down there, but the consul told us yesterday afternoon that they'd rather he stayed out of the country. Apparently, they're afraid that if he's brought to trial, a lot of things they don't want the people to know would be brought out."

"Just like here at home," Lynn commented. "You like Mort, don't you?"

"More than that. I guess you could say we're going steady."

"I'm glad. He's the kind of brother-in-law I'd like to have. Did you talk to Father?"

"I've been putting it off," Laurel confessed. "He must have read about Lisa — and me, too — by now but he hasn't called."

"No Malone except him is supposed to make the headlines and, with three daughters on the front page in so many days, he's probably chewing nails." Lynn laughed. "I'm going to see him at ten o'clock, though, and I'll give him a few more to chew."

"Good luck! Tell Paul I'm happy to have

him back as a brother-in-law."

III

Shortly after Laurel hung up the telephone, it rang again. This time Kelley Parnell was calling.

"Congratulations on making the headlines, Laurel," she said. "I tried to call Lisa just now but they told me she's still in one of those big steel tanks in that new laboratory. What do you call it?"

"Hyperbaric —"

"I never was good with scientific terms. Dex says I was born to make babies so I guess I'd better stick to something I enjoy — at least at the beginning. Those Pentids you left for little Dex did the trick. He's running around like usual this morning, but I'm still worried about Lisa."

"You don't need to be. Lynn just talked to her in the chamber and she's safely over the bends. In fact, she seems to have made a new conquest in there, a Naval officer."

"I met Commander Fuller at the reception. He's a second Burt Reynolds except for the red hair. Maybe Lisa's met her match at last."

"I only saw him through a glass porthole in the wall of the hyperbaric chamber last night, but he's handsome all right. Mort says he's the hottest man the Navy has in Undersea Medicine."

"Hold on for Dex," Kelley told her. "He wants to talk to you about something."

Dexter Parnell came on the telephone a few moments later. "Do you have any idea how long the LeMoyne house will be quarantined, Laurel?" he asked.

"No. That's a job for Dr. Prentiss and the Health Department now. Baby DuVall is coming around, though. When Mort Weyer and I left Biscayne General around three o'clock this morning, there'd been no new admissions with symptoms resembling malignant malaria for forty-eight hours."

"Doesn't that mean there's no chance of an epidemic any longer and the house can soon come out of quarantine?"

"That depends on whether the baby's grandfather is a carrier and any more *Anopheles Gambiae* are hiding with him in the LeMoyne house. With the picture of the mosquito in the *Herald* this morning, though, everybody in the area will be warned to look out for them. By the way, how did Father take the news about the

Historical Society option?"

"You won't believe this but he didn't blow his top."

"Maybe he's remembering Dr. Downing's warning about running up his blood pressure."

"Could be, but I don't think so. In fact, I'm not real sure he didn't know about it already. You didn't call him, did you?"

"I haven't seen Father, or talked to him, since Friday night at the reception. Why would you think he already knew about the option?"

"Theo's got several stooges working in Liberty City. He calls them real estate agents and won't even tell me who they are but they have been able to buy some pieces of property I had trouble getting. One of them could have heard the story about the option and the stolen gold from the minister you say talked to Dr. Prentiss and told Theo about it. He knows better now though."

"How can you be sure?"

"I told him the rumor was false and there was nothing to it."

"What are you worrying about then?"

"Something about the way Theo took the news of that option makes me think he's up to something. I don't want complications with the Department of Housing and Urban Development that could make them think twice about approving the housing project — or get me into questionable legal activities without my even knowing what's going on."

"Have you asked Father about it?"

"Yes, but he only laughed. And I like that even less than knowing he's got stooges working behind my back."

"I can't help you, Dex. Father doesn't confide in any of his daughters — and me least of all since I discovered the invasion from Africa and started this whole business about the quarantine."

"Let's hope he isn't up to something, then. By the way, Art Jones tells me the Haitian government is going to request that you be part of the commission the WHO will be sending down there to head off an epidemic of malaria carried by that fancy mosquito you found on old Jock and at the house. A vacation at government expense yet — some people have all the luck."

"Hunting *Anopheles Gambiae* in the mountains of Haiti where the consul said the plane from Africa crashed won't be any vacation, Dex. But at least it won't be as hot as Zaire was last year."

"Give your mother our love and congratulate Lisa for us on coming out of that diving accident alive," he said. "Good-by."

IV

Lynn didn't get to talk to her father until after Grand Rounds. She waited until he came into the auditorium where she was to show her film on microsurgery and describe briefly the technique, hitherto unused to her knowledge, by which she had been able to reestablish the flow of blood through a severed coronary artery to a vital portion of the heart.

"It isn't too late to announce the new operation, even if you don't find a subject for it while the seminar is in progress, Father," she suggested.

"What gave you that damn fool idea?" he growled.

"The last artificial heart we put in – the one in the pie-bald calf – we filmed it, remember? I had to do a lot of microsurgery for that operation and we could substitute that film instead of the one I'm going to show today demonstrating the technique."

"And let somebody else steal my discovery?"

"You'd still have the record for the first experimental operation."

"It's the first successful case on a human that's going to put me ahead of everybody else in cardiac surgery, Lynn, not an operation on a calf. Besides, that's already been done at the National Institutes of Health."

"By showing the film today," she insisted, "we could get a manuscript together in time to publish the technique in the next issue of the *Journal of Experimental Surgery*."

"*I* developed that heart, Lynn. All you did was add those Dacron flanges to the openings by using the adhesive technique I had already developed for putting the valves into place."

Lynn stared at her father in amazement for a moment, then began to laugh.

"What's so damn funny?" he demanded.

"So that's the reason you won't let the experimental technique be published? You don't want the world to know anyone else — even your own daughter — played any part in it!"

"I was operating on hearts before you were born," Malone snapped. "Why should I share the credit now?"

"No reason at all. In fact, I should be thanking you — and I do."

"For what?"

"Making me see where my real duty lies – to the man I love."

"Paul Rogers? He couldn't even –"

"Become another Theodore Malone? I'm glad he didn't. Paul has asked me to go to Tampa with him as the microsurgeon on his staff and as his wife."

"You're free to go, but don't ask for my blessing."

"I won't, but I'd like to leave one thought with you. You see, I'm the only other person besides yourself who knows how to build an artificial heart that works and how to put one in. If I go to Tampa, Paul and I may just be lucky enough to find a suitable case before you do. If we do, and you see it first in newspaper headlines and on television, just remember that you taught me how to make medical headlines."

V

Paul Rogers was waiting for Lynn when she finished answering the questions several surgeons had raised about the lecture.

"Are you going to the luncheon?" she asked.

"Not if you'll let me take you somewhere else."

"I wish I could but the luncheon is my final duty for the seminar – and probably my final official act at the Institute."

Paul's face suddenly brightened. "Am I hearing what I think I'm hearing?"

"Yes. My resignation from the Institute goes in tomorrow."

"Then you'll be free to go back to Tampa with me?"

"After I've had a few weeks to get my thoughts together and convince myself that Mother will be happy with only Lisa and Laurel in Miami."

He took her arm and held her close to him as they walked to the bank of elevators leading to the ground floor.

"We'll take the next one down," he said when a group of doctors held the elevator for them. "I want to talk to Dr. Rogers about something."

In the empty elevator, he took her in his arms and kissed her. "Between us we're going to make the Tampa Institute the best damned place to have your heart fixed in the country – no, in the world," he told her. "What made you change your mind about staying on at the Institute?"

"Father practically threw me out, when I suggested substituting a filmed version of our last artificial heart operation on a calf in place of the one I just showed on microsurgical technique. He's determined not to make any mention of the heart implant publically until he finds a patient he can operate on before the TV and newspaper cameras."

"He'll still have to give you credit as co-developer of the technique, particularly that part involving microsurgery."

"Not the way he sees it."

"Never mind. You're going to love Tampa, darling, and I'll see that you get all the credit you deserve – plus my love."

"I guess that's all any woman could want, especially a woman surgeon. But I still have deep roots here in Miami, Paul, plus an already established reputation as a cardiac surgeon. Accomplishing something like that isn't very easy for a woman."

"You can have it in Tampa, too."

"I'm sure you'll give me all the credit you can but one of these days you're going to be another Theo Malone –"

"God forbid!"

"Another Cooley – or a DeBakey then, while I'll wind up being only Paul Rogers' wife. As much as I love that, I guess I inherited enough of my father's drive to want to feel that I've accomplished something as a woman surgeon."

VI

At mid-morning, Laurel stopped at the Critical Care Unit and examined Baby DuVall. She was pleased to find him sleeping quietly, with no sign of either fever or the malarial chills that had wracked the small body. She'd promised Mort Weyer to help arrange the furniture in his small apartment overlooking the Miami River, near where the first settlement in this area, Fort Dallas, had been started as an army station during the Seminole War of the 1830s. It was after twelve on Sunday afternoon, when they quit work for lunch and walked to a nearby Pizza Hut for a leisurely meal. As Mort opened the door to his apartment when they returned, he heard the telephone ringing and hurried to answer it. It was Artemus Jones.

"I've been trying to reach you for an hour, Doc." The union organizer sounded tense — a strange thing for him.

"What's up?" Mort asked.

"Trouble's going to start in Liberty City

any minute now and I need a fi – A shot of methadone – so I can stay calm until it's over."

"Is a Sunday injection on your schedule?"

"No, but this is an emergency, Doc. If I can keep my cool this afternoon, I may be able to stop another riot that could destroy everything we've accomplished since the other one."

"I still don't understand."

"This one is centering around Jock LeMoyne's house," Art explained. "A lot of people around there got excited when they read in the morning paper about a mosquito carrying the kind of malaria that killed old Jock and the baby."

"He's out of danger now, thanks to Dr. Malone's knowing what to do."

"That's good news. But when a house people think is haunted suddenly sprouts quarantine signs and the Health Department starts spraying the whole neighborhood for a mosquito that the newspaper says can cause thousands of deaths, people who aren't educated enough to understand what's happening begin to be upset. They've known for months that Jock was protecting refugees but they didn't stop him because he always saw that they were moved inland. Usually it was to farms and small towns around Lake Okeechobee, where they didn't compete for jobs. But when they read in the *Herald* this morning that Jock is dead, they figured everything is going to change and some want to burn down the house."

"Henri DuVall is probably hiding out there, but he doesn't speak much English, so he wouldn't understand what was happening," Laurel protested.

"Worse than that," said Art. "Somebody — and I think I know who it was — started the rumor that whoever's hiding in Jock Le-Moyne's house has a lot of gold —"

"From what the consul told us, DuVall couldn't have had many Krugerrands to start with," said Mort. "And after paying Le-Moyne to pick him and his family up in a boat, he couldn't have many left."

"*We* know it, but the people don't who are firing themselves up with whiskey and grass. If you'll meet me at the clinic and give me that shot of methadone, maybe I can talk them into believing the truth."

"Have you called the police?"

"Come now, man. The police don't listen to labor organizers — particularly a black one. Let 'em find out about this for themselves."

"I'll meet you at the clinic in half an hour and give you the injection," Mort said without any more hesitation.

"Make it twenty minutes; this is a real emergency." The line went dead and Mort turned to Laurel. "I've got to go to the clinic and give Art Jones an injection of methadone. Want to go with me?"

"For the rest of my life, from the looks of things. What's this all about anyway?"

On the way, Mort recounted for Laurel the gist of his conversation with the labor leader.

"I wonder why the workers waited until this afternoon to start a riot," she said. "The story appeared in the Miami *Herald* early this morning."

"There were radio and TV broadcasts about it last night, too. I doubt that riots have much to do with logic, though," he added as he parked the car beside Artemus' flamboyant convertible outside the Liberty City clinic. "Maybe Jones can tell us."

Artemus Jones, for once, wasn't inclined to be loquacious. When Mort finished giving him the injection, he rolled down his sleeve and started for the door.

"Dr. Malone and I were wondering what started the riot — if there is one," Mort said as he and Laurel followed Jones out to the car. "You wouldn't maybe be conning me into giving you an extra shot of methadone, would you?"

"Trouble's been building since the neighbors learned that old Jock is dead but the fine Machiavellian touch was added a couple of hours ago, when the story about the stolen gold was planted to make sure the crowd would get excited and attack the house."

"Who would do that?" Laurel asked.

"Dexter Parnell!" Mort exclaimed. "He needs that property to finish out the land for the housing project your father is involved in. With the house burned down, the Historical Society wouldn't be interested. Parnell could buy it from Jacques Le-Moyne's heirs — if any exist — for a lot less money than if Jock were alive and he had to force it to be sold under the doctrine of eminent domain, if a judge would issue the order."

"Dex knows Henri DuVall is probably hiding out in the LeMoyne house," Laurel protested. "He wouldn't stir up a riot to burn it when he knew a life, or lives, could be lost." Her face suddenly brightened. "You've got a mobile telephone in your car,

Mr. Jones. Can I call Dex with it and find out the truth?"

"Okay! But I'm pretty sure I know that truth already and it doesn't involve Dex."

Laurel made the call, a short one. When she came back, her face was flushed. "Dex bawled me out for even suggesting he had a part in placing that rumor about gold. He's leaving right now for the LeMoyne house to help stop the riot."

"Then I'd better get going." Art Jones headed for the car. "Take my advice and stay away from that part of Liberty City. In one of these fracases a white face is the first target."

"How about you?" Mort asked.

"I follow Teddy Roosevelt's doctrine of speak softly and carry a big stick." Artemus Jones lifted a high-powered rifle with a telescopic sight that was propped against the other seat. "This is my hole card. Thanks for the shot, Doc."

The motor of the convertible roared and it shot away from the clinic with a spattering of gravel from the tires.

"What do you think?" Mort looked inquiringly at Laurel.

"I guess we'd better do as he advi —" She stopped suddenly. "Dex said on the phone, when I called him from the *Herald* building that he told Father about the rumor that someone who'd escaped from Haiti with a lot of Krugerrands stolen in South Africa had paid Jacques LeMoyne to help him escape by picking him up with the boat that LeMoyne kept in the Keys. Dex told Father the rumor was false but I remember him saying now that Father has some stooges in Liberty City who answer only to him."

"Then Theo Malone could have planted the rumor," said Mort, "hoping the rioters would attack the house and maybe burn it down?"

"I guess it's not beyond him," Laurel agreed. "We'd better go and tell Artemus Jones that possibility. If he can convince the crowd that they're being manipulated, he might even stop the riot before anybody is hurt."

Chapter 13

Lisa Malone awakened about two o'clock from an after-lunch nap in the luxurious V.I.P. section of the hospital, to which David Fuller had ordered her transferred early Sunday morning. Roberto Galvez was standing beside the bed, looking like a boy caught with his hand in the cookie jar. The sight of his face made her start laughing.

"What the hell's so funny?" he demanded.

"Do you have any idea how you look?"

"Not as well as you do, I'm sure. You're beautiful."

And she was. Lisa had seen to that immediately after being transferred. One of the nurses had brought a blue nylon pajama and robe set from her apartment and also her cosmetic kit. After changing from the hospital gown she'd been wearing in the hyperbaric chamber, she had brushed her. blond hair and tied it back with a blue ribbon. The cosmetic kit had also provided the necessities for removing practically all signs of what she had endured the night before.

"I came to say good-by," said Galvez. "My plane leaves for Caracas at five o'clock."

"Did you get to the final luncheon?"

"Yes. Your father gave his usual peroration. Has he been in to see you yet?"

"No. And I don't give a damn if he never does."

"Lynn was at the luncheon — with Paul. I understand that she's going to Tampa to work with him."

"That's good news. Do you feel okay now?"

"Depressed — by the thought of how near I came to killing you. Commander Fuller really chewed me out this morning."

"You deserved it." Lisa gave him no mercy. "I was paralyzed for a while, until Da — Dr. Fuller, caused me to have an oxygen convulsion that moved the nitrogen embolus out of my brain."

"He told me about it. You owe him your life."

"All because you got high on cocaine before we started that last dive and failed to seat that valve properly," she said bitterly.

"I'm sorry. Can you forgive me?"

"Never. In fact, I'll be happy if I

don't see you again —"

"But, we —"

"I have no patience with people who put my life at risk because they're hopped up on hard drugs like cocaine, Roberto. After yesterday, I don't think I'll even smoke grass again."

When the door closed behind him, Lisa found herself wondering how she'd ever been interested in Galvez. Although six feet two and strikingly handsome in the dark Latin way that was attractive to many women, he was nothing compared to David Fuller's healthy maleness.

I'm in love! she told herself with a sudden sense of wonder. *In love for the first time in my life. And it's wonderful!*

II

"Turn right at the next street crossing, please," Laurel told Mort before they had covered more than a block on the way to Liberty City.

"Okay," he said, pulling into the curbside lane. "I'd just as soon you weren't at the scene where the riot's going to break out anyway."

"We'll go there, later. First I've got to talk to my father at his apartment in Biscayne Terrace."

"Why in the world —?"

"If he deliberately got people in Liberty City stirred up to riot by having agents he pays spread the story about refugees in the LeMoyne house having gold, I want to know it."

"Maybe Art can convince them it isn't true."

"That isn't the most important thing right now. I've got to give Father a chance to stop what he's started before it's too late."

"But how?"

"By telling the truth or, better still, going there himself. He's been pretending to be the great humanitarian by building the low-rent housing project, so the rioters will know him. If he tells them the truth, they might listen."

"That's a long shot," said Mort as he pulled the small car to a stop in front of the marquee at the entrance to the building housing the luxurious Biscayne Terrace Condominiums. "Want me to go up with you?"

"No. He hates you already, so your being there would only anger him."

"You can say that again. I'll wait."

"You *can* do something, though," she said. "There's a telephone just inside the foyer. Call the police and tell them there's going to be a riot at Jacques LeMoyne's house."

"But we promised Art —"

"We didn't *promise*. He just said he didn't want them to know, but I think they should. While you're at it, call the Fire Department, too, and have them send a Rescue Squad ambulance, in case somebody gets hurt. They know you so they won't ask questions."

She was gone up the covered walk leading to the entrance before he could get out on the other side of the car. When he came into the foyer, he saw the floor indicator of the elevator moving upward and watched until it stopped at the penthouse. Then going to the phone she had indicated, he called the Fire Department for the ambulance and then the police.

"We just got word that a crowd is massing near that old house in Liberty City, Dr. Weyer," said the operator at the Police Department switchboard. "The dispatcher has ordered a half dozen cars into the area, but there's been a bad accident on the Palmetto Expressway across town and cars are piled up everywhere. It may be a while."

Taking a seat in the foyer, Mort waited with his gaze on the elevator indicator that still stood at the letter P, marking the penthouse.

Theo Malone himself had answered Laurel's ring. He'd taken off his shirt and his muscular chest, with the fringe of white hair, was bare. He also carried a half empty glass in his hand.

"Laurel!" he exclaimed. "What the hell are you doing here?"

"I've got to talk to you."

"Then talk out here in the hall," he said, pulling the door almost shut behind him. "And make it short. Elena's taking a nap."

"Out here is fine," said Laurel. "I wouldn't want her to hear the truth about you."

"What the hell are you talking about?"

"That rumor you had your stooges start in Liberty City this morning — about Haitian refugees with a lot of stolen gold hiding in Jacques LeMoyne's old house."

"You're crazy! I don't know anything about any gold. As for stooges in Liberty City, I've got a couple of Negroes buying up property where we're going to put up a housing unit but they're only real estate agents."

"A couple of men you pay to stir up trouble out there so you'll be able to buy the property for half what it's worth and build yourself a tax shelter," Laurel snapped. "Dex told me this morning that he'd told you about the gold rumor being false, so you also knew that a Haitian refugee named Henri DuVall is hiding there. He'll probably be killed by the mob your *real estate agents* stirred up or be burned to death if that tinderbox of an old frame house is set afire during the riot."

"Is that why you came up here?" Malone demanded angrily. "To involve me in something I don't know a damn thing about?"

"You know about it, all right. One thing your daughters learned to recognize early is when you're lying, because you lied so much to us and to Mother while we were growing up. I came to give you a chance to do at least one decent thing in your life, by calling off your agents. Or, better still, going out to the LeMoyne house yourself and calming the rioters."

"Me talk to a bunch of welfare bums and dope addicts?" Malone started to laugh. "That's what I get for letting you go off to Africa for a year. You've come back a damned bleeding heart."

"Then you're not going to help prevent a possible tragedy?"

"You're damn well right, I'm not." The pulse at Theo Malone's temple was throbbing as his anger built. "Don't threaten me, either, Laurel, or I'll give you the thrashing you deserve. Believe me, I'm still man enough to do it."

Laurel shook her head slowly. "I guess I was wrong in believing you'd do one decent thing to make up for some of the lousy things you've done – to Mother and to your daughters. But if that poor refugee out there at the LeMoyne house is killed, you can be damned certain I'll swear out a warrant for your arrest on a charge of conspiracy."

"It wouldn't stick," he sneered.

"Maybe not, but it will make the headlines. *'Doctor's Daughter Accuses Father of Murder'* – think how that's going to look on the front page of the *Herald*. And how your new wife's family is going to feel about you then. They might even decide not to donate all that money I hear they promised to give your Foundation."

"Get the hell out of here!" Malone snapped. "And stay out of my sight from now on!"

"That will be easy, at least for a month or two." Laurel turned and pressed the elevator button. "There's a good chance that the WHO will want me to go to Haiti with a commission to direct a campaign to eradicate *Anopheles Gambiae* and malignant malaria from the area where the plane from Africa crashed."

The elevator doors swung open and, stepping inside, she pressed the button that closed them. But she couldn't close from her mind the sight of her father, his temple arteries throbbing and his face beet red with anger.

If I threw him into a stroke or a heart attack, she couldn't help thinking, *I wonder if I could ever forgive myself, even knowing what I know about him.*

III

Lisa Malone woke up again when she felt gentle fingers seeking the pulse at her wrist. She looked up to see David Fuller, freshly shaved, and wearing a crisp, summer Navy uniform, standing by the bed. An examining basket containing the instruments for a routine physical was on the bedside table.

"I was wondering whether you'd deserted me," she said.

"Not a chance of that unless you want it, and then I wouldn't obey the order. Remember, I'm your superior officer."

"Did you get some sleep? I know you didn't get much those long hours after midnight when you were holding me in your arms."

"Who could want to under the circumstances? While you were being transferred from the tank to this V.I.P. suite, I stopped and gave your friend, Galvez, a lecture. Then I went to my apartment, shaved, and took a shower before getting in a couple of hours of sleep."

"Roberto stopped to tell me good-by, but I gave him his walking papers. The next time I dive, I'll make sure my partner hasn't been sniffing cocaine."

David Fuller sat on the edge of the bed and took her smaller hand in his own. "The next time you dive it will be with *me*. That's an order."

"Aye, aye, sir. I never thought I'd let any man order me around; not even Father has ever been able to do that. But coming from you, I sort of like it."

"You're going to like it more as time goes

on," he assured her. "Right now, though, I need to do a brief neurological examination to see whether you have any sequelae from the embolus."

The examination was brief, but thorough.

"Everything okay?" Lisa asked when he finally put the examining instruments back in the basket.

"I still haven't tested the *orbicularis oris* muscle. One side of it was paralyzed briefly, too."

"You're the doctor."

When he leaned over to kiss her, she reached up to put her arms around his neck, making that particular examination anything but perfunctory.

"How are the muscles around the mouth?" she asked, when she finally released him.

"Coming along fine. Of course, I'll have to give them some exercise from time to time as part of your rehabilitation program."

"Do I need one? I feel wonderful."

"You'll like this program," he promised. "Medically, you'll need a few days of rest in the hospital. The skeletal muscles on the right side are still a little weaker than on the left and the reflexes somewhat more active. Both of those go with some temporary damage to the brain cells on the left that were briefly without oxygen, but they should be back to normal soon."

"How about the *orbicularis oris?*"

"Performance in that area is already well above average," he assured her with a twinkle in his eyes, "but we won't take a chance on its losing power. Now about your further rehabilitation —"

"Short term or long term?"

"Both."

"Aren't you taking a lot for granted? After all, we've only known each other a little over forty-eight hours."

"Look what's happened in that time. Your sister, Laurel, said a female Good Samaritan is hidden inside that lovely body by the shell of sophistication you've built around it. I think I know why you built it, but I'd still like to find the real person inside."

"Clue me in, please."

"Like your sisters, you're essentially a strong-minded woman, something you inherited from your father."

"The only thing, we hope."

"Perhaps. Anyhow, resenting the way he treated your mother was a driving force making you all try to exceed him — Lynn as a surgeon."

"And me as a lecher?"

"Maybe, but that's all behind you now —"

"Can you be sure?"

"I'm willing to bet my own happiness — and yours — on it. We faced death together last night and won, so from now on you don't need to prove yourself all the time, like a knight of old —"

"Or Don Quixote tilting at windmills," she said on a somewhat bitter note.

"Say what you want to about Quixote but he was still an idealist — and so are you beneath the lovely outer shell. Until last night you were so busy hiding your real self in the running battle you girls have always carried out with your father, that you couldn't let your real self emerge. The first convulsion cracked the shell, when you thought you were going to die, however, and the second finished the job."

"You were the only one there to see it," she reminded him.

"I'm glad. I was very much attracted to you Friday morning when we met so precipitously, although perhaps only as —"

"A sex object?"

"That, of course. But when the shell cracked in the Hyperbaric Laboratory, I got a glimpse of the real Lisa Malone inside. That's the one I want to know more about."

"How do you propose to go about it?"

"I'd say three months of an old-fashioned courtship should do the job." He'd taken her hand again. "We'll go diving a few times and explore that reef you promised me. Besides, we can always wade the shallow areas of Biscayne Bay around Crandon Park and some other places looking for interesting marine life. I'll never forget the time — I must have been around twelve — when my family came to Miami at Christmas. We stayed in a motel at the edge of Coral Gables — they were cheaper out there — and spent the days wading or swimming. Once I found a baby octopus hiding in an empty conch shell and took it back to school in a jar of formaldehyde to show my class in Biology. I was the hero of the class for two days."

"My biggest treasures were a starfish two feet across and a small shark I caught in my bare hands, while Lynn and I were swimming one day off Key Largo. Father keeps a twenty-four-foot boat at the marina on Key Largo. You'll love our cottage there, particularly if you like to ski."

"I love it."

"On a long weekend, we can even take the boat out into the Gulf as far as Dry Tortugas; it's only a run of maybe five or six hours. Fort Jefferson's only claim to fame is its location – plus the fact that Dr. Samuel Mudd, who set John Wilkes Booth's leg after he escaped from Ford's Theater the night he shot Lincoln, was a prisoner there. The Keys around it are called Dry Tortugas and are fascinating."

"Are there any hotel accommodations?"

"Hardly, but the boat has a head and the seats in the half-cabin are comfortable beds. There's a big ice chest, too, and a Coleman stove for cooking the fish we'll catch."

"Sounds wonderful."

"You haven't lived until you've lain on one of the Dry Tortugas Keys at night and watched the sky."

"See what I mean!" he exclaimed. "You're going to like this old-fashioned courtship I've outlined for you."

"What comes next?"

"A wedding, of course. What else? For a honeymoon we'll fly to the Mediterranean, where the Cousteau team will be diving off Carthage. I've been invited to go with them to explore a Phoenician ship from Tyre or Sidon that went down in the Bay of La Kram forming part of the harbor of ancient Carthage."

"When was that? Pre-med courses didn't leave me much time for studying history."

"Me neither, until I got fascinated with it while I was diving with the Cousteau team at Thera. Carthage was founded in 814 B.C. and the wreck must have happened pretty soon afterward."

"How do you know it's still there?"

"Divers have seen it; you'll love diving for ancient treasures." Lost in description of what he was depicting, David hadn't looked at Lisa until a muffled sob brought his attention back to her and he saw a tear course its way down her cheek.

"What's wrong, darling?" he asked, putting his arm about her shoulders.

"What you've been saying reminds me of the years I've thrown away – on vodka, grass, and men like Roberto Galvez."

"You put all those behind you last night when that convulsion cracked the shell you were showing the world. And you put the shell behind you, too." He leaned forward to kiss away the tear. "There, it's gone."

"Wait a minute and I'll shed another one," Lisa said, a little huskily. "Besides, it's time for some more exercise of the *orbicularis oris.*"

IV

Mort and Laurel heard the shouting before they came in sight of the LeMoyne house on foot, having been forced to park a half block away. As yet, neither the police nor the Rescue Squad ambulance Mort had requested were in sight.

The tall form of Artemus Jones stood well above the heads of the crowd milling around in the street across from the building. When they came within earshot, they could hear Jones trying to placate the mob, several of whom, Laurel noted, carried bottles filled with gasoline, the mouths stopped with cloth wicks to make the typical Molotov cocktail.

As yet, there had been no surge of people across the street toward the shabby three-story frame structure with its rusty tin roof. One group, however, carried a log with which they would easily be able to break open the gate and also the doors of the old house.

A car raced down the street, its tires squealing as the driver put on the brakes and drew to a stop near where Laurel and Mort were standing. Dexter Parnell leaped from it.

"What's the situation here?" he demanded.

"We think Henri DuVall's inside," said Mort. "Theo Malone has had his stooges stir them up with a tale about a fortune in gold that DuVall is supposed to have brought from Haiti."

"I told your father yesterday all that was only a myth, Laurel," Dex protested.

"So did I, not more than fifteen minutes ago," Laurel said bitterly. "He denied it but I could tell he was lying."

"The stubborn old fool! If there's another riot in Miami, the Department of Housing and Urban Development will withdraw its support from the whole housing project, and it will never be built."

"This whole situation is like a bomb," Mort commented. "One of those Molotov cocktails could be the fuse that sends the house up in flames."

"And Henri DuVall with it, if he's hiding somewhere in the house," said Laurel. "Do either of you speak French?"

Both men shook their heads.

"There goes any chance we might have of talking DuVall out then. If we could convince DuVall that the Haitian authorities don't want him back, he might give himself up."

"The police should be here soon," said Laurel. "Maybe they'll have a bullhorn and somebody who speaks French."

Art Jones had moved closer to them while she was speaking and was near enough to hear.

"You called the cops after I left, didn't you?" he said accusingly.

"Of course. This isn't the jungle."

"You'd better believe it *is*," said the union leader. "The only chance we have of saving DuVall now is to get into the house as fast as we can. Most of these people here know me and they'd hardly set the place afire if they knew I was inside."

"I'll go with you," said Laurel.

"Me, too," said Mort.

Before they could start across the narrow open space separating the house from the crowd, however, a siren sounded in the near distance. And with a sudden shout of anger, a tall black man holding a bottle with a wick in one hand and a cigarette lighter in the other, ran across the open street to the gate to the yard.

"Abner! Don't!" Artemus Jones shouted but it was too late.

The tall black lit the wick and, when it burst into flame, threw the bottle in a powerful high arc that attested to his skill as a baseball player. It smashed into a window on the second floor of the old house and a sudden geyser of flame filled the room.

"The whole building will go now," Dexter Parnell shouted. "There's a fire box at the corner; I'll turn in an alarm."

He was too late, however, to avoid the tragedy that followed. As Artemus Jones tried to tackle Abner, the tall, almost emaciated figure of Henri DuVall suddenly appeared at another window of the house. Holding a highpowered rifle in his hands, DuVall used the butt to smash the casement window open. Then putting one foot through it on the windowsill to support his knee he raised the weapon and the report of a rifle shot echoed across the group of rioters.

The tall figure of Artemus Jones was a natural target as he tackled the black man he'd called Abner and at the impact of the bullet, Jones's body spun around and fell in the street. For a single instant the watching rioters were frozen into immobility by the sheer horror of what they had just witnessed. Not so, however, Henri DuVall. Leaning farther out of the casement window he had pushed open, he raised the rifle and fired again, this time aiming at the tall black who had thrown the fire bomb. At just that instant, however, Abner dropped to the pavement and the bullet struck a metal sign behind where he'd been standing, ricocheting over the heads of the rioters with a whine like some malignant spirit in flight.

From the group of blacks, the crack of a second highpowered rifle sounded just as DuVall was bringing up his weapon to fire once again. Striking him in the throat, the bullet smashed his spinal cord as it penetrated his neck, and the rifle dropped from suddenly nerveless hands. DuVall's body, already half out the open window to get off the second shot, pitched completely out and cartwheeled with agonizing slowness as it fell the two stories to land, with the oddly flat sound of a completely inert object, on the cement walk.

With shouts of triumph, the rioters holding the log ran across to batter down the front door but never got a chance to enter the building. From behind them, a barrage of Molotov cocktails was thrown by the angry mob through the windows, causing flames to suddenly appear in a dozen or more places.

"Stay back and direct the ambulance,"

Mort Weyer called to Laurel as he ran across the street to where Artemus Jones was lying, the ominous dark stain spreading from beneath the body giving mute evidence that the bullet had gone through his chest.

The whine of an ambulance siren briefly drowned out the steadily increasing roar of the flames racing through the doomed building. The vehicle came to a sliding stop close to where Mort was bent over the body of Art Jones and two technicians poured from it, pulling open the back to drag out the stretcher.

"We'll take over now," one of the technicians said authoritatively, as they moved quickly to where Mort was kneeling beside the wounded labor organizer.

"I'm Dr. Weyer," said Mort. "It's a through-and-through wound."

"Sorry, Doc, we didn't recognize you," said the chief technician. "Tell us what you want us to do."

"Put him on the litter on his side," Mort directed. "He's probably been shot through the heart and we need to get him to Biscayne General immediately. There's a big wound of exit at the back so I'll need an occlusive dressing."

"Right." As one technician went to the

ambulance for the first aid kit, Laurel appeared with a police sergeant beside her.

"The Fire Department's right behind us, Mort," she said. "How's Jones?"

"A heart wound. We'll be leaving for Biscayne General in a few minutes. Please clear a path for us."

"Right," said the policeman. "Sorry we didn't get here earlier but someone gave us the wrong address."

"I'll follow the ambulance in your car; give me the keys," Laurel told Mort. "I've already notified Biscayne General on Artemus Jones's mobile telephone to be ready."

"Good!" Mort handed her the keys to his car. "Tell the hospital to have your father or your sister Lynn on tap and ready to operate. I'm going in the ambulance to control the loss of blood as much as I can before we get there."

A Fire Department chief's red limousine whined to a stop before the burning house just as Laurel finished telephoning Biscayne General, using the mobile telephone in Art Jones's car. Behind it was a fire engine and a hook and ladder wagon.

"Anybody hurt here?" the fire chief asked.

"Artemus Jones was shot through the heart

and is on the way to Biscayne General," Laurel answered. "A man with a bullet in him is lying against the wall that's burning the fastest. He fell out of the second-floor window when somebody in the crowd shot him after he shot Jones. I'm a doctor and I'm due to follow the ambulance to Biscayne General but I'll take time to examine the other man, if you'll have your firemen bring him over here away from the flames."

"That wall could fall any minute, Doctor," said the chief. "I can't risk sending men over there to drag out a dead man."

"He may not be dead," she protested. "Besides, aren't you going to try to save the house?"

"Ain't worth saving," the fireman said with a shrug. "We had orders last week to let it go, if it started to burn."

"Orders?" She stared at him unbelievingly. "From where?"

"Upstairs. I don't know who issued the order but I wouldn't risk my men to save what's been a firetrap for years anyway."

"I take it that the 'fix' is in, then," said Laurel bitterly, but the chief only shrugged.

"I don't have the least idea what you're talking about, Doctor. Didn't you say you were needed at the hospital?"

371

"Yes, and I might as well go, for all the good I could do here. I'm pretty sure Henri DuVall is already dead."

Chapter 14

"Who were you talking to in the hall just now, Theo?" Elena asked when Malone came back into the master bedroom of the apartment after talking to Laurel.

"It was Laurel."

"I thought I recognized her voice; I like her very much," said Elena. "You both sounded excited, though. What were you talking about?"

"Laurel's got a chance to go to Haiti with a WHO commission to study malignant malaria there. She wanted to talk to me about it."

"The paper said this morning that a commission would be sent and Dr. Prentiss had requested that she be part of it."

"I don't know about that, but I told her to go. It's a chance for her to achieve a solid position in the field of Tropical Medicine."

"Your daughters are very smart," said his young wife. "I wish I were more like them."

"You're exactly what I need," Theo Malone assured her. "Don't worry; I'm happier than I've been in years — and all because of you. Why don't you take a shower while I do some thinking. We can find something more exciting to do later."

On the balcony outside the master bedroom of Theo Malone's penthouse apartment in Biscayne Terrace, ten stories above the ground, the surgeon stood with a powerful pair of binoculars gazing northward in the direction of Jacques LeMoyne's house. Malone couldn't distinguish the building itself because of intervening structures but he wasn't looking for that alone. What he hoped to see was a plume of smoke against the afternoon sky that would tell him his immediate troubles from that source had ended.

Elena Malone, fresh from her bath and looking lovely in a negligee, came out on the balcony.

"You've been out here with those binoculars for a half hour, Theo," she complained. "What's going on?"

"Something's about to go up in smoke in Liberty City."

"How could you know that?"

"I arranged it. You should know by now,

Elena, that I never leave anything to chance."

The girl shivered and some instinct made her draw away from her husband, whom she adored but had never really understood.

"Sometimes I wish you'd leave a few things to chance. It's sacrilegious to play God, Theo. I'll ask Him to forgive you when I go to Mass this afternoon."

Theo laughed. "Just don't tell Him my plans. I don't like them revealed until I'm ready to put them into effect."

"What plan could possibly include burning something down?"

Theo only laughed and reached out to draw her close. "Nothing you should concern your pretty head about, my dear. It involves things like insurance, the changing values of land, and the generosity of HUD."

"What's HUD got to do with us?"

"In a few minutes, a mob is going to set fire to the last house we need to own before we start the housing project. The block that house is in lies in the middle of a slum —"

"It's not worth much, is it?"

"Maybe not by most standards, but the government will pay me and my partners well to build rent-subsidy housing in that area. Insurance companies and the federal government will finance building the unit and it will bring income to me as long as I live and afterward to the Malone Foundation."

"Don't say that!" she protested. "You'd be in better shape than men ten years younger if you'd watch your blood pressure and do something about it. Dr. Downing told me Friday night at the reception that you're in grave danger of having a stroke almost any minute if you get excited."

"Harris Downing's an old maid! If he had his way, we'd sleep in separate rooms and enjoy each other maybe once a week." He chuckled and drew her close. "In fact it's not such a bad idea, once that fire gets going."

"I still don't under —"

"You don't need to, my dear; just leave everything to me. When this is all over, I'll be a great benefactor by building a housing unit that will pay us in tax write-offs and government subsidies for the next twenty years. I'll let Dexter Parnell wrangle with government agencies during the time it's being built so you and I can enjoy a real honeymoon. How would you like to go around the world?"

"I'd love it — with you."

"Doctors in a dozen of the leading medical centers have been pestering me for years to hold seminars there on cardiac surgery. By arranging lectures in most of them, I could charge the whole trip off on taxes."

"Let's start soon, Theo. I worry so much about what's been happening the last few days. Lisa almost drowned −"

"She brought it on herself, scuba diving when she'd been drinking the night before and probably smoking marijuana, too."

"How could you know that?"

"She deliberately skipped coming to the reception, knowing her absence would cause talk."

"And embarrass you?"

"My daughters' activities have long since lost the power to do anything but make me mad, Elena. They know that, so they keep on doing the things that will."

"Surely not Lynn − or Laurel."

"Lynn operated on a patient that should have been mine − and made the headlines."

"But you forgot to take your pager when you went with me to my parents' wedding anniversary. Lynn couldn't have reached you."

"That's her story but she could have kept on drawing blood from the area around the heart to keep it going until she could locate me."

Elena didn't argue, having long since learned that arguing with Theo Malone about anything could bring on one of the towering rages against which Dr. Harris Downing had warned him repeatedly. Loving him, she was afraid of the consequences.

"You must be happy at least about Laurel making the headlines with this malaria business and probably being chosen to go to Haiti and fight it there. I remember her from high school; she always stood out in every sport."

"Laurel's the worst of all." Theo Malone's face suddenly beetled with color. "She's built up a *cause célèbre* over an old wino who's been holding up the housing project by refusing to sell us a rotting old house that's about to fall down. If Dex had been positive enough, we'd have owned it long ago and the contractor could already have been pouring the foundation, so I had to take hold."

"That's why Laurel came here just now, isn't it? To get you to stop whatever you're doing?"

"Nonsense. She's only trying to get back at me for leaving her mother."

"And I'm responsible for that," said the

young wife sadly. "I've confessed my sins and asked for forgiveness but I still feel guilty."

"The only thing you're guilty of is being young and beautiful – plus having a body that can give an old man back his youth night after night." Malone leaned down to kiss her and squeeze the breast he was caressing with his left hand. "As soon as I see that pillar of smoke I'm looking for, we can try making it day after day, too."

"There it is!" Elena cried suddenly, pointing northward.

Theodore Malone directed his binoculars toward where a plume of smoke had suddenly appeared in the afternoon sky and was rising rapidly. It thickened steadily at the base and in the powerful binoculars, he could see the red glow of flames. For some fifteen minutes, he watched while his heart pounded with exhilaration and satisfaction.

"That should take care of the LeMoyne house, along with some other things," he said finally, putting down the binoculars. "Go break out a bottle of that wine I've been saving for a special occasion, Elena."

"What special occasion is this?"

"Everything's working out just as I planned. Tomorrow you can start planning the trip around the world."

Even the best laid plans can change and these did – suddenly. Just as Theo Malone was enjoying the sight of his young wife's beautiful nude body on the king-size bed with its satin sheets, the pager he'd dropped with his clothing suddenly beeped. Seizing the small instrument, he started to throw it across the room but years of habit overcame the impulse. A naked bear of a man, he padded to the telephone and rang the hospital paging operator.

"What the hell do you want?" he demanded.

"Dr. Mort Weyer just called, Dr. Malone," she said. "He's on his way in a Rescue Squad ambulance with a heart wound patient and says you'll want to operate –"

"I'll be there right away. Tell Dr. Sanchez to have the main Cardiac Operating Room set up immediately."

"I'm paging Dr. Rogers, too," said the operator. "She's sailing on the bay this afternoon."

"Don't bother her then; if she answers, tell her I won't need her." Theodore Malone hung up the phone.

"Aren't you coming to bed?" Elena Malone asked.

"Not quite this early, my dear," said her husband as he headed for the door, stuffing his shirttail in his pants. "Opportunity just knocked — maybe the opportunity of a lifetime."

II

Lynn and Paul Rogers had rented a yawl at the Miami Yacht Club after the final seminar luncheon was finished. They had sailed down Biscayne Bay past the old lighthouse on Cape Florida and were almost back to the yacht club slip, when Lynn suddenly pointed shoreward.

"Look at that smoke to the east of us; it must be close to Liberty City. I wonder if another riot has started."

"So what?" said Paul, resenting the interruption in what had been a lovely afternoon.

"That looks like the area where Father and Dex are going to build the housing unit. They already own most of the property and, if a fire swept through there, it would save them a lot of demolition expense."

"Theo already has one fortune. Why would he want another?"

"You know better than that, darling. If

anything, or anybody, tries to stop Father from doing something he's got his heart set on, he'll stop at nothing until he's won out."

"Just as he refused to give you credit for your part in developing the artificial heart. Let Theo Malone take care of his own problems."

"I'm glad I brought my portable CB. Maybe I can find out from the hospital operator what's going on," she added as she reached for the switch and picked up the microphone. "This is Dr. Lynn Rogers," she told the marine operator. "Will you connect me with Biscayne General?"

When the hospital operator came on the line, Lynn listened a moment, her forehead creased by a frown, then switched off the CB.

"Anything wrong?" Paul asked.

"That fire we can see is the Jacques Le-Moyne house in Liberty City going up in smoke, according to the hospital operator. Mort Weyer is bringing in an emergency heart wound and Father just answered his page, taking the call. He's on the way to the hospital now and ordered the Cardiac O.R. made ready but told the operator that if I called, to tell me he wouldn't need me."

"How could he know that when the patient hasn't even reached the hospital yet?"

"He's determined to keep me out of the surgical picture."

"They wouldn't have called him for anything but a serious wound," said Paul. "Would he be bullheaded enough to start putting in the artificial pump, whether it's actually needed or not, so he can claim to have performed the first successful artificial heart transplant in a human being?"

"Probably. He bawled me out for suturing that damaged coronary a few nights ago because he wanted the patient kept alive until he could get there and implant the artificial heart, without letting me try to suture the severed coronary artery under the microscope."

"In that case, we'd better get to the hospital in a hurry." Paul reached for the starting rope on the small outboard motor hanging from the stern of the yawl, designed to bring in the boat in an emergency.

III

Art Jones was gasping for breath by the time Mort and the Rescue Squad technicians got him into the ambulance. The technician who wasn't driving immediately placed an oxygen mask connected to a respirator over Jones's nose and mouth, starting oxygen under pressure to combat the lung collapse following loss of the section of chest wall taken out by the path of the exploding bullet.

Air was whistling from the large wound in the back of Art Jones's chest – made by the bullet when it exited – every time the respirator pumped oxygen into the collapsed lung. Mort could also see part of the heart itself, contracting steadily but spurting blood at each beat. The occlusive dressing he had strapped over the wound controlled much of the air leak, coupled with the oxygen under pressure that was being pumped into Art Jones's lungs, but the patient could not long stand the gush of blood from his heart with each pulse beat.

After strapping the oxygen mask in place, the technician had placed a blood pressure cuff on Art Jones's arm and was listening with a stethoscope to the beats as they came from beneath the inflated cuff.

"How is it?" Mort asked.

"Ninety over fifty, but falling steadily."

"You don't carry emergency blood for transfusion, do you?"

"No, Doctor."

"Plasma?"

"Wait a minute. We've got some of that new chemical blood substitute —"

"Fluosol?"

"That's the one. Dr. Lisa Malone brought a few cases of it back from Japan, and persuaded the Director of Public Safety to put a couple of flasks on each of the Rescue Squad ambulances. She thought we might be able to use it in hemorrhage cases instead of the glucose solution we almost always start before we get to the hospital."

"Break it out and get me the largest I.V. needle you have," Mort directed as the technician was opening the package of Fluosol. Moving forward, he tapped the ambulance driver on the shoulder and, when the man nodded, spoke into his ear:

"Get Biscayne General on your radio and tell them to rush all the Type O blood they can find in the blood bank up to the Cardiac Operating Room. Our only chance to save him is to replace most of what he's losing through those wounds in his heart with Universal Donor blood."

The driver reached for the radio microphone as Mort moved back to the stretcher. The pulse at the now unconscious Artemus Jones's wrist was thready and fast but it was still there, giving the union organizer at least a fighting chance, if he could be gotten to surgery in time.

"Here's the needle, Doctor," the technician told him. "Nineteen gauge."

"Fine! Hand me the end of the Fluosol tube as soon as I put the needle in."

Without trying to find a vein in an arm or hand, all of which would certainly be collapsed from the falling blood pressure, Mort pulled back Art Jones's shirt on the right side, exposing his upper chest. Exploring the depression below the collarbone, he shoved the needle in as deeply as it would go, seeking to penetrate a large vein, the subclavian, that carried blood from the arm to the superior vena cava only inches from the heart itself.

Mort felt a thrill of exhilaration when blood spurted back through the needle but didn't take time to congratulate himself for hitting the large vein directly. Picking up the end of the plastic tubing attached to the flask of Fluosol, he connected the metal flange tip of the tube to the larger needle he had just inserted, opening a direct pathway for the blood substitute, or any other fluid, to the heart itself.

"Let it go wide open," he instructed the technician, and the man lifted the flask of artificial blood as high as he could to make it run in faster.

By the time the ambulance pulled into the loading area for the Biscayne General Emergency Room, one flask of Fluosol had already poured into Art Jones's circulation and a second was half empty. Mort had strapped the needle in place while the fluid was pouring in but he still stayed beside Art Jones's left shoulder as the stretcher was moved from the ambulance, holding the needle to prevent the possibility of its being pulled from the vein.

"Don't try to transfer him to a hospital stretcher," he told the nurse-practitioner responsible for triage. "He's been shot through the heart and is losing blood but I've got a needle in his subclavian and we're putting in Fluosol as fast as we can."

"Dr. Malone just went up to the Cardiac O.R., Doctor," said the nurse. "He said for us to send the patient directly to the twenty-first floor."

"Good! I'll stay with him until he's on the table."

The anesthesiologist, a plump doctor with thinning hair, named Potter, met the stretcher bearing Art Jones in the corridor outside the main operating theater of the Malone Heart Institute and helped transfer the wounded man to a waiting operating table.

"I see that you're giving him Fluosol," he said.

"Started it in the ambulance in the subclavian vein through the largest needle I could find," said Mort. "He's got at least two holes in his heart; I could see one of them in the wound of exit at the back of his chest before I put on the occlusive dressing."

"We'll switch to Type O blood right away." The anesthesiologist reached for Art Jones's pulse. "You probably saved his life by giving him Fluosol."

"Thanks to Dr. Lisa Malone," said Mort. "The Rescue Squad technician told me she persuaded the Director of Public Safety to put Fluosol in the ambulances."

"Practically had to hold a gun to his head to do it," said Potter laconically, as he connected the tubing from a plastic bag of Type O blood to the needle in the patient's chest, "but that's our Lisa."

"He also had twenty milligrams of methadone intramuscularly about an hour and a half ago."

"Good God! That dose would put me in coma. Why so much?"

"Jones was a heroin addict but switched to methadone when the government project started," Mort explained. "He was hoping to be able to disperse a mob at the LeMoyne house before the riot developed into a real melee and asked me to give him his daily dose at my clinic this afternoon so his nerves would be under control."

As Potter pushed the operating table into the center of the theater, Mort stepped back so as not to interfere with the bustle of masked and gowned figures in pale green preparing for surgery.

"Dr. Malone is scrubbing," Dr. Potter told Mort. "You can describe the wound and Jones's condition to him. The door to the lounge and scrub room is next to this one."

Theodore Malone, wearing pale green operating pajamas with a mask hiding most of his features except the beetling eyebrows and the dark eyes, was scrubbing at a basin in the adjoining room.

"Well?" he asked as the younger doctor came into the scrub room.

"I just brought Artemus Jones in from Liberty City," said Mort. "He was trying to calm the rioters who'd been told that a fortune in Krugerrands was hidden in Jacques LeMoyne's old house, but a Haitian refugee hiding out there shot Art through the heart. Two units of Fluosol were in the Rescue

Squad ambulance so I put a large needle into Jones's subclavian vein and started pouring it into him."

"Pretty darn sure of yourself, aren't you?"

"I know my business. You should have learned that yesterday morning."

"Any possibility of saving him?"

"My guess is you'll find a hole in each ventricle, plus one in the septum between them, Doctor. I saw the posterior one before I closed the wound of exit as best I could with an occlusive dressing. It looked pretty big to repair."

"You do know your business," Malone conceded, but not very graciously. "Maybe I've underestimated you."

"I'm going to marry your daughter, Laurel, if she'll have me."

"Maybe I should be the one to decide that." Mort hadn't realized Laurel had just come into the scrub room. "Henri DuVall is dead, Father, and the LeMoyne house is almost destroyed. I thought you ought to know that before you operate on Art Jones."

"Why in hell should I?" Malone did not interrupt the ritual rhythm of scrubbing his hands and arms as far up as the elbows.

"Because, as I told you earlier, I'm pretty sure you used your agents in Liberty City to stir up the people there so they'd burn down the house and make the land valuable only to you and Dex for your tax shelter."

"Stop talking drivel," Malone snapped. "You can't prove any of that cock-and-bull story you've dreamed up."

"I agree about the proof at least. The Fire Department chief on the scene practically admitted he had orders from higher up to let old Jock's house burn, if anybody managed to set fire to it. Art Jones was convinced, too, that you'd somehow arranged for the fire to start but he wanted the project as badly as you do — though for a different reason."

"Stop babbling and come to the point."

"The point is this," she said. "Even though Art Jones may be as convinced as I am that you've stirred up the riot with that story about the gold, he wouldn't be likely to testify against you."

Malone glanced at the small sandglass on the shelf above the scrubbing basin and saw that the last of the sand had run itself out.

"Get out of here, both of you," he snarled as he moved to a soaking basin of antiseptic solution. "I've got to operate on a patient with a damaged heart."

"I just thought you'd like to know that

you're probably in the clear so you can save Art Jones — if you can and want to," Laurel told him. "Let's go, Mort."

IV

As Theo Malone turned to push open the door into the operating room itself with his hip to avoid touching it with his scrubbed hands, Lynn and Paul Rogers came in from the Doctors' Lounge. They were still wearing bathing suits under terry cloth robes, not having taken time to change after leaving the sailboat at the yacht club dock.

"I'm here, Father, if you need me," Lynn said breathlessly.

"You're no longer a part of the Institute." Theodore Malone glared at her as he held the door to the operating room partially open. "Didn't I make that clear when you told me you were going to Tampa?"

"But you may need —" The final "me" was cut off by the closing door.

Lynn was the first to speak. "You and I need some clothes, Paul," she said. "Let's put on operating pajamas and go into the observation gallery overlooking the O.R."

"We'll hold some seats for you in the

gallery," Laurel promised. "As soon as word gets out that the Great God Malone is about to perform a difficult heart operation, the place is bound to be jammed."

Chapter 15

As in most new teaching hospitals, the main operating theater in the Malone Heart Institute had been built with an elevated glassed-in gallery extending across the section just opposite the center. Accommodating twenty-five observers, the gallery was equipped with loudspeakers connected to the microphones in the room below and especially the small throat microphone, worn by the surgeon, with its cord plugged into an outlet in the floor.

By the time Laurel and Mort Weyer reached the gallery by way of a staircase from the corridor below, information about the dramatic procedure about to begin was already being relayed by the hospital grapevine that was far swifter than electronic communications. Being the first to arrive, however, Mort and Laurel found seats at the front and also held two more for Lynn and Paul.

Below them what might have appeared to the uninitiated to be a scene of utter confusion was actually – to those with any understanding of what was going on – a picture of controlled order, control resting absolutely in the surgeon himself. As Malone thrust his hands into sterile gloves held for him by a nurse, the technician slapped small circular electrocardiographic terminals on Art Jones's chest outside the area where Ernesto Sanchez was preparing the operative field and connected them to the monitoring system. Immediately a picture of the patient's heartbeat, faint and almost imperceptible, appeared upon the bank of monitors against one wall.

"Towers," Malone called to an assistant resident who had just finished sliding his hands into sterile gloves. "Cut down on the vein in front of the ankle and get in a cannula so you can start another transfusion."

Meanwhile, the anesthesiologist had just finished putting an intratracheal tube into Art Jones's windpipe and was connecting it to the anesthesia machine. Thereby he created a closed system by which a respirator pump could inflate and deflate the patient's lungs, even when his chest was opened. The two television cameras focused on the operating table were now manned by technicians, not only recording on tape the events that were taking place but also relaying them to monitor screens in the adjoining auditorium, which was now filling with the overflow from the gallery.

"Can you get a catheter electrode into the right heart through that needle Dr. Weyer put into his subclavian?" Malone asked the anesthesiologist.

"It's too small, but I can probably cut off the flanged end of the needle and slip a small trocar over it."

"Do it, then," Malone ordered as he was moving toward the table itself while a circulating nurse followed him, quickly tying the strings of his gown behind his back and plugging the cord from his throat microphone into the outlet on the floor.

"Since I don't know yet whether the wounds in the heart can be closed, I will first open the chest and examine it." Malone was addressing those in the gallery. "We can also accomplish manual compression of the heart while the decision is made whether to put him on the heart-lung pump."

Ernesto Sanchez had finished prepping and draping the patient and as Malone stepped up to the table, the instrument nurse slapped a scalpel into the surgeon's hands. Meanwhile, Dr. Potter had been moving swiftly. Cutting off the needle Mort had inserted just below its flanged end, he shoved a larger needle called a trocar over it through the chest wall and into the artery beneath, using the smaller needle as a guide. Through this, after removing the smaller needle, he now inserted a catheter-electrode, combining a channel through which blood could flow with a metal electrode by which the stimulus of a pacemaker-defibrillator could be directed to the heart muscle itself. When he switched the tube from the transfusion bag to the catheter, blood immediately began to flow into Art Jones's circulation.

His eyes on the monitor where the electric pattern of the heartbeat was being recorded, Dr. Potter pushed the catheter-electrode steadily deeper, stopping when he felt resistance as it touched the inner wall of the heart. At the same moment, the picture being recorded on the monitor suddenly became clearer and the range of the heartbeat considerably better.

"The electrode is in place," Potter announced. "Shall I start the pacemaker, Dr. Malone?"

"Not as long as the heart has a regular

pattern of its own."

With one stroke, Theo Malone brought the blade of the scalpel straight down the length of Art Jones's sternum, laying open skin and tissues beneath to expose the breastbone itself. Reaching for the oscillating saw with which to divide the bone, the surgeon began to cut almost completely through the sternum, being careful not to go deep enough to injure the heart itself, which lay just beneath.

"I'll say this for your father," Mort told Laurel. "He can go into a chest faster than any surgeon I ever saw."

"He can do anything faster than any surgeon you ever saw," said Lynn. She and Paul, wearing green operating pajamas over their swimsuits, had filed into the seats Laurel and Mort had been holding for them. "I see that the pump technicians are busy, too."

Mort glanced to one side of the room, where two men were busy charging with blood the vital machine that would substitute for both heart and lungs, if Malone decided the task of repairing – or removing – Art Jones's heart demanded the substitution of the pump in place of the vital organ.

"What happened in Liberty City this afternoon?" Lynn asked Laurel.

"A mob attacked Jacques LeMoyne's house, thinking some gold coins were there. A refugee named Henri DuVall, grandfather of the baby I've been treating in the Critical Care Unit, was hiding there and apparently thought they were after him. He shot Art Jones while Art was trying to quiet the mob, but one of them killed DuVall."

"Father never liked Jones," said Lynn. "And he hates unions."

"He'd still have no reason not to save Art," said Laurel.

"And a lot of reason to do it," Lynn agreed.

"What do you mean?" Laurel asked.

"We've had three artificial hearts powered by nuclear energy working in calves at the ranch for the past six months," Lynn said in a low voice. "Father was hoping to implant one while the seminar was in progress."

"What did you just say about an artificial heart, Dr. Rogers?" Jack Parker, the Miami *Herald* feature writer, who was sitting just back of her.

"Nothing, Mr. Parker," Lynn said flatly. "If you say I did in your account of this operation in tomorrow morning's *Herald*, I'll swear you're a liar."

II

Theodore Malone had finished sawing the breastbone almost through from top to bottom. Picking up another instrument, shaped like a hoe with a foot projecting slightly beyond its blade, he worked the foot beneath the sternum at the upper end of the incision and reached for the steel mallet handed him by the instrument nurse.

"The Lebsche knife is invaluable in completing a median sternotomy," he informed the gallery in a tone that — to Lynn's surprise — was tense, something she'd never before detected during the hundreds of operations in which she had assisted her father. "It enables us to cut through the bone without danger of injuring any structures beneath it."

At the patient's ankle, Roberts, the assistant resident, had already exposed a dark-colored vein through a small incision and was threading in a short nylon catheter attached to a plastic bag of blood for transfusion by transparent plastic tubing. While the blood started running in, he swiftly placed a circular tie around the vein holding the catheter in place. Blood from two sources —

the catheter-electrode Dr. Potter had inserted into Art Jones's chest, plus the one in his ankle – was now flowing and the improvement caused by its presence was obvious in the rising curve of the blood pressure chart on the monitor.

Dropping the Lebsche knife back on the instrument table, Malone picked up the spreader, an instrument consisting of two flanged arms which could be separated by means of a ratcheted screw. Tucking an arm beneath the edge of the cut breastbone while Ernesto Sanchez fitted the other into the opposite edge, Malone began to twist the ratchet handle rapidly, separating the jaws and enlarging the opening into the patient's chest where the sternum had been split.

The heart was now visible in the depths of the wound. It was beating rapidly but feebly and, when the surgeon lifted the wounded vital organ to inspect the back side, even those in the gallery could see the gaping hole in the thinner wall of the right ventricle.

"Can he possibly close those wounds in the myocardium?" Mort Weyer asked Lynn, who was sitting beside him in the front row of the gallery.

"With luck, he might," said Lynn. "But

the bullet must have penetrated the septum between the right and the left ventricles, too. Closing that with Dacron or fascia from the thigh means making an incision into the ventricle itself and for that the patient needs to be on the heart-lung pump."

Ignoring Lynn's threat, the *Herald* reporter had been scribbling rapidly on a pad of copy paper while she was speaking.

"Take a look at the lower left ventricle," Paul objected. "It's so much lighter in color than the upper part that I'd say it's almost bloodless."

"Which almost certainly means the left main coronary artery inside the heart muscle itself has been injured or severed," Lynn agreed.

"Would repairing that be like the one you sutured last Thursday night, Dr. Rogers?" Jack Parker asked.

"Compared to what my father is facing now, Mr. Parker, Thursday night was easy," said Lynn. "The artery involved here has probably been torn by the bullet while mine was severed cleanly by a switchblade knife."

"So what will Dr. Malone do?" Parker insisted. "Put in that artificial heart you mentioned just now?"

Theo Malone saved Lynn the trouble of

answering. He was holding Art Jones's heart in his hand, keeping the posterior wound closed as best he could by squeezing the torn edges of the muscular ventricle together.

"This patient has four heart wounds, any one of which would have been fatal ten years ago," he said. "Today, we could probably repair the three involving the heart muscle and he would have an excellent chance to live. Unfortunately, one of the main arteries supplying blood to the heart itself is almost certainly damaged, too." He touched the blanched section of the left ventricle to which Paul Rogers had referred only a few moments earlier. "That means the blood supply to the most important part of the main section of the ventricle has been damaged causing much the same effect that would result from coronary thrombosis. In my judgment, the injury to the coronary artery is too massive in itself to justify trying to repair the other three wounds."

Malone paused for an instant, while silence gripped the room. Then he said quietly: "What this patient needs is a new heart. Without one, he will die."

Again, silence, then the calm voice of the surgeon sounded: "Finding a donor for a transplant on such short notice is, of course, impossible. The only answer then is a machine, an artificial heart that can take over all the functions of the damaged one. Fortunately, I have succeeded in developing just such a pump. It has been working successfully in three calves for over six months."

"The son-of-a-bitch," Paul said softly. "He isn't going to give you any credit at all, Lynn."

"That isn't important," she said quickly. "Nothing matters now except that it might save a life."

The announcement had hit those in the gallery – except Paul and Lynn – like the bombshell that it was.

"Another Malone Miracle!" the *Herald* reporter exclaimed. "They're happening almost every day."

III

"I'm going to put him on the pump," Theodore Malone announced. "Put your hand under the heart Ernesto, and keep that posterior wound closed as well as you can. Roberts, assist me while I put a cannula into the femoral artery. Pump ready?"

"It will be by the time you have the cannula in, Doctor," said the senior technician.

"It had better be." Malone reached for the scalpel and moved down to Art Jones's groin, which had been shaved and prepped while Dr. Roberts was opening the ankle vein.

"Blood pressure falling," the nurse watching the monitor reported.

"Squeeze that heart, Ernesto," the surgeon barked. "Keep the blood flowing until we can get him on the pump."

Ernesto Sanchez immediately began to compress the now almost immobile heart rhythmically, trying at the same time to control the surge of blood from the wound in the right ventricle.

"I'd better start the pacemaker, Dr. Malone," said the anesthesiologist. "Dr. Sanchez needs all his attention to keep the posterior wound closed."

"Start it then!" Malone was cutting deeply, but expertly, into the patient's groin to expose the femoral vein and artery coursing there.

When Potter flicked a switch on the pacemaker-defibrillator, the almost inert heart suddenly leaped in Sanchez's hand, as the muscle was stimulated into contraction from the electric shock being delivered to it by the metal electrode pressed against the inner wall of the right ventricle. As the heart once more started to beat rhythmically under the electrical stimulus, Sanchez was able to control the larger wound in the posterior wall much more effectively. Meanwhile, blood being poured from a steady progression of transfusion flasks into the patient's circulation began to absorb oxygen through the air sacs of his lungs. Immediately, too, the blood pressure line on the monitor started rising steadily.

In the gallery, the low voice of a senior medical student talking to a pretty first-year enrollee could be heard: "Once the heart-lung pump is connected to the patient's circulation," he was telling the fascinated girl, "both heart and lungs will be by-passed and the machine will take over."

"But how?" she breathed.

"Oxygen flowing into the pump permeates the red blood cells circulating through it and they are then pumped out into the circulation."

"How long can he be kept on the pump?"

"Quite a while. Open heart operations often take five to ten hours or more."

"Not when the Great God Malone is operating," another student interposed. "He does things in minutes that would take other surgeons ten times as long."

The proof of the student's statement was being dramatically illustrated at Art Jones's groin, where Theo Malone had already exposed the finger-size femoral artery that normally supplied blood to the leg. Making a small slit in the wall, he inserted a cannula, passing it rapidly up to the aorta, the great vessel that took blood from the left side of the heart with each beat and carried it to the rest of the body.

At the heart-lung pump, a nurse deftly removed the small plastic bag covering the sterile end of a tube leading to the machine. Holding it so Theo Malone could pick it up without contaminating his hands, she extended it to him and he quickly connected it to the cannula which now extended up the femoral artery into the main artery channel of the aorta.

"Can I use that cannula you've got in the subclavian for the venous connection to the pump, Dr. Potter?" Malone asked.

"I think you'd better try, as a temporary measure at least," said the anesthesiologist. "His brain cells have certainly been deprived of oxygen to a dangerous point and they need all of it they can get."

Malone moved back to the chest wound while the assistant was securing a tight fit around the cannula in the femoral artery, using a single suture placed through the wall of the artery itself.

The nurse holding the covered end of another tube going to the heart-lung pump removed the plastic bag, handing the sterile end to Malone. He, in turn, passed it to the anesthesiologist, who attached it to the cannula that extended into the right side of the heart.

"I'll have to stop the pacemaker while I pull the cannula back out of the heart," Dr. Potter warned, but Malone only nodded.

"Once the pump takes over, we won't need the damaged heart anymore," he said, and reached for a clamp with which to shut off the flow of blood from the almost flaccid heart into the aorta, allowing the blood now pouring into the main arterial channel from the heart-lung machine to enter the arterial system.

Moments later, a second set of clamps were in place obstructing the large veins – called the vena cava – that brought the blood returning to the heart.

"Roberts." Malone spoke to the assistant resident who was still working in the groin wound clipping the suture he had placed in the femoral artery. "Put a second cannula into the femoral vein in case the one we have in the subclavian isn't able to handle the entire return flow of the blood."

"Yes, sir." With a blunt-ended hemostat, the assistant resident started dissecting the large thin-walled vein lying in the depths of the wound beside the much thicker walled artery.

"Line pressure one hundred," one of the pump technicians reported. "Oxygen tension rising."

"Urine output 1 cc. per minute," a nurse watching the flask into which urine was dripping from a catheter in the bladder reported.

To one unfamiliar with the physiology involved, the single factor might have seemed unimportant. Actually, however, kidney function was one of the best possible indicators of the efficiency of the circulation.

"Respirator and pacemaker off," Dr. Potter announced.

"The patient's vital functions have now been taken over by the heart-lung pump." Malone's voice filled the gallery where a tense group of people were watching.

"The patient is just lying there, not breathing and with his heart not beating." The senior medical student had raised his voice a little as he explained what was happening to the pretty first-year student. When Malone stopped speaking, the student's voice was audible throughout the gallery, causing a brief spurt of laughter.

"It's enough to make you believe in robots," she breathed.

With all flow of blood to and from the heart now cut off, its functions had been assumed by the mechanical action of the heart-lung pump. Theo Malone moved swiftly, cutting the connections of the heart to the rest of the circulatory system but leaving a small cuff of heart tissue around each opening.

"Get the artificial heart ready," he directed and the instrument nurse lifted the sleek machine of stainless steel from a basin of heparin solution in which it had been soaking.

The purpose of immersing the artificial heart in heparin was to make certain that its inner surfaces would be covered with the anticoagulating agent and thus not tend to cause clotting when the blood started flowing through it.

"What you are seeing is something never before constructed successfully." No one could miss the note of pride in the surgeon's voice. "In essence, it is simply a double-chambered pump of stainless steel, powered by nuclear energy. The power pack will be placed later under the skin at the upper part of the chest."

Malone had been cutting away the now dead heart while he talked, moving with swift, skilled strokes. With the last cut, it came away in his hands and without even glancing at it, he dropped it into the basin held by a waiting nurse.

"Blood heparinized?" he asked.

"Everything going well, Doctor," a pump technician answered. "Oxygen tension near normal."

No one who knew where to look could have failed to see that the report was correct. The color of the blood flowing through the heart-lung pump and the plastic tubing carrying it to and from the body was now very close to its normal red hue.

Taking the artificial heart from the nurse, Malone fitted it tentatively into the cavity formed by removing the damaged natural organ. Little space was left but the watchers could see that the openings from the steel heart, with their soft Dacron flanges, could be fitted easily against those left when the heart was removed.

"I will suture the venous connections first," Malone announced. "The flanges you see at the pump orifices are made of Dacron, cemented to the steel. Dacron is now widely used to patch surgical incisions made into arteries in order to remove material clogging them, mainly cholesterol plaques. Fortunately the Dacron flanges can be sutured directly to the cuffs of living tissue I have left around each of the openings from the heart I have just removed, thus making a blood-tight connection between the great vessels and the new heart."

"He isn't going to give you credit for constructing the Dacron flanges either," Paul told Lynn.

"I didn't expect him to; I just hope he can get the suture lines tight. It's a lot easier to do under a microscope the way I would have done it."

"And the way you should be doing it now."

Lynn shrugged, but didn't answer. She was watching closely as Theo Malone attached the synthetic fabric to living tissue with rows of carefully placed sutures.

"The first connection is now complete," Malone announced on a note of triumph. "I will now suture the pulmonary artery and vein to the new heart before finally attaching the aorta. First, though, I will insert a catheter through the flange of tissue left from the excised heart so the artificial heart can be flushed out with heparin solution to remove air and prevent clotting before finally taking the patient off the heart-lung pump."

The catheter he used was small, inserted through a large needle which was then removed, leaving the small rubber tubing in place but attached to a large syringe filled with a clear fluid lying on the instrument table.

"If he's going to have trouble, it will come now," Lynn said softly in Paul's ear. "The aortic connection is hard to suture because you can't lift the pump high enough to reach the posterior line of sutures easily."

"Does the microscope help there?"

"A great deal. Through it you can use smaller needles and other instruments, along with smaller bites in the tissue." She suddenly gripped Paul's shoulder. "Something's wrong, Paul! Look at Father's right hand."

A quick glance showed Paul what she

413

meant. For the first time since the operation had begun, Theo Malone's right hand had begun to tremble. When the instrument nurse held out the needle holder with a suture in place for him to begin attaching the Dacron flange to the aortic cuff, he dropped the instrument on the table.

"Wipe my forehead," he directed, and a nurse standing behind for just that duty reached up quickly when he turned his head, applying a pad of soft gauze to his forehead to absorb the sweat that had suddenly popped out there.

"Maybe he's just realized he needs your skill in microsurgery but is too proud to ask for help," said Paul.

"No." Lynn's voice was suddenly urgent. "It's more than that. His right arm is jerking."

"Good God!" Mort Weyer, too, had seen what was happening − and recognized the cause. "He's having a stroke!"

"Lynn! Take over!" Theo Malone's words were barely distinguishable as he staggered back from the table.

"Come on, Paul! Help me!" Lynn started up the steps for the door at the back of the gallery where a metal stairway led down to the main operating floor. But even before

414

the door closed behind her, Theodore Malone was already falling like a felled ox to the tiled floor of the operating theater.

"Mort!" Paul said before following Lynn. "Take charge of Dr. Malone and get Harris Downing over here as fast as you can."

"Right."

Mort was behind Paul at the door as it opened, which allowed them to run down the circular metal staircase together and out into the corridor below. As Paul opened the door to the Doctor's Lounge and the adjoining scrub room, Mort pushed open the main doors of the operating theater, whose occupants had been gripped by a sudden panic. A moment later, Lynn appeared in the doorway between the operating theater and the adjoining scrub room, tying the strings of a mask behind her head.

"Ernesto!" Her voice had the ring of authority needed to quiet the panic in the theater. "Don't try to suture, just move the microscope into place for me. Dr. Weyer will take care of my father."

Moving into the room but being careful to stay as far away from the sterile zone around the operating table itself as he could, Mort knelt and felt for the pulse at Theo Malone's temple. It was full, bounding, and rapid, harbinger of a serious accident to the circulation of the brain, but at least an indication that the surgeon was still alive.

"Get a gurney," he directed the nurse who had been mopping Malone's forehead only seconds before. "A low one."

Seizing Theo Malone's inert body beneath the armpits, Mort began to drag it toward the door. He was almost there when a stretcher, accompanied by two orderlies, was pulled through. The three men quickly lifted Malone's flaccid body to the stretcher and pushed it from the room.

Meanwhile, Ernesto Sanchez had regained a measure of composure and was directing the circulating nurse as she wheeled the operating microscope on its mobile frame into place. Adjusting it until the magnifying objective was directly over the area where Malone had been about to start the final suture of the aortic cuff to the Dacron flange around the corresponding opening in the steel pump, she locked it in place.

"Scrub with me, Paul," Lynn begged as he came into the room with its line of basins against the wall. "I need all the help I can get."

"Of course." He tied the last of the strings holding his own mask in place and reached for a brush. "Mort Weyer's looking after your father. I told him to call Harris Downing."

"It's a stroke, isn't it?"

"A severe one, from the looks of it, but Mort Weyer will know what to do. So will Harris Downing."

While the stretcher was being removed from the operating room, Mort Weyer had quickly evaluated the situation and concluded that the whole clinical picture was that of a classical attack of what was called apoplexy. The paralysis of the facial muscles and the tongue on the left side that had been apparent in Theo Malone's barely intelligible plea to Lynn to take over. The sudden fall too, when the surgeon became unconscious, plus the flaccidity apparent in the muscles of the right side when Mort dragged Malone's body from the operating theater — all spelled the rupture of an artery deep within the brain.

The most likely criminal was an S-shaped vessel called the lenticulostriate artery. A weak spot in the arterial system of most human brains, it had no doubt ruptured under the rising blood pressure from the sheer nervous tension of trying to complete the operation that was to be the crowning event of Theo Malone's career. Flooding vital channels in the nervous system leading from the thinking brain, the cerebrum, to the lower and far more ancient medulla, the stroke had felled Theo Malone as effectively as would have a bludgeon directed at his head.

Inside the elevator leading to the new Critical Care Unit, Mort wrapped a blood pressure cuff around Theo Malone's upper arm. The figure he read off the dial when he took it made him blink. It was 250 mm. of mercury, nearly twice the normal blood pressure and dangerously high for anyone, especially a man of Malone's age.

As the stretcher was pushed through the door to Critical Care, the nursing supervisor for the unit appeared. "This way, Doctor," she said, recognizing Mort. "The first room on the right."

"Call Dr. Harris Downing, please," said Mort. "And give me a cutdown set. I'm going to bleed him."

The supervisor started calling orders to assistants as she directed the stretcher into one of the glass-walled cubicles. Meanwhile, a younger nurse was opening a sterile tray beside the stretcher with a scalpel, small hemostats, suture material, and dressings on it. Tearing open the shirt of the operating pajamas Theo Malone was wearing, the supervisor started slapping small round sensors for the intricate monitoring system against the surgeon's chest, attaching each to one of a sheaf of different-colored wires hanging from a cable attached to a column beside the bed.

"His systolic's 250 and he's already hemiplegic," Mort told the graying, and obviously very experienced nursing supervisor. "I'm going to bleed him with a scalpel to try to lower the pressure before more blood escapes into his brain tissues."

"I still remember enough from the old days to be able to catch blood." The nurse moved to a cabinet beside the bed and picked up a small metal kidney basin.

Picking up the scalpel, Mort didn't bother to make any surgical preparations to the skin. Using a maneuver thousands of years old, he chose a clearly visible vein in Theo Malone's forearm and, with a single stab of the scalpel, slit the wall. Blood spurted in an arcing stream at least a foot high but the nurse supervisor was nimble and caught it in the kidney basin as it arced downward, spattering her uniform and Mort's shirt but still keeping the major portion of it in the basin.

"Haven't done this in thirty years," she remarked. "Where did you learn the technique of bloodletting, Doctor?"

"Bellevue!" Mort put the tips of the stethoscope in his ears and started pumping up the blood pressure cuff again to determine the height of the systolic level. "We sometimes had to use pretty primitive medicine up there."

The systolic — the upper pressure reached by each beat of the heart in the arterial system — was starting to fall, he discovered. It still stood at 220, however, a significant lowering, but not enough.

"About 200 cc. are out," the gray-haired nursing supervisor reported.

"Let's go for 500."

Slowly the pressure in the damaged artery system crept downward to 190, then 180, and finally, 150.

"Looks like about 500 to me, Doctor."

"Good." Mort reached for a gauze pad from the cutdown tray. "We'll stop there and see what happens."

Pressing a gauze sponge against the small wound in the vein, Mort quickly strapped it into place with adhesive.

"He's been asking for this for years, particularly since he took that gorgeous Cuban girl for a mistress," said the nursing supervisor. "I could have warned him."

"He wouldn't have listened."

"I know. Theo Malone never did — except to his desires."

Something in her tone made Mort Weyer glance at her sharply. For the first time he realized that she must have been a stunning beauty in earlier days, the kind for whom Theodore Malone would naturally make a play — and probably had. Tall, high-cheeked, almost regal, she had the kind of quiet confidence that came with vast experience in handling and understanding the needs of the sick — and seeing that they were met. Then he noted the plastic nameplate she wore over her left breast pocket and recognition struck him like a blow.

"Mrs. Helen Parnell, RN," said the plate, and beneath it was the legend: "Supervisor, Critical Care Unit."

"You must be Dexter Parnell's mother," he said. "I can see the resemblance now and I remember his telling me his mother was in charge of the Critical Care Unit."

"I'm very proud of Dex, in spite of the

row he had with Dr. Malone," said Helen Parnell. "He's married to a fine girl and I have a houseful of grandchildren."

Mort was remembering something else now, something Laurel had said only yesterday: "Dex is probably a half brother to us Malone girls. Helen Parnell was Father's first mistress and is still one of Mother's best friends."

"Maybe the reason why doctors like him succeed so often is because they're driven with such an intensity of purpose that everything else in their lives is burned out, so to speak," he said.

The nurse shrugged. "Is it worth the acclaim to have so many people hating you — particularly your own daughters?"

"His first wife doesn't."

Helen Parnell smiled. "Mildred Malone is a saint; too bad she married a demon. Still, he wasn't like he is now in the old days. We were all at Hopkins together; I was in training there when he was studying medicine. That was long before Mildred developed that spinal cord tumor and became only half a woman."

"Half a woman could never be enough for a man like him."

"I guess the Theo Malones of the world

shouldn't really be tied down by marriage. No one woman could fill both his intellectual needs — what there were — and his physical ones, which are gargantuan."

Mort was beginning to understand why, even though Helen Parnell was no longer as beautiful as she must have been in a healthy maidenhood, the gray-haired nurse could once have been very close indeed to Theo Malone. And her tone, even after what must have been years of neglect and eventual abandonment for a younger woman, still held a note of sorrow that her once proud lover had been reduced to a stertorously breathing hulk of flesh by the frailty of his circulatory system.

While Mort was working on Theo Malone, reducing the blood pressure as rapidly as he could in order to try to stem the tide flooding an important part of the surgeon's brain, a technician had been rapidly inserting small needle electrodes into Theo's scalp and connecting them to the electroencephalograph. When she switched on the monitor, Mort was startled to see a jumbled bedlam of waves appear where normally a regular procession should have been moving across the face of the instrument, a picture that could only mean severe brain damage.

"He's not likely to live long with that pattern," Helen Parnell said quietly. "I've never seen one so disturbed before."

"If he does, it will only be as a vegetable," Mort confirmed.

"And for him that would indeed be a fate even worse than death."

Chapter 16

In the scrub room outside the operating theater, Lynn rinsed the suds from her hands, letting the water drip back off her elbows so it wouldn't contaminate her now surgically clean hands. Stepping through the open door into the operating theater, she accepted a sterile towel from the nurse waiting to hold her gown and gloves.

"How is he, Joe?" she asked the pudgy anesthetist, but he only shrugged.

"He's got amazingly normal brain waves, so he must be alive. Other than that he's only a body connected to a heart-lung pump and dependent on it for whatever small life currents are actually registering on the EEG."

Paul came in to receive a sterile towel as Lynn shoved her hands into the gloves the nurse was holding out to her. "Move to retractors, please, Ernesto," Lynn directed. "Dr. Rogers will assist me."

Theodore Malone's new brother-in-law obeyed, obviously happy to be rid of the responsibility. As Paul moved into place across the table from where Lynn had taken her position behind the operating microscope, she studied the operating field briefly through it. Her plan of action obviously decided upon, she reached for the delicate needle in a slender holder with a suture streaming from it, handed her by the instrument nurse.

Carefully, but with great skill, Lynn began to suture the opening at the cut end of the aorta; here something over an inch in width, attaching it to the corresponding cuff of Dacron around the aortic mouth of the metal pump. Having placed the first suture uniting the aortic opening to the Dacron cuff surrounding a similar opening of the pump, Lynn expertly tied it with two secure knots, the long remaining strands of which were immediately clipped by scissors in Paul Rogers' hand.

"Nice going," he said softly. "You can suture my heart any day."

Lynn was busy placing the second in a row of sutures that would ensure a blood-tight connection between the steel pump and the great aortic channel through which blood would flow to all the vital structures of the body — if the pump functioned properly when the nuclear power was turned on. She did, however, pause for a brief fleeting smile of thanks before starting with the rest of the sutures.

Meanwhile, the senior medical student in the gallery was busy describing what was happening to his feminine compatriot.

"You're witnessing something that's never been done on a human patient," he said in a tone of awe. "A human being is being connected to a steel heart."

"Watching something like this is so exciting, it gives me goosebumps," said the girl.

Watching – and hearing the low-voiced comments by the two students – Laurel Malone had to admit that what she was seeing gave her goosebumps, too. She couldn't help wondering what Mort Weyer was doing just now and, however badly she'd hated Theo Malone for much of her life, she was glad her father was in expert hands at this critical moment.

II

Mort Weyer and Helen Parnell were still watching the jumble of helter-skelter waves in Theodore Malone's electroencephalographic picture, when Dr. Harris Downing, puffing from the exertion of hurrying from his apartment in Biscayne Terrace — where he'd been watching a baseball game on TV — came into the Critical Care Unit.

"What happened to Theo?" he asked as he reached for the patient's pulse, an instinctive action by any doctor when coming upon a situation with which he was not yet familiar.

"The stroke hit him while he was operating," said Mort, "putting a steel heart pump into Artemus Jones."

"The labor organizer?"

"Yes. Jones was shot by a Haitian refugee living in Jacques LeMoyne's old house when the rioters tried to break in."

"They've burned the place down." Downing was regaining his breath. "I saw it on a local TV program just a few minutes ago."

"Jones's heart was shot through-and-through with a rifle bullet that exploded on the posterior side. I was there and came with the Rescue Squad; we gave him Fluosol most of the way."

"That stuff Lisa brought back from Japan?"

"Yes, sir."

Downing was examining Theo Malone as they talked, listening to his heart while Helen Parnell was repeating the blood pressure examination.

"I'm sure we wouldn't have been able to get Jones to the O.R. alive if we hadn't had the blood substitute in the ambulance," said Mort.

"I suppose Theo finally got a chance to put his artificial heart into a human subject. Was Lynn there?"

"Yes, but he wouldn't let her help him. I don't know why."

"Two reasons," said the internist. "He must have learned that Lynn is planning to join Paul Rogers in Tampa. And, second, he wanted the glory for himself."

"Dr. Malone had gotten to the most difficult part of the surgery – where he would have to suture the aorta to the steel heart –"

"The part where he needed Lynn the most," Harris Downing commented.

"Just then his right hand started shaking. All he said was 'Lynn! Take over!' Then he collapsed."

"I'd been warning him," said Harris Downing. "Anything that sent his blood pressure up –"

"It was around 250 when I first took it before bringing him down here."

"Enough to damage the lenticulostriate artery beyond healing and turn him into a vegetable," the internist commented. "The poor damn fool! I kept warning him!"

"But against taking a young bride!" Helen Parnell's voice was harsh. "Not against attempting to do something even he couldn't do — the final suture of the artificial heart without Lynn's expert help."

"Whatever!" Harris Downing turned to Mort Weyer, "What have you done so far, Doctor?"

"When we got him down here, I stuck a scalpel in an antecubital vein and bled him as fast as I could. Mrs. Parnell caught 500 cc. It reduced the systolic to around 150, but it hasn't changed things."

"And it isn't going to, considering the appearance of that EEG pattern. The hemorrhage must have literally blown his cerebral circulation apart from the looks of it."

"I agree, Doctor," said Mort. "If you don't need me any more right now, I'll run up and see what's happening in the operating room."

"We can do nothing more here but wait — for the end," said Downing. "Damn it! If Theo hadn't been so stubborn and insisted on always having his own way, that magnificent brain of his might have been able to function for at least five or maybe ten years

430

longer at least. And who knows what new discoveries could have come out of it."

III

In the gallery overlooking the main operating theater, Laurel looked up when Mort slid into the seat beside her.

"How is Father?" she asked. "Or should I ask?"

"Dr. Downing is with him but the EEG pattern is all shot to hell. How are things going here?"

"Perfectly. I've seen a few microsurgeons operate but Lynn has them all beat."

"What about Paul?"

"He's leaving the glory to Lynn but he's supporting her all the way."

"I hope we'll be supporting each other," said Mort, as he reached for her hand. "All the way."

"It's an idea worth considering," Laurel said with a warm smile. "We'll discuss it later."

In the brilliantly lighted operating theater below, Lynn had just completed placing the last suture and Paul had clipped the end.

"I'd like to start taking him off the pump

431

now, Joe," she told the anesthesiologist.

"Any time."

"Connect the nuclear power unit, please, Ernesto," she told the Cuban surgeon who'd taken little part in the operation since Lynn and Paul had approached the table, but didn't seem to mind.

Picking up the flat metal package that formed the nuclear power plant for the artificial heart, Sanchez handed Lynn each of the several terminals, colored differently so they could be easily identified. While she made the connections to the motor in the artificial heart, the instrument nurse had been letting heparin solution flow into the catheter inserted through the cuff of heart tissue and thus into the artificial heart itself.

"Heart filling, Dr. Rogers," she reported.

"Let it flow until I tell you to stop." Lynn continued attaching the colored leads to terminals on the solid center of the artificial heart where the nuclear-powered motor was located.

"Slowly," she told the nurse. "How much so far?"

"Two hundred."

"Let a little more in, then disconnect the catheter." She turned to Dr. Sanchez. "Start the pump, please, Ernesto."

When the young Cuban surgeon touched a tiny switch on the central surface of the heart, it began to hum quietly in the place where a living heart had been before.

"Venous pressure rising," one of the pump technicians reported.

A small amount of air and bloody froth escaped from the catheter. When it changed to a small red stream, indicating that any air which might have been trapped inside the metal pump was now removed, Lynn removed the clamp that, until now, had allowed blood from the heart-lung pump to flow through the patient's circulatory system.

"We can now come off the heart-lung pump," she said a moment later, when the steadily rising pressure level in the connection indicated that the artificial heart had now taken over the function formerly handled by the damaged one Theo Malone had removed.

Blood from the humming steel heart, with its power source of nuclear energy, was now flowing into the pulmonary artery, leading to the lungs, where it would receive oxygen — if the whole procedure was successful.

"Get ready to close the femoral cannula," Lynn directed tersely, as the blood pressure being recorded on the wall monitor from a needle inserted into a small artery in the arm rose steadily.

"Congratulations!" Paul said quietly. "It's working like a Swiss watch."

"But no spontaneous respiration yet." Lynn's voice was taut. "That will be the real test."

"Arterial pressure, 130," the technician watching the monitors reported.

"Close the femoral cannula, Ernesto," Lynn said, and the Cuban surgeon applied a clamp, shutting off all flow of blood to and from the heart-lung machine.

"The patient's condition is now being maintained solely by the artificial heart," Lynn announced, and a wave of applause came from the gallery. "It is driven by nuclear energy but the battery will need to be replaced only about once every five years."

"Incidentally," she added on a note of justifiable pride, "we have had three pumps of this type working very satisfactorily in calves for more than six months, although this is the first instance of its use in the human body."

"And acting as well here as in the experimental laboratory," Paul added.

"One hurdle yet remains," Lynn said. "We

have to obtain spontaneous respiratory function."

"You just did; he's trying to breathe on his own," the anesthesiologist reported, and another wave of applause swept through the gallery. "Congratulations, Lynn!"

"Let's hope they're not premature, Joe. Is it safe to take him off the respirator?"

"I'll switch to oxygen without the closed respiratory system," he said. "That should tell us very quickly."

On the monitor reporting respiration, a pattern of sharp up and down changes suddenly appeared, showing that the lungs — though still protected by the tube connecting them to the anesthetic machine — had indeed resumed their natural functions.

"There's your answer," Dr. Potter reported.

"We can start to close now," Lynn said quietly to Paul and accepted from the instrument nurse the drill which would place holes in the breastbone, allowing it to be returned to its normal position.

IV

In the gallery, the *Herald* reporter had been scribbling frantically on a wad of copy paper. Now he sprinted for the door leading from the gallery. Lynn Rogers looked up and saw him, however, before he reached it.

"Mr. Parker!" Her sharp command stopped the reporter with his hand reaching for the doorknob. "When you write up the first successful use of an artificial heart in a human body, don't forget to state that the instrument itself was devised by Dr. Theodore Malone and that implantation was complete before he became ill and asked me and Dr. Rogers to take over."

"Right!" the reporter stated as he reached for the door.

V

"DR. THEODORE MALONE ACHIEVES SURGICAL MIRACLE," the headline in Monday's Miami *Herald* read. A subtitle added, "Implants First Artificial Heart," but no mention was made of Lynn's or Paul's part in completing the operation. By that time, however, Theodore Malone, whose genius had made the surgical miracle possible, was dead from the rupture of the lenticulostriate artery deep within his brain.

Chapter 17

Tuesday afternoon, a somber group gathered in the Biscayne General Tower in the spacious office of Mr. Alexander Brinton, Superintendent of the Medical Center. The funeral that morning had been one of the largest – if not the largest – in Miami's history, attended by highly placed personages from all parts of the world who had been saved by Theodore Malone's skill. Present also were famous surgeons from great medical centers, many of whom had been trained by Malone, with the éclat that training had given them.

Now that the funeral was over and the family had been notified by Mr. Brinton that he had been appointed executor under the will, they had gathered in his office to hear the details. Mildred Malone was there in her wheelchair, with Laurel and Mort Weyer – the latter at Laurel's request. Lisa was with Commander Fuller and Paul

Rogers had delayed his departure until five that afternoon, to be with Lynn, now the titular head of the family. Elena Sanchez Malone, in black, and the only person present who was weeping, was attended by her father, a distinguished-looking Cuban, who headed one of the wealthiest families of émigrés in the United States. Both of them sat on the other side of the room away from the rest of the family.

"I will skip the usual preliminary legalese and go to the core of Dr. Malone's will," the administrator began. "None of you will be surprised, I am sure, to learn that he left all of his possessions to the foundation that operates the Malone Heart Institute, making it one of the richest organizations of its type in the world. Since the will was written before Dr. Malone's recent marriage, it is my duty" — he turned to Elena — "to advise you that, as his wife, you may contest in the courts the fact that you are excluded from any benefits under the will."

"My daughter has decided to make no contest, Mr. Brinton," said Renaldo Sanchez. "It is enough that Dr. Malone's fortune shall be used for the benefit of the sick."

"Thank you, Señor Sanchez and Mrs. Malone, both in my capacity as administrator of Biscayne General and also as Chairman of the Malone Foundation, which finances and operates the Institute," said Brinton. "Are there any questions?"

Laurel asked the only one. "Does the will in any way affect the trust fund my father established for my mother at the time of their divorce?"

"It does not," said Brinton. "The trust will continue until your mother's death and then the remainder of the corpus will revert to the foundation." He looked around the group. "Are there any other questions?"

There were none.

"Then you're all free to go except that the trustees of the foundation, who will meet immediately after we finish, have requested Dr. Lynn Rogers to remain."

"I'll be back," Lynn told the administrator as the others were filing out. "I think Dr. Rogers would like a last look at our prize patient before he leaves this afternoon."

"Of course," said Mr. Brinton. "Good-by, Paul."

"Good-by, Alex. It was nice seeing you again."

In the Critical Care Unit, Lynn and Paul entered the glass-fronted cubicle where Artemus Jones had been placed after he'd

439

been brought down from the main operating theater of the Institute. Every parameter being recorded on the small monitors in the room and also upon the larger ones at the nursing station occupying the center of the triangular new unit showed an excellent report — save one. The screen where normally the electrocardiographic tracing of the patient's heartbeat would be recorded was blank. In its place, only a low hum came from the nuclear energy activated pump that kept blood moving on its otherwise normal course through his body.

Instinctively, Lynn reached for Jones's pulse, but drew back with a wry smile. "It'll take me quite a while to get used to its not being there," she admitted. "The pump in the steel heart is a rotary."

"He looks as if he might become conscious any minute," said Paul.

"Do you suppose he will?"

"I don't know."

"Don't go counting me out." The voice was Art Jones's, though somewhat hoarse from irritation by the tube that had been placed through his larynx during surgery to keep his lungs functioning under pressure while the chest was open. And when he opened his eyes, his gaze was clear.

"How long have you been conscious?" Lynn asked.

"Maybe an hour."

"Why didn't you let us know?" Paul asked. "Everybody has been on tenterhooks waiting to see —"

"Whether I might wind up as a vegetable?"

"Well, yes."

"No way, Doc. From what I've heard the nurses saying, you must have done a heart transplant —"

"Not a transplant as you know it, but a stainless steel heart," Lynn corrected him. "Right now, you're the only person in the world with one."

"Well, what do you know," Art Jones said with a chuckle. "I don't even know my real last name and here I am one of a kind. I guess that ought to get me into the *Guinness Book of Records*."

"I'd bet on it," Lynn assured him.

"That's one bet I won't take, Doctor," said Jones. "It would cost me too much to lose."

At the chart desk Paul glanced at his watch. "You'd better get going, Lynn, they'll be waiting for you upstairs. I'll make a note on the chart and tell Laurel and Mort. Jones is a special friend of theirs."

She stood on tiptoes to kiss him. "Wait

441

for me at the airport until they threaten to close the gate in your face. I may still make it there in time to tell you good-by."

II

Mildred Malone, Laurel, and Mort Weyer met Elena and her father as they were waiting for one of the Institute elevators to take them down to the ground floor. Instinctively, Laurel reached out her hand to the young widow.

"That was noble of you, Elena, not claiming a wife's portion of my father's estate," she said warmly.

"I promised him that," said the Latin beauty. "Nobody who knew him would doubt that he loved the Institute more than anything – or anyone."

"Especially more than any woman. I learned that long before you came into the picture, Elena." When Mildred held out her hand, the younger woman seized it and pressed it against her tear-wet cheek.

"Thank you," she said. "Thank you for understanding."

Two elevators came to the floor simultaneously. The Sanchezes entered one, while

Mildred Malone, Mort, and Laurel took the other.

"Can you come to dinner tonight, Dr. Weyer –?" Mildred started to ask but Mort cut her off as he held the "Open" button so Laurel could push her mother's chair into the elevator.

"It's Mort – or Mortimer, if you wish," he said.

"Mortimer over my dead body," said Laurel as she pushed Mildred Malone's chair into the second elevator. "But please come to dinner. A telegram came this afternoon from the WHO. They want me to leave to-morrow for Haiti with the rest of the com-mission."

"You're going to have to accept the name, Mortimer, at least once," Mort told her.

"Where?"

"On a marriage license. If it's not correct there, all our children will be bastards."

III

Lisa and David Fuller paused outside the marquee over the entrance to Biscayne General. "Miami can be the most beautiful place in the world on a day like this," he said, "with a girl like you."

"There's one place more beautiful."

"Where?"

"Father's — our — cottage on Key Largo. Are you off tomorrow?"

"I'll arrange to be."

"Then let's have breakfast together in the hospital cafeteria; they open early for the nurses going on and off the morning shifts. Afterward we'll drive down to Key Largo for that scuba dive over the reef I promised you."

"Why not leave now and breakfast on Key Largo?"

"The damned rehabilitation schedule you've got me on, that's why. You're not getting me into bed before it's finished — those were your own words."

"And I won't go back on them."

Lisa chuckled and reached for his hand. "You're hoist on your own petard, my friend. But darned if you don't look good on it."

IV

Flight 214F from Miami to Tampa had already been called when Paul Rogers saw Lynn hurrying through the Eastern Airlines lobby of the Miami airport and thought — for the thousandth time at least in the years since they'd faced each other across a cadaver on their first morning as medical students at Johns Hopkins one September day long ago — that she was the loveliest thing in the world.

"How long do you have?" she asked breathlessly.

"Five minutes — with luck. Have you decided to go with me?"

"Better than that. You can come back here if you wish — as Director of the Malone Heart Institute. The board authorized me to offer you the position less than a half hour ago."

"That's *your* right. Didn't they offer it to you?"

"They might have, but I told them at the start I wasn't a candidate and that unless they gave it to you, I'd go to Tampa with you."

"You could have had it for yourself."

"Maybe yes, maybe no. The point is, I didn't want it."

"Why?"

"I want other things more."

"Name one."

"Motherhood — for openers. And that, I'm

445

pretty sure, is already on the way."

"I don't understand —"

"You should; it was your doing. After the divorce, I never took the pill and I didn't start again when you came to Miami for the seminar. You don't have any choice now except to make an honest woman of me."

"Last call for Eastern Flight 214F for Tampa and Atlanta," the announcer's voice came over the loudspeakers. "All passengers should be aboard."

"Except one!" Paul shouted to the startled attendant as he raced for the gate. "You'd better be on this same flight next Friday evening for Tampa, Lynn," he called back. "I'm going to need someone to help me pack, so I can come home again."